T0037494

ALSO BY HOLLY JAMES

Nothing But the Truth

HOLLY JAMES

THE DÉJÀ GLITCH

A NOVEL

DUTTON

DUTTON

An imprint of Penguin Random House LLC
penguinrandomhouse.com

Copyright © 2023 by Holly Rus

LIBRARY OF CONGRESS CATALOGING-IN-PUBLICATION DATA
has been applied for.

ISBN: 9780593471586 (paperback)
ISBN: 9780593471593 (ebook)

Printed in the United States of America
1st Printing

BOOK DESIGN BY KATY RIEGEL

For my parents.
Happy fortieth anniversary.

THE DÉJÀ GLITCH

CHAPTER
1

GEMMA PETERS DID not like parties.

Her idea of a good time consisted of a book and a blanket, perhaps a cup of tea. The loud, raucous bar where she stood was draining her battery faster than a Netflix binge would her phone. Nonetheless, she was dutifully wearing her party smile and positive attitude. She only had to last another hour until her alarm went off, set for a strict departure time of ten p.m. so that she could head home to give her dog his meds and be in bed by ten forty-five like a responsible adult. It was a weeknight, after all. No doubt the party would last until the small hours of the morning because her best friend Lila regarded mundane schedules with the same importance as spam calls.

If a fizzy glass of pink champagne—bubbly, beautiful— were a person, it would be Lila.

Speaking of champagne, the birthday girl suddenly materialized in front of Gemma, pushing the tiara that had begun to slip from her silky hair back into place and shoving a glass of bubbles into Gemma's hands.

"You need another!" Lila screamed at her from inches away. Despite her skin being misted with remnants of the night's festivities, her makeup remained impeccable. Gemma chalked it up to the stockpile of free, high-quality beauty products causing small avalanches on every available surface in Lila's apartment. Companies sent them to her in exchange for a review on her YouTube channel or a post on her Instagram. @Lila_in_L.A. had over two hundred thousand followers.

Lila held a matching champagne glass in her own manicured hand, and Gemma knew by the gloss in her eyes that she had had plenty to drink.

I don't think I need another, but thank you, Gemma thought about saying, but she knew that refusal would only result in playful pouting, a reminder that it was Lila's birthday, and accusations of being a party pooper. So instead she would take the glass and discreetly leave it on the bar while Lila sauntered off into the clutches of her more spirited guests. The routine was as old as their friendship.

Except Lila went off script. She did not smear her painted lips against Gemma's cheek in a parting kiss and gush an inebriated tribute to their bond. She expectantly watched Gemma floating, glass in hand, like an awkward iceberg in a sea full of mostly strangers.

"What?" Gemma asked.

"Drink it!" Lila commanded with an upward sweep of her hand. The bangles on her wrist tumbled midway to her elbow.

Gemma's face filled with warmth as if they were back in

their dorm room years before and Lila was asking her to choke down a mouthful of pilfered peach schnapps.

"I will," Gemma said with a shy shrug of her shoulders.

"No, you won't. You're going to wait until I turn around and then leave it on the bar and hope I don't notice. I know you, Gemma Rose Peters." Lila narrowed her eyes and pointed a finger. "Drink it."

Gemma cast her a glare and took a tiny sip. She reasoned that her morning didn't really start until nine a.m. the next day; a slight champagne headache was nothing she couldn't remedy with a jog and a fresh cup of coffee beforehand. "I wasn't aware your thirties was the decade of renewed peer pressure. Why are you being so insistent?"

Lila smugly smiled and cocked out a hip. She dug her thumbs into the bodice of her strapless dress and yanked it up, adjusting her sizable chest and doing a little dance. Her dark hair swept her shoulders in a fan made shiny by a host of products with exotic names that Gemma had never even heard of. "Because you're gonna need it." She pressed her fingers to the glass's round base and tilted for another sip.

The sharp bubbles sloshed against Gemma's lips as she sputtered. "Lila!"

Lila giggled and leaned into the bar to grab a napkin. The Westside lounge hit all the Los Angeles stereotypes: crowded, dim, peddling overpriced cocktails with pretentious ingredients like beets and house-made organic syrups, and full of attractive people slipping in and out of the shadows. Lila brushed against the man beside her. He turned and raked his eyes from her head to her toes, crushed as they were at a needlessly severe angle in shoes Gemma wouldn't dream of wearing, and obviously liked what he saw. He smiled and opened his mouth to say something right as Lila turned back around and blindly whipped him in the face with her hair.

Gemma stifled a laugh.

"You're fine," Lila said, and dabbed Gemma's lips with a small black square of rough paper. Despite her similarities to a glittering disco ball, Lila had a surprisingly maternal side to her. "But you do need to finish your drink."

A mother with an expansive booze collection.

Gemma took another tiny sip. "Again, I ask, why?"

"Because I know you, and I know you'll need some liquid courage to go talk to that guy at the end of the bar who hasn't stopped staring at you for an hour."

Lila casually tilted her head, and Gemma's eyes shot to the end of the room. At almost the same instant, her whole body flushed, and the alcohol went straight to her head.

"Oh no, I'm not—"

"Yes! Yes you are!" Lila cheered. "Listen, I've checked him out: he's clean, no ring, looks our age, maybe a little tired around the eyes, but that probably just means he's got a good job and works hard, and he's got the best quality a girl could ask for . . ." She suggestively trailed off, beaming, and slowly swaying back and forth on the toes of her ridiculous shoes.

Gemma gulped at her drink simply for relief from the arid desert that had suddenly appeared inside her mouth. She swallowed too hard, and the bubbles burned her throat.

Talking to guys in bars was not her thing. It was Lila's thing, hence the birthday party in a bar full of guys. Her best friend stood before her with a devilish glint in her eyes, and Gemma wanted to call it a night early and go home.

She risked another glance at the mysterious man in the corner, and he was in fact staring at her.

Heat flushed her body anew. From the distance, a good fifteen feet, she could not make out any of the features Lila had listed, except for the fact that he was very good-looking.

Had she said he was good-looking?

Gemma couldn't remember, but she did remember the last item on the list.

"What's the best quality a girl could ask for?" Her words came out sounding like she was in a trance. She suddenly felt as if gravity had shifted, and something was pulling her toward the stranger at the end of the bar.

Lila circled around to stand behind her so that they both faced the man. She propped her chin on Gemma's shoulder and spoke right beside her ear. "That even with everyone in here, he's looking at you like you're the only person in the room."

Gemma heard the smile in her friend's voice and felt a rush of affection that Lila, *look at me* Lila, would still play wingwoman at her own birthday party.

Not that Gemma wanted a wingwoman. She did not currently have space in her life for a brooding stranger making eyes at her from the shadows. Not even one with the kind of tousled hair that did the wind favors by letting it blow it around and eyes that seemed to shine in the dark.

Nope. No room for that.

But Lila appeared to be making room whether Gemma wanted it or not.

She poked Gemma in the ribs and nudged her forward. "Go."

Gemma stumbled a hesitant step, feeling that gravitational pull tug her forward at the same time her feet stubbornly refused to leave the ground. The opposing forces did not mesh well.

"Consider it your birthday present to me," Lila said.

"I already gave you a present."

"Well, then go get yourself one. *Go.*"

Lila's interest in her love life had increased exponentially during the year since Gemma's last breakup. While Gemma found solace in solitude, an ease about caring for herself and her geriatric mutt Rex and no one else, Lila encouraged her to join the dating race at every turn.

You're a catch, Gem. I don't know what you're waiting for.

In truth, Gemma didn't know either, if she was waiting for anything at all. But with pink bubbles bursting in her brain and the sudden, inexplicable shift in the earth's tilt, she wondered if all she had been waiting for was the guy in the corner staring at her like she was the only girl in the room.

"Atta girl," Lila quietly cheered when Gemma took a purposeful step forward.

Warm bodies pushed against her as she fought her way like a fish swimming upstream to the other end of the bar. The room was hot and thick with indecent desires. A fug of perfumes and heavy air squeezed in from all sides and reminded her why she preferred books and blankets to a night out.

But then she arrived on the other end of it all, and the intriguing stranger gently smiled at her. She instantly forgot her distaste for the whole scene. She made note that Lila had been right about everything: clean, no ring, same age.

Despite the shine in his blue eyes, he did look a little tired, but Gemma was tired too. Perhaps he was worn out for the same occupation-related reasons.

The expectant look on his handsome face told her that she had exceeded the amount of time that was reasonable for walking up to someone and not saying anything.

"Hi," she said, and sounded even to herself like a rusty old tool that hadn't been out of the box in ages. "My friend sent me over. It's her birthday." She cringed as his eyebrows rose. It sounded like she had been sent over on Lila's behalf.

The fact that he didn't immediately look over her shoulder for the curvy brunette in question won him a point. Everyone in the bar knew it was Lila's birthday thanks to the tiara and intermittent cheering with every round of drinks.

"Happy birthday to your friend."

"Thank you. I mean, thank you for her." She cringed again. In her defense, she didn't spend too much time talking to other people, not at her job in the production booth at a radio show, and especially not to attractive ones with secrets in their eyes. Other than the nights Lila succeeded in dragging her along, she didn't go out much.

She couldn't put her finger on it, but there was something about him. A flicker of familiarity like a scent tied to a memory that couldn't quite be placed.

"Not really your scene?" he asked without a hint of judgment.

She quietly laughed, feeling exposed for being so obvious. "No, not at all."

"Mine either."

"Then what are you doing here?" The words slipped out more in surprise than anything. He was obviously alone, not even avoiding a party like she was. She hoped she didn't sound harsh.

Thankfully, he shrugged and gave her half of a smile that she suspected would have wobbled her knees at full wattage. "Waiting for someone special."

It felt like a line, and despite herself, she fell for it.

She sank onto the stool next to him, which was somehow empty in the bustling crowd.

"I'd ask what you are doing here too, but you've already told me as much with the birthday party. Can I get you a drink?" he asked.

She looked down at her waning pink champagne bubbling with only half the gusto of when Lila had handed it to her. She imagined it had gone warm in her nervous hand. She set the glass on the bar and decided to see where saying yes to this friendly stranger would lead her.

"Sure."

"Great. I actually have a talent for guessing people's favorite drinks."

He had started with a line and shamelessly moved to a gimmick, and Gemma normally would have called him on it or rolled her eyes, but something about him left her willing to follow his lead.

"Oh, really?"

"Yes, really. Watch, I'll show you."

He threw up a hand and waved at the bartender. Gemma noted how long his arm was and that he wore a vintage watch on his wrist. She saw no discernible tattoos in the band of skin between his watch and the rolled-up sleeve of his shirt, which of course didn't mean that he didn't have them elsewhere. She had grown accustomed to expecting ink on men in L.A., especially ones hanging out in bars like this.

"You strike me as someone who prefers a classy cocktail, probably something bitter."

She bit her lip instead of telling him he was right.

"Am I warm?" he said with a smile at the look on her face.

The bartender, a man who indeed did have tattoos decorating his arms, materialized and nodded at them.

The man with the watch and shining eyes and killer smile—who still didn't have a name—gave Gemma a coy grin before turning to place the order.

"Two Negronis, please."

Gemma's mouth popped open. She managed to close it by the time the bartender nodded and whisked off.

"How'd I do?" the man beside her asked.

"That's my favorite drink," she confessed, too shocked to summon any flirtatious banter.

He proudly shrugged a shoulder. "Told you I was good at it."

She shook herself and regained her bearings. "Maybe it was a lucky guess."

"Or maybe not," he said with a grin.

Right then, a pop song that instantly took Gemma back to the free-spirited, early days of college came on the house speakers. Every lyric came back to her even though she hadn't heard the song in ages. She knew if she caught Lila's eye, she'd get a knowing wink and they'd mouth the chorus to each other across the room.

"Did I miss something?" the man asked, and Gemma realized she was grinning like a fool.

"Oh, I just love this song. I haven't heard it in a long time, and it always puts me in a good mood."

"Is that so? Well, looks like we're stumbling into all sorts of luck tonight."

The bartender returned with their drinks.

He lifted his in toast. "To luck and all the good fortune it brings."

Gemma lifted her glass to clink his and paused. "Wait. I don't even know your name. I feel like it's bad luck to share a toast without knowing."

"Fair." He held her gaze. His eyes searched hers long enough to make her feel like he was waiting for something.

"Are you not going to tell me your name?" she asked with a laugh.

"Yes. Sorry." He shook his head. "I'm Jack."

"Gemma," she said, and clinked her glass against his.

"Pleasure to meet you, Gemma."

"Likewise, Jack."

She sipped the harsh, citrusy bite of her drink and loved the way it burned her tongue. Jack did his best, looking like he'd prefer something else.

"Not your drink?"

"Afraid not," he said with a laugh and a shake of his head. "You must be tough to like these things."

She almost snorted. "I don't know if *tough* is the right word. My grandmother used to drink them. They remind me of her."

"Was she tough?"

"Oh, the toughest. I wish I had half her strength."

"Sounds like an amazing woman, but don't sell yourself short. You were tough enough to walk over here, weren't you?"

She sipped again. "Are you suggesting I should be intimidated by you?"

"Not at all. I just get the sense you'd rather be somewhere else, and that socializing with some stranger in a bar is not high on your list of favorite things." He said it so sincerely, as if he knew her well enough to understand that it was the truth, that she found herself leaning closer.

"Don't sell yourself short either. I didn't walk over here for lack of alternative activities."

"No?" he said with great interest. "What brought you over, then? Aside from your friend who sent you."

That was an excellent question, and one Gemma still did not know the answer to. Though sitting beside him, she only felt that mysterious pull with more force. She wasn't sure she would be able to resist if she tried.

She thought of the best way to sum it all up and landed on one word.

"Curiosity."

"And? Do you like what you've found?"

She took another sip. His smile and the liquor along with the sweet memories the song had looping through her mind had her in a very warm, happy place. "I have to say I do."

"Excellent."

They slowly sipped their drinks, chatting and casually learning about each other. He was a television screenwriter, which Gemma did not find the least bit surprising, given where they were. What she did find surprising was that he did not name-drop anyone or anything. He spoke of his work with pride but as exactly that: work. When she told him that she produced a local radio show, a job she loved despite having had a rough day that day, he leaned in with interest, asking all about the host and the guests they'd interviewed. The topic turned briefly to their families, a subject Gemma skirted other than for one member. By the time she was telling him her younger brother spent half the year in sub-Saharan Africa working at a wildlife conservation institute and actually had been due home that day for an extended visit but missed his flight, their knees were touching beneath the bar.

The sound of her phone screaming from her clutch yanked her out of the moment. She apologized and pulled it out, shocked to see that the alarm she had set for her self-imposed curfew was clanging like a school bell. They had been talking for almost an hour, and she hadn't even realized.

"I have to go," she told him with disappointment in her voice.

Jack looked equally disappointed. "Someone waiting on you at home?"

She stood from the stool and dug a few dollars out of her clutch to leave as a tip. "Yes. An old dog who needs his meds before bed."

Jack smiled with obvious relief. "Well, I wouldn't want to be responsible for any veterinary emergencies." He stood up next to her, and she realized she'd had no sense of his height since they had been sitting the whole time. His eyes hovered several inches above hers. She found herself suddenly snared in them as she looked up. Even if she had wanted to break free, she couldn't have.

"It was nice to meet you," she told him.

"You too. I'll walk out with you."

Gemma had half a mind to offer to meet him after she went home and tended to Rex, but a long night out was not in her plans. She felt him walking closely behind her as they worked through the crowd, and she didn't mind at all. She punched a rideshare order into her phone and saw a swarm of cars nearby on her screen, ready to pick her up in minutes. Before she made it to the door, she scanned for Lila. She caught her eye over at the other end of the bar where she was tossing back shots with a gaggle of other painfully cool influencers who had joined the party. Gemma waved, and Lila blew her a kiss. Then Lila curled her hands into a heart and pointed at Jack with a thumbs-up. Clearly, she thought they were leaving together.

The thought pushed a rush of warmth into Gemma's cheeks as they stepped outside into the balmy evening. West L.A. teemed with nightlife: cars whizzing by, clusters of friends clutching one another and laughing, thumping bass pouring from the doors of venues where Lila was likely to end up at some point in the night. All of it both exhilarated and exhausted Gemma.

But mostly exhausted.

She saw the car she had called whip around the corner and approach. Her moments with Jack were quickly coming to an end.

He turned to her on the sidewalk, and while she expected him to ask for her phone number, or even her last name, he instead got a strange look on his face. Almost as if he was in pain.

"Gemma, before you go, I just want to—"

He cut off like he didn't know how to finish.

Her car came to the curb behind them. The driver lowered the window and called her name into the knot of people milling around the sidewalk.

"What is it?" she asked Jack, suddenly concerned over his distress.

He took a determined breath. "I'd like to test a theory, if you don't mind."

She frowned at him. "O . . . kay—?"

Before she got the whole word out, he stepped forward and slipped a hand around her waist. He used his other hand to reach for the nape of her neck and paused with his lips inches from hers. Whatever his theory was, it obviously involved a kiss, and Gemma found herself more than willing to help him test it out.

She pressed her lips to his, answering his request for permission, and almost lost her balance when they made contact. Thankfully, his hand around her waist kept her upright. She wondered, fleetingly and through a consuming haze, if anticipating her reaction was the exact reason he'd placed his hands where he had.

It felt enormous. The pull of his lips, the soft push of his tongue against hers. She had only known the guy for an hour, but the contact felt like a lifetime of intimacy wrapped up into one showstopping kiss. Gravity shifted again, and the center of everything became the points where their bodies touched. It was the best kiss of her life, and it ended as abruptly as it had started.

Jack released her, face flushed and lips shining. She could hardly see straight, but he held her gaze with an intensity she was seeing in his eyes for the first time.

Her driver called her name again, and she hardly heard it for all the blood rushing in her head. Her heart was pounding.

Jack gave her a pleading look in their final moment to-gether. "Please remember me, Gemma."

He let her go, and she was too stunned to think what an odd thing that was for him to say.

CHAPTER
2

GEMMA WOKE TO a soft, wet nose pushing into her palm that was hanging over her bedside. Rex, the most faithful man in her life, woke her like clockwork every day. She relied on his elderly bladder as her alarm.

"Yes, I'm up," she mumbled, though she still lay flat on her back blinking at the ceiling. She patted his furry head with one hand and flopped the other into the downy fluff of her comforter. Lila had gifted her the free sample after she gushed about it to a few hundred thousand Instagram followers as *the best blanket* you could buy for your bed. Gemma actually owned a fair amount of free stuff courtesy of her friend's influencer status.

Rex took the friendly pat as invitation to jump up onto the bed. He stood over Gemma and shoved his muzzle into her hair, taking a few snorting sniffs and licking her ear.

"Yes, good morning to you too. Come on, let's go outside." She sat up and pushed back the covers. Rex gingerly walked to the edge of the bed and lowered himself to the floor two paws at a time. Jumping up was fine but getting back down was hard on his knees.

Gemma climbed out of bed and combed her fingers through the scruffy hair on his head that she sometimes spiked into a little mohawk. The shelter had told her he was some kind of terrier-Lab mix. She had considered doing one of those doggie DNA testing kits now that they were readily available, but his wiry black hair and adoration of water was convincing evidence that the shelter had gotten it right all those years ago.

She passed him to take her own bathroom break before she pulled on a hoodie and stepped into flip-flops to take him outside. One thing her NoHo apartment building did not have was a yard, and Rex's ultra-regular bathroom schedule kept her climbing the building's staircase four times a day: once as soon as they woke, again before she left for work, then again as soon as she got home, and finally once more before bed. On the rare occasion he gobbled up something unseen on the sidewalk or she let him indulge in table scraps that she shouldn't have, she found herself re-grettably descending the stairs in a middle-of-the-night zombie daze to prevent having to shampoo her rugs.

Rex waited by the front door like a perfect gentleman, tail swishing and eyes bright. Gemma slipped her phone into her hoodie pocket and unhooked his leash from the peg on the wall. Their bathroom breaks were not long; she paid a dog sitter good money to drop in midday and take him for a real walk while she was at work. Trips one through four down the stairs culminated in a slow stroll along the sidewalk until Rex found his preferred bush and they turned back home.

They made it to the lobby, a nondescript utilitarian room with a wall of mailboxes and a perpetually empty reception desk, and passed through the glass front doors. Outside, the flat, modest expanse of North Hollywood greeted them with another day of sun. Palms and telephone poles lined the street, backlit by a blue-gray sky that only L.A. could paint. Gemma's lungs had grown accustomed to smog; she hardly noticed it. But on days she craved fresher air, she loaded Rex shotgun in her Prius and cruised up the coast to Malibu or took him on a hike in Temescal Canyon.

Their street still slept for the most part. They wouldn't run into anyone else until their second trip down the stairs in a few hours. Then it would bustle with babies in strollers, Rex's neighborhood canine friends, exercise enthusiasts out for a jog. On their first trip, they could really only rely on Mr. Weaver to be stationed in his yard across the street.

"Morning, Mr. Weaver!" Gemma called on cue to the man she considered the human form of Rex. They were both old, gray around the muzzle, and friendlier than most people.

"Morning, Gemma! Hi there, Rex." He gave them a wave from his patchy front lawn.

He stood out in his front yard every morning to, from what Gemma could tell, monitor his uninspired grass. The whole neighborhood was on water restriction thanks to California's never-ending drought. The difference between lawns on their street and the lush, emerald cushions stretch-ing the yards over the hill in Bel Air and Brentwood was that here they actually followed the water conservation rules.

Mr. Weaver stroked his chin with a determined look on

his face like he might be able to will his lawn into a greener existence. He looked up at the cloudless sky advertising a zero percent chance of rain and dropped his arms with a shrug. "At least it's another beautiful day. Sunny and seventy-five, can't complain!"

Gemma was struck with an acute sense of déjà vu as his words echoed in her mind. She watched Mr. Weaver for a moment, puzzled, and feeling like she was trying to grab something slipping through her fingers. She could swear he had said those exact words in that exact way before, like notes repeated in a song she had heard many times.

"Need something there, Gemma?" he said when he caught her staring.

She shook her head to clear the webby thoughts clouding her mind. She convinced herself that she was groggy and still waking up, and that Mr. Weaver *had* said those exact words before because it was sunny and seventy-five degrees in L.A. almost every day. This sunny, early-summer day was no exception.

She felt Rex tug on his leash and looked down to see that he had chosen the tree that dropped lime green pollen that occasionally made her sneeze for his morning mark.

"No," she told Mr. Weaver. "We're good. Have a nice day!"

"You too, Gemma. Bye, Rex!"

On her way back up the stairs, she pulled out her phone to check the weather to double convince herself that what Mr. Weaver had said wasn't out of the ordinary and she wasn't imagining things.

Sure enough, Los Angeles: sunny with a high of seventy-five degrees every day this week.

Still, his words felt familiar in a way beyond a casual and redundant statement about the weather.

She couldn't shake the feeling, so she grounded herself in reality by texting her best friend.

Lila wouldn't wake up for several hours yet, but at least she'd have a happy birthday text to greet her.

Gemma typed one out filled with every party emoji her keyboard had to offer. They were going to celebrate later with dinner and a night out on the Westside, and honestly, the thought of keeping up with Lila on a regular night exhausted Gemma, let alone on her birthday. Nevertheless, she would put on her party smile and positive attitude for her best friend.

Then, for good measure and to soothe the anxiety bubbling in her veins at the thought of her little brother miles in the sky on a plane somewhere over the Atlantic, she peeked at the last message he had sent her before boarding a flight out of Lagos. She had stopped trying to calculate all the time zone changes, but she knew he landed in New York that morning her time, and after a layover, he would arrive in L.A. in time for her to pick him up that afternoon. He would be a jet-lagged mess, starving because he hated airplane food, and insufferably grumpy. But she hadn't seen him in half a year. His inevitable crankiness would not interfere with their reunion.

West Coast, best coast. Here I come!

She smiled at his message and couldn't wait to wrap her arms around his lanky body, grown lean and tough from living in a tent for six months. He would return to L.A., and she would fatten him up like a housecat with lunch dates and weekends at her complex's pool before the cycle started over again in another six months.

The bug for global conscientiousness had bitten him hard after college. His work in wildlife conservation had taken him around the globe, from Greenland to Australia and now to Africa for the past few years. She wasn't exactly sure what he did in Lagos, but he came back tan and down two pants sizes every time. She had hoarded all the homebody genes in the family while Patrick lived to roam free.

His message had come in during the middle of the night while she slept, and she couldn't text him back because he never bought the in-flight Wi-Fi. She would have to be patient until he landed.

Rex's morning walk always woke her enough to make it through her workout before needing coffee. Back inside, she unclipped his leash and dropped a scoop of kibble in his bowl before heading to her room to change. Once she was strapped into her shoes, sports bra, and Lycra, she left to go down to the building's gym.

It was nothing to swoon over, but it got the job done. The oblong room with a view of the parking lot housed two treadmills; a pair of ellipticals; a wall of stretchy, bouncy resistance equipment; and a few racks of weights that Gemma avoided to the best of her ability. The cramped room sometimes grew muggy depending on who was in there punishing the equipment. The wall of thick air that hit her as soon as she opened the door informed her that her morning run would not take place in isolation, but she hadn't expected it to.

The only other person she regularly ran into each morning

22   HOLLY JAMES

was hard at work on one of the treadmills, earning the title Lila had bestowed upon him: Hot Guy in 202.

Gemma did not know his real name, but she knew that he looked excellent in a tank top, had arms like a romance novel cover model, and ran five miles in an impressive forty minutes.

His feet hit the belt in a syncopated rhythm with his breathing. His focus was on whatever he was watching on his phone mounted on the treadmill. He wore earbuds and didn't acknowledge Gemma when she climbed onto the treadmill beside him. Which was fine because she wouldn't want someone interrupting to chat while she was running, and, despite Lila's appeals, she did not want him to become anything more than Hot Guy in 202 to her.

Gemma's last relationship had not ended well, and even with it having been a year, she was not looking to change her single status anytime soon.

She put in her own earbuds and jabbed the treadmill's screen to program her usual workout.

The screen flashed an angry red *ERROR* message that startled her as if someone had shouted at the same time it felt familiar.

She frowned and backed out to the main menu to reprogram her workout and got the same *ERROR* message.

"That one. Is. Busted," Hot Guy in 202 huffed from beside her.

Gemma jumped at the sound of his voice both because she had never heard it before and because the room was otherwise silent, aside from his feet and breathing.

"I'll be. Done. In ten minutes," he said, and went back to watching his phone.

Gemma considered sitting back and watching him run for ten minutes while she waited her turn, but she didn't have the spare time in her morning. Instead, she crossed the room to the ellipticals and flipped on the TV overhead. She normally stared at the parking lot while she listened to an audiobook and envisioned far-off places, but the opposite wall offered the chance to watch the morning news while she exercised.

The TV came on muted with closed captioning scrolling across the bottom. She got to work pumping the pedals on the machine and watched a reporter with slick black hair and a News10 fleece give an update. He stood on a neighborhood corner with palm trees and a row of houses over his shoulder. It was a standard L.A. neighborhood, except for the fact that the street behind him gushed with water high enough to touch the belly of every car parked on it bumper to bumper.

The whole, strange scene somehow looked startlingly familiar.

Gemma scanned the words along the bottom to see what he was saying as he motioned at the street with a hand.

". . . neighborhood in Burbank where a water main broke sometime, we think, around four a.m. Now, you can see there is substantial flooding in the area, and crews are working to drain the water before there is any structural damage."

"What a waste," Gemma muttered like a drought-wearied native. Her first thought at the sight of all that water was how green Mr. Weaver's lawn could be if they diverted it to his house instead of washing it down a drain.

Her second thought was that she had had that exact thought before.

She grabbed the TV's remote and unmuted, knowing it wouldn't bother anyone because Hot Guy in 202 was listening to his own program and they were the only two people in the room.

"There have been no reports of damage yet," the reporter went on, "but as you can see behind me, residents are concerned about their property."

The camera panned to a man on the sidewalk, water up to his knees, holding keys in his hand and looking like he didn't want to risk opening his car door and flooding the interior to move it. Behind him, two children splashed around like they were at a water park.

Gemma got the distinct sense, somehow, that she knew the little girls. They spun and kicked in the water, twirling each other around like it was the best day of their lives and sending droplets glinting in the morning sun. The taller one suddenly stopped, a flash of excitement on her face, and the microphone picked up what she said in the second before the camera panned back to the reporter. The words were in Gemma's head, exactly, inexplicably, and came out of her mouth in a whisper at the same time they appeared on the screen.

"Dad, can we get the inner tubes?"

The blond news anchor in the studio chuckled when she came back on-screen looking polished in her navy dress. "Looks like not *everyone* is disappointed with this turn of events, Mark."

Gemma stared at the TV in shock. That same gluey sensation she had gotten when Mr. Weaver talked about the weather clouded her mind. She thought for a second that maybe she had somehow turned on the previous day's news and hadn't remembered that she'd seen the story before, the little girls splashing in the water, but it said *LIVE* right there in the screen's corner.

She grabbed her phone and quickly searched for the story online. A smattering of results showed reports from local outlets and county and city organizations within the past hour.

She stared back at the TV.

It really was happening live.

Gemma decided to turn off the TV and return to her planned audiobook for the rest of her workout.

By the time she got back to her apartment, she was furiously trying to convince herself that she must have already listened to chapters 14 and 15 in her audiobook and forgotten because how else would she have known the big plot twist? It was a good twist, and she couldn't have just . . . figured it out, could she have?

No, she told herself. She must have fallen asleep listening the night before and subconsciously stored the information.

She headed for a cold shower to snap herself out of the strange morning and felt refreshed on the other side. When she wound up in her kitchen dressed for work in jeans and her favorite white blouse that she'd picked for that day's special occasion, ready to fill her to-go tumbler, she noted to her dismay that she had run out of coffee.

"This day is off to a start," she told Rex. He monitored her morning routine from his gray velvet pouf in the living room. "Maybe I should go back to bed."

He let out a little whine and rested his chin on his paws.

Gemma sighed. "You're right. One of us has to go to work."

She crossed the room to pat his ears and decided to stop off at the coffee shop around the corner on her way to the radio studio.

BY A SMALL miracle, Gemma found parking half a block away from the coffee shop. It was one of those serendipitous L.A. moments where the end of one person's journey coincided precisely with the beginning of hers. She supposed the odds couldn't have been too slim, given the city of four million people and all the coming and going, but any time it happened, she felt like the parking gods were smiling down upon her.

Inside, the shop buzzed with the early-morning clamor of productive people fueling up to set out into the world. A handful of devotees braced against the noise with headphones as they hunched over laptops to work on whatever creative venture had brought them to the City of Angels. Every single person in line with Gemma was on their phone, tapping, scrolling, or talking as if connection to something elsewhere was keeping them alive.

Gemma opened her texting thread with her brother, expecting to have heard that he landed and wondering if the message had somehow slipped through without her noticing. But she only saw his message from before. She tried to ignore the nervous spike it put in her blood.

To her dismay, she did have a new message from her father. It was short, and she could see the whole thing in the preview without even opening it.

Looking forward to seeing you.

She did not return the sentiment, so she left the message unread.

As much as she loved her brother, he was the harbinger of a family reunion she'd rather forgo. Something sweet inextricably linked with discomfort. Like a hangover after a frivolous night with Lila, she couldn't have one without the other. Her father's efforts to spend time with her were directly related to his advancing age, but she didn't share the view that getting older was justification for reconciliation. Especially not after the lifetime of selective attention he'd paid her. But Patrick held a different view, so she begrudgingly put on a neutral face and went along on his biannual visits.

Sometimes she wished she had a normal family and that living in the same city as her father was a comforting resource instead of a chronic ache she tried to ignore.

"What can I get you?" the barista asked when she arrived at the front of the line.

Gemma shook her thoughts and ordered an iced coffee for herself and, feeling generous, got a round of lattes for her coworkers. It was a big day for them. She would be in the booth with Carmen, her co-producer, and Hugo, their sound tech, as Marsha, their boss and the show's host, interviewed Nigel Black, her childhood and current personal idol and the biggest guest they'd ever had. The thought of being in the same room, even if separated by a piece of soundproof glass, made her giggle in delight. Not only was she a huge fan, but she had also pulled an exhausting number of strings and called in favors she did not wish to mention to get a rock legend on the show. She couldn't wait to hear his iconic, gravelly voice answering the questions she had written for Marsha to ask as if it were the two of them having a conversation instead. If she played her cards right—and worked up the nerve—it might even be her hosting someday.

She stepped aside after she ordered to wait in the crowded wing with other patrons. Conversations bubbled around her, many one-sided as people spoke to invisible microphones stowed in their earbuds. The tall, thin woman beside her let out a loud bark of a laugh at nothing apparent, and then Gemma saw the tiny white pegs hooked in her ears. She marveled at how strange they all would have looked to anyone from twenty years before.

Her own phone rang, her brother's name flashing across the screen. Where she expected to feel a surge of warmth, the sight of it shot a sense of unexpected anxiety through her as if she were somehow anticipating bad news.

"Hey! There you are," she greeted him, nonetheless. She pressed her phone to her ear because her earbuds were buried at the bottom of her purse.

"Hey, Gem," Patrick said. Jet lag slowed his voice like thick syrup, but Gemma detected an edge to his tone.

"What's wrong?"

"Gemma?" a barista called over the squeal of milk mercilessly being steamed into boiling froth. The young man with flannel sleeves rolled to his elbows wedged four to-go cups into a cardboard tray and slid it across the counter.

Gemma threw up a hand to let him know she was the customer coming to collect. She pushed her way through the herd of phone tappers and squeezed her own phone to her ear with her shoulder. The crowd was distracting her, but a flicker of familiarity danced like a flame in her brain. She repeated her question to her brother.

"Patrick? What's wrong?"

She smiled at the barista with a nod and grabbed her tray before turning back into the busy room.

"I'm stuck in New York."

"You're what?"

Gemma turned sideways to slip through a gap in the line and head for the exit. She could hardly hear him through all the noise—on her end and his.

"My first flight took off late, and I missed the connection." He audibly yawned, and Gemma envisioned him running a hand through his shaggy blond surfer hair and scrubbing his baby face. They shared fair hair and brown eyes, though Patrick's tended toward an enviable shade of hazel. "I'm trying to get another, but I might check into a hotel and sleep for a week."

"What?" Gemma fought her way toward the door, phone squeezed to ear, one hand holding the tray and the other balancing the cups from the top, and purse swinging from her arm. Her heart sank at the thought of waiting longer to see him, and she got the sense she'd had the same sinking feeling before. "Don't do that!"

He laughed. "I'm kidding, Gem. Don't freak out."

"I'm not freaking out."

"Yes, you are. I can hear it in your voice. I've known you for twenty-five years, remember?"

"Aren't you twenty-six now?"

"Am I? I don't know. I've lost count."

She smiled, missing him more. "Just come home."

The noise on his end grew louder. She imagined him in a crowded New York airport, bedraggled and wrinkled, surrounded by a steady stream of travelers threatening to swallow him whole.

"I'm working on it." His voice drifted as if he had held the phone away.

"Patrick?"

"Yeah, I'm here. I'm reading this board . . ." He trailed off, then came back with a burst of energy. "Oh! I'm gonna go see if I can get on standby for this 11:45."

Gemma pulled her phone away to check the time and did some quick math. "That's in a half an hour. Aren't they already boarding?"

"Yep. Gotta go!" he blurted, and disappeared into a muffle.

"Okay! But please—"

The words *tell me if you get on* dissolved on her tongue because he had ended the call.

She looked down at her phone with a frown and looked up right in time to see a broad-shouldered man with tousled brown hair staring at his own phone crash straight into her.

"Whoa!" she blurted as they collided in a fantastic display of exploding to-go cups and spewing coffee. Frothy brown liquid—*hot* liquid—splashed her chest like a wave and splattered the floor. The cups clattered and rolled. An ice cube from her drink found its way into her bra. The kind of mortifying, deafening hush that only follows a loud, public accident swept the room as she struggled to gain her balance. To top it all off, she slipped in the seeming *gallons* of liquid that had somehow managed to drain from the four reasonably sized cups.

The man reached out, struggling on his own, and gripped her arms in a desperate effort to keep both of them from hitting the floor.

"I'm so sorry!" he said as they just managed to stay on their feet. "I wasn't watching where I was going. Are you okay?"

She was a dripping, sticky, possibly burned mess. Her favorite blouse was ruined. She'd have to change and was going to be late for work now. An insistent ice cube was getting intimate with her left boob.

But all of that disappeared when she heard his voice.

She knew that voice.

She looked up and saw eyes that she knew too. Shining, slightly tired blue eyes that looked like they held a secret.

She blinked and shook herself. It was impossible. She had never seen him before but also felt like she'd known him for years.

He stared at her, searching with an earnestness that warmed her face.

The feeling of something familiar slipping through her fingers returned, except the familiar thing was holding on to her with a substantial amount of force, she realized. As if he didn't want to let go.

"Do I . . . ?" The words slowly left her mouth, and she wasn't sure where they were headed.

His eyes brightened. He leaned forward like he desperately wanted her to continue.

The rest of the coffee shop returned to life around them.

Chatter resumed. The milk steamer squealed. An irritated barista came over to mop up the mess, her face set in a scowl that implied she was the true casualty of the collision.

But Gemma tuned it all out. She couldn't stop staring at the stranger staring at her.

"Do you what?" he asked.

The look on his face, Gemma couldn't quite place it, and it didn't look appropriate for having smashed into someone carrying four cups of coffee and living to tell the soggy tale, but she swore it looked like . . . hope.

Her thoughts had veered off into an irrational place. She kept careful inventory of the people she knew; she could count most of them on four hands, and she was certain on a very confident level that she did not know this man. But at the same time, the familiarity about him was as striking as a brilliant sunset. She could not ignore it.

The only way forward that she could see was to ask.

"Do I . . . know you?"

To call the look on his face relief would have been an understatement. Sheer joy blossomed, lighting his eyes and lifting his lips into a smile. Gemma got the distinct sense that she had seen the look before. He squeezed her arms where he still held them and nodded.

"Yes, you do."

CHAPTER
3

THE MAN LOOKED like he wanted to kiss Gemma right there in the crowded coffee shop. Strangely, she had a curious feeling that they had in fact kissed before.

But that was impossible.

Gemma didn't go around kissing men and then forgetting about it. Certainly not ones with soft pouty lips and big blue eyes. She would *definitely* remember doing that.

And did she remember it?

Flashes of familiarity nipped at her brain like parrotfish on coral. She knew this guy but didn't remember him at the same time. And he obviously knew her—the look on his face almost matched the blind relief of homecoming that she expected to see on Patrick's face in a matter of hours.

And that left her in a very odd position.

Despite their already humiliating coffee collision, she didn't want to embarrass him by telling him he had the wrong girl. Nor did she want to embarrass herself by admitting she did not know who he was despite whatever previous meeting had him gazing at her like the promised land.

Gemma forced herself to feel the floor beneath her feet

and shifted to reclaim her balance. She removed her arm from the man's hand and politely laughed. "I'm sorry, but I can't seem to remember—"

He all but lunged at her. "*Yes!* Yes you can, Gemma. I see it in your eyes."

At the sound of her name, she stepped back. Their encounter had crossed from charming-meet-cute-misunderstanding to downright concerning in a snap.

"How do you know my name?"

"Because I know you. And you know me! I'm Jack." He pressed his hand to his chest and reached for her with his other. His words came out in a rush. "We met last night at your friend's birthday party. Well, technically it's tonight, and technically it hasn't happened for you yet, but we know each other, I swear."

Gemma pulled from his grip and stepped farther away. She knew L.A. attracted some weirdos, but this guy was pushing it.

A desperate, startled look shot across his face. "Okay, I know that sounded absurd, but let me explain." He stopped reaching for her and calmly held up his hands like she was a frightened animal about to bolt. "I'm sorry if I startled you, but weird things have been happening to you today, right? You've been remembering things? Feeling like they've happened before?"

The fact that he knew that made her want to run away at the same time it made her want to listen.

He recognized the willingness on her face; he had her ear at least, if only hesitantly. He slowly nodded. "It's because it *has* happened before." He waved his hands between them like he was casting a spell over a cauldron. "This. Us."

Gemma glanced around the room. The spectacle they had provided with the coffee fountain was already old news. But even with everyone having gone back to business and appearing to ignore them, she searched for knowing eyes, because she had obviously stumbled into some kind of hidden-camera prank, and someone was watching. It was the only explanation for this handsome stranger having plowed into her, called her by name, and then insisted that they knew each other. The fact that he knew about her otherwise strange morning was admittedly more difficult to explain. But she would not succumb and make a fool of herself. Even if she wanted to throw herself at him, grip his lovely forearms—had she seen that vintage wristwatch before?—and confess that he was completely right, she would not turn herself into a viral video for the sake of a joke.

She gathered herself and searched for a reason to end their confrontation. "Sorry. I have to call my brother," she said when she realized she was holding her phone. How she had not dropped it in the collision, she wasn't sure. And how it avoided a sticky, scalding latte bath was nothing short of a miracle.

She turned to step away, and he lunged at her again.

"No, you don't, Gemma. Your brother doesn't make it."

She wheeled on him in horror. "*What?!*"

Visions of a fiery plane crash must have been written all over her face because he visibly backpedaled.

"Oh god, no! Not like that! Sorry. I mean he takes another flight and gets stuck in Atlanta, or Dallas, or Salt Lake City. One time in San Francisco and tries to rent a car to drive the rest of the way. I meant he never makes it *here*, to L.A., anytime today. At least he never has before."

The synapses in her brain had instantly fired *disaster* as soon as he said Patrick didn't make it. She was so quick to worry about her brother's safety that she completely forgot to wonder how this stranger could have impossibly full knowledge of his travel plans.

She reeled for the third time in what felt like as many minutes.

"How do you know my brother is trying to fly here?"

Jack took a big breath as if in effort to calm them both. He held her gaze with his bright, pleading eyes. "Because I told you: this has happened before."

She watched him with growing uncertainty at the same time she felt he was sure he knew what he was talking about. He spoke with enough conviction to mean either he was telling the truth or he was completely delusional. Despite herself, Gemma hoped for the former, even though it might make her delusional as well, because she didn't want to think that this handsome man was trapped in some unfortunate prison of his own mind's making.

"Please," he said. "Let's go sit down and I can explain." He gestured to an empty table in the window.

Gemma felt like a stranger was offering her a ride off the street. *Don't get in the car* had been beaten into her head like every young woman's. This wasn't a car, but indulging him felt as precarious as buckling up with a potential madman behind the wheel.

He sensed her reluctance and sighed. He checked his watch and gave her a weary look. "I was hoping I wouldn't have to do anything like this so early on, but your brother is going to call you in about thirty seconds and tell you he missed that 11:45 flight, but he's trying for another."

Gemma gaped at him, her mind a scramble of impossibility. Silence stretched between them while her heart pounded in her ears. She was tempted to walk out the door and forget everything about their strange encounter, but the certainty in his voice glued her to the floor.

Thirty seconds expanded into an eternity. She did and didn't want Patrick to call. All at once, it could explain everything and nothing.

Jack watched her, holding his breath.

How could he have any idea? she wondered as her phone buzzed to life in her hand.

Patrick Peters.

She stared at it in shock before numbly lifting it. "Hello?" Her voice was a hoarse whisper.

"Hey, Gem." He was out of breath. "I missed that 11:45, but I'm trying for another."

Her first thought was that her brother, her beloved little brother who did appreciate a good joke, was in on the elaborate hoax. Maybe he was already in L.A., sitting in the same coffee shop and watching her fall victim to whatever scheme had been hatched at her expense all for a laugh.

But she could not think of why anyone would want to play a trick on her.

All she knew was that the man in front of her had predicted exactly what was happening, right down to the very words Patrick said.

"Gem? You there?"

Her mouth hung open like a flytrap. "Yeah," she said with a stunned shake of her head. "I'm here."

"Good. Thought I lost you. Well, the good news is I'm officially on standby now. There's another plane in an hour, and if one of these unfortunate souls doesn't show up on time, I'll have a seat." The signature pep of caffeine inflected his speech. Gemma was certain he'd downed a coffee since their last call.

She was still floundering.

"Unless there's no hurry and I can kick it in New York for a few days . . ." Patrick said in her silence, the hope in his voice unmistakable.

"No, no, please come home," she pleaded, and she felt like she had said the words before.

He sighed. "All right. Thoughts and prayers for standby. I'll let you know if I have any luck."

Jack was staring at Gemma with a knowing, if not slightly patronizing look on his face.

"Wait, Patrick—" she blurted before he vanished into the airport chaos. "Where was that 11:45 headed?"

"L.A., duh," he said with the air of his younger self.

Gemma had a sudden vision of a gangly teenager wearing an obscure band's tee shirt and dirty Chucks. There was a high probability Patrick was wearing the same thing, his signature uniform, at that very moment.

She couldn't help the smug smile that spread across her lips. She aimed it at Jack and hoped he could hear her brother all but shouting over the background noise on his end and proving him wrong. "Right. Of course it was."

"Layover in Dallas, though," Patrick said. "Gotta go!"

Jack tilted his head with his own smug smile and motioned to the empty table in the window. "Shall we?"

Gemma lowered her phone and closed her mouth, which had fallen open again. She stepped over the puddle the barista had smeared into gritty brown sludge in an attempt to clean it up and swiped a few napkins from the cart by the door. Less reluctant than she had been thirty seconds before, she followed Jack to the table.

He sat across from her. Their knees bumped beneath the small wooden surface. The feeling shot a jolt of recognition to a fold buried deep inside her brain.

She shook it away, looked down at the damage to her shirt, and dabbed her still-dripping chest with the napkins. At least the ice cube in her bra had melted.

"Sorry about that," Jack said. "I know that was your favorite shirt."

She stopped dabbing and looked up at him.

"Sorry. I'll stop saying things like that. I can see it's not working in my favor."

"Definitely not. Now, explain to me how we know each other again? Or, how you *think* we know each other?"

He spread his hands out on the tabletop and took a deep breath. Gemma noticed the vintage watch again and how it seemed to clash with his otherwise modern, casual appearance. It looked like something a man who wore a suit and tie to work would sport. Jack wore jeans, and a tee shirt that had been a shade of light blue that set off his eyes before it was splotched with pale brown latte. The shape of the stain on his chest looked like it could have been the other half of the Rorschach test on hers.

"Gemma, we've met before. Many times. I know this seems impossible to believe, but that interaction we just had? That wasn't the first time we've crashed into each other. It happens every day—*this* day. I know that's your favorite shirt because I've ruined it, over and over."

She blinked at him, at a loss. "What does that mean?"

He pressed his hands into the table and held her gaze like he was desperately gripping it with a fist. "It means that I know your name, and I know that's your favorite shirt, and I know your brother is stuck at JFK trying to get home to you because it has all happened before. This day has happened before. We have lived it before."

His explanation ended and left an expectant energy lingering in its wake. He watched her as if he wanted her to solve the rest of the puzzle. To put the implausible pieces together and be the one to speak the impossibility aloud.

She knew what he was talking about. She had seen it in plenty of movies, read it in many books.

A time loop.

The fictional circumstance that left someone cycling through the same day over and over for any host of reasons. Key word: *fictional*.

Because time loops weren't real. Not unless you were an unpleasant TV weatherman who needed to learn a lesson on a holiday honoring a rodent.

Jack read the skepticism on her face. "Listen, I know that sounds absurd—it is absurd! But I promise you, it's happening. How else would I know those things about you?"

She considered his valid question and reasoned that he could have overheard her phone conversation with her brother, and the barista had called her name for her order. But the fact about the shirt? She didn't think she'd ever mentioned this being her favorite shirt to anyone. She wasn't prone to declaring her love for inanimate objects online like Lila, so she had no idea how he could have known, even if he had somehow found her private social media accounts.

A chill suddenly shook her body. The thought of what

he already admitted to knowing about her was disturbing enough, but she realized that if what he was saying about living the day on repeat was true—which it *wasn't*—he probably knew all sorts of personal things about her.

She crossed her arms over her chest, feeling defensive. "Maybe you're stalking me."

"No." He shook his head. "I'm not, I swear. The first time I met you was exactly like today: I was looking at my phone, you were talking on yours, and we crashed into each other and spilled coffee everywhere."

He spoke with such bald honesty that she couldn't help humoring him.

"And then what?"

He sat back in his chair, relaxing a little that she hadn't jumped ship yet. "And then usually some variation of us apologizing and you leaving ensues."

She mulled it over and agreed it sounded plausible since leaving was exactly what she intended to do in the very near future.

A thought suddenly struck her.

"Wait, if you knew that was going to happen, why did you still crash into me?"

"Because I needed to see if you recognized me, to see if you remembered me."

The desperation in his voice was as plain as the day was sunny. She almost felt bad for him, this strange, beautiful man telling stories of impossible realities.

"Why not just ask me, then?" she said, and looked down at her ruined shirt. It could have been spared, if only.

"Would you have believed me?"

By the way he said it, she got the sense that he had perhaps attempted to just ask her before in one of his alt-realities and received unfavorable results.

"No," she said. "But I also don't believe you now, so it seems the only loss here is of my favorite shirt and fifteen minutes of my morning."

"Gemma, wait," he said when she started to stand. "Please. This is the furthest we've ever gotten. Hang with me on this." He reached out a hand, pleading like he was fully aware of how unhinged he sounded. His lips curved into a half smile that suddenly yanked her into a memory.

Except the memory was half dream.

A crowded bar. A bitter drink. A familiar song. That smile. And the best kiss of her life.

Feeling her whole body tingle with a sensation she couldn't name, almost as if her limbs had gone to sleep from lying on them wrong, she slowly sank back into her chair.

Jack nodded at her, letting his lips fill out the other half of his smile. "Do you remember?"

She did not want to expose herself by answering. She cleared her throat with a shake of her head, searching for her bearings. "Okay, so if all this has happened before, what changed? Why is today different?"

The full wattage of his smile broke out, and she was glad she had sat down. "Because I tested a theory."

She could not deny that her interest was piqued.

She nodded at him to continue.

He gazed out the window for a moment, watching the street. She studied the line of his jaw, the light brown stubble on his chin. He had a classic look about him, and she wondered if he was an actor. The thought sent her spiraling into another tunnel of doubt: it was all made up, someone had hired him to prank her, and he was doing an excellent job of getting her to fall for it.

But the thoughts dissolved when he turned back and gave her a look too sincere to be faked.

"Gemma, I walk through this day every day, over and over. I've turned every stone and looked in every corner, trying to find my way out of it, and I can't. It's all the same dead ends no matter what I do. The only glitch—the *only* thing that varies in the slightest—is you. It took me a while to realize it, but you're the key. You have to be. Every time I run into you, I feel the earth tilt, like gravity is shifting, and I think you feel it too. It's like we're on a collision course with each other—literally—and I think . . . I think we're meant to do more than apologize and walk away." He softly chuckled and ran a hand through his hair. It was cut somewhere between short and shaggy and fell in a messy, shiny tumble that made Gemma bite her lip. "But the problem is, you always walk away. Some days, it takes longer than others, and sometimes I can convince you to stick around for a while, but you never stay. Not really. I've been trying to get you to remember me, but your memory is wiped every morning, just like everyone else's, which feels *really* unfair since you're the only person I've ever met who I've actually wanted to have remember me." He faded out with a soft, sad laugh and stroked his chin.

Gemma stared at him. It was either the most romantic or the most irrational thing she had ever heard, and she realized, profoundly, that the difference between those two options might be less than she'd thought.

"Then why do I remember you today?"

The words slipped out. She was under the spell of his

story, momentarily untethered from reality and wanting to buy into his explanation for the morning's confusion and the undeniable pull she did in fact feel toward him.

He smiled again. "I think because we kissed last night."

Gemma flushed, startled. "We *kissed*?"

He nodded. "We did. Finally. At your friend's birthday party. I wanted to see if that would make you remember me; it's part of my theory. And by the looks of today, it worked. Kind of."

Gemma was reeling all over again. The vision she'd had moments before that felt like a dream—the bar, the kiss— had actually happened, if he was to be believed. She could barely wrap her mind around it.

"What do you mean, 'kind of'?"

He sighed and leaned back again. "Well, you seem to remember me to some extent, but you weren't aware that today is a temporal anomaly until I told you, right?"

She had no idea what was right or wrong, but the term suddenly jarred her out of the fantasy like a whole bag of ice cubes down her bra. It sounded like something he'd found on a subthread of a subthread on a conspiracy website.

She arched one dubious brow at him. "A *temporal anomaly*?"

He held up his hands. "Okay, I can see that I'm losing you, but give me a chance—"

She checked the time and saw that she needed to get to work. She had wasted enough energy on this stranger and his sci-fi theories of déjà vu gone wild. She kicked herself for almost buying it. Good guys didn't just fall into your lap and tell you wild, swoony stories about your being the key to their rescue like some warped fairy tale. Good guys probably didn't even exist. Or if they did, she had yet to meet one.

She stood with more resolve than she had the first time. "Listen, Jake—"

"It's Jack."

"You seem like a nice guy—strange—but nice. I wish I could help with whatever is going on, but I have to go."

He scrambled out of his chair quickly enough to send it scraping across the floor. A few heads turned. "Wait, Gemma, please."

A small headache had taken root at the base of her skull, and she realized that despite being bathed in it, she hadn't actually had a single sip of coffee that morning.

"Goodbye, Jack."

He trailed after her, making a scene almost as embarrassing as the coffee incident. "Don't leave, please! Just let me try—"

She stopped and pivoted to face him. He almost crashed into her again. "Listen, I don't know what you do all day, but *I* have to get to work. I have a busy, important day, and I'm already going to be late since I have to go back home and get a new shirt since you ruined this one!" Her voice rose and turned a few more heads. She hadn't realized how annoyed she had grown, and she frankly didn't care that she was taking it out on him.

To her shock, Jack stood there grinning rather than looking affronted that she had snapped at him.

"Why are you smiling?"

He folded his arms, stretching his stained tee shirt over muscles Gemma had not previously noticed. "You're not going to be late for work."

"What are you talking about?"

"Check your phone."

She hated to humor him, but he had been right about her brother calling.

She looked, and her carefully monitored inbox showed a new message from one of her VIP contacts: her boss, Marsha.

Hey gang,

Bradly has a stomach bug, so I'm out this morning. Run one of the canned shows from last month. I'll try to be there for Nigel Black this afternoon, but no promises. Might have to cancel the interview.

—M

Gemma read the brief email and felt the ache in her head throb. Canceling Nigel Black, rock legend and personal idol, would be a disaster. She'd spent months wrangling him. He was in L.A. for one night for part of his comeback tour—an event that had sold out in minutes, much to her despair. It was a miracle she even got him on their calendar. But the personal blow to her hard work aside, the takeaway was that Jack had been right: she wasn't going to be late for work because work had effectively been canceled for the morning. Carmen would be in the studio already, always early, and she'd plug something canned into the program without anyone aware the show had been taped weeks before. And the worst realization of all, the whole unfolding scenario felt somehow familiar.

She looked up at Jack.

"Boss's kid still sick?" he said with an annoyingly proud grin.

She scowled at him and turned for the door, ready to get away.

"You know I'm right, Gemma! This is really happening!" he called behind her.

She stepped out onto the sidewalk and let the sun kiss her face. The warmth and the semifresh air washed away her frustration for a quick second. Traffic rolled up and down the street, but she could still find a gap to dash through to her car. She took two steps in that direction before she got an overwhelming, inexplicable urge to stop walking.

She froze right before a teenager on a skateboard came scraping down the sidewalk, barreling out of nowhere, and sped past her fast enough to throw her hair sideways and miss her by inches.

"Sorry, lady!" he called over his shoulder.

Gemma's heart leapt up into her throat and she gasped. She hardly had time to recover before Jack was at her side, gripping her arm in excitement.

"You moved!" he shouted at her. His eyes sparkled in the sun. "You knew that was going to happen, didn't you?"

She stumbled for balance. She couldn't say if she had known consciously, but like with what Mr. Weaver said about the weather and the little girls playing in the flooded street—and, if she was being honest, the feeling she got when she first saw Jack—it felt wildly familiar.

She turned on Jack with another glare. "Wait. Did *you* know that was going to happen, and you didn't warn me?"

He gave her a guilty shrug. "I don't know the rules about what we can mess with."

"So, you were going to let me get hit by a speeding skate-boarder?" she shouted at him, and stomped away.

"You wouldn't have gotten hurt! He just kind of elbows you as he goes by!"

She was halfway across the street and didn't want to hear any more. Apparently, the busted treadmill and empty coffee bin were signs of what was to come before she had even left the house. She would have stayed home had she known she would have scalding lattes poured all over her and nearly been run over by a skater. Not to mention met a strange, handsome man whose considerable charm was quickly evaporating.

A thought struck her as she reached her car. She opened the driver's door and turned back to face the other side of the street. Thankfully, Jack hadn't followed her. He stayed on the opposite sidewalk as if the traffic between them were a moat he could not cross.

"If you don't know what you are allowed to mess with, why are you messing with me?" she shouted over the passing cars. A stoplight down the street had turned green, releasing a wave of noise.

Jack cupped his hands to yell over the rush. "Because I told you! You're the key, Gemma!"

CHAPTER
4

GEMMA CLIMBED IN her car and slammed the door. She had no idea what Jack meant. She wasn't the key to anything, especially not this mysterious time loop he seemed to believe they were stuck inside.

But what about everything he knew? Her shirt, her brother, her morning getting canceled. And they had *kissed*?

None of it made sense.

She pulled into traffic, needing to clear her mind and get some perspective on it all. And she knew exactly who could give it to her.

But first, she had to check in with work.

She poked her touch screen console to pull up Carmen's phone number.

"*Yell*-o," she answered in her husky voice after a few rings. Gemma pictured her in the studio leaning back in a chair with her combat boots kicked up on the soundboard. Hugo, their sound tech, would show up and scold her, and she would flick his ear. Working in close quarters on a daily basis made them all feel a bit like siblings.

"Hey. Are you good to cover this morning? I saw Marsha's email."

"Already covered, Gemstone."

She heard a slurping sound and knew Carmen was finishing one of the protein smoothies she favored for breakfast. Few things annoyed Hugo more than a straw sucking air at the bottom of an empty cup. Gemma didn't mind it.

"Great. I have something I have to take care of, so I won't be in for a while."

"Well, when the cat's away . . ."

Gemma smirked and switched lanes to head toward the freeway on-ramp. "That's not it. I actually have something to deal with."

She heard a shuffle and a *thunk* and pictured Carmen rocking forward to put the chair's feet on the floor. "Everything all right?"

She honestly didn't know how to answer, though she appreciated the concern. There was the fact that she was still damp with coffee, and that her brother was not on his way home, not yet at least. And the whole potential *stuck in a time loop* thing.

"Yes," she said, because she hadn't planned to explain it all to Carmen. She needed to tell someone a little safer than her coworker—even a coworker whom she considered a friend. She needed the protection of unconditional support first.

"If you say so. What are we going to do with Nigel Black if Marsha can't do the interview?"

She chewed her lip at the thought of what would happen

with that particular predicament. "Not sure yet, but let's hope we don't have to cancel."

"Well, *you* could always do it, you know . . ."

"Ha," Gemma said flatly as she accelerated onto the freeway.

Music lived in her blood. She played a few instruments, sure, but she would never be onstage. She had never wanted that, and the mere thought of such exposure terrified her anyway. What existed in her veins was a passion for the *people* in music: the stories, the history. The human experience tied up in creating the most universally relatable art form. She wanted to talk to those people, to hear what they had to say and then share it. The closest she'd come was producing a small but up-and-coming live radio show in the heart of the entertainment industry—which was miles closer than most would make it—but she had yet to work up the nerve to actually interview someone on air. Starting with Nigel Black, her favorite singer of all time, would be like climbing Everest without so much as ever going on a hike first. But still, the thought was exhilarating.

"I'm serious," Carmen said. "You scripted the interview, and we all know you're a closet fangirl."

She was right on both counts, but she didn't know Gemma's history with Nigel. She didn't know he was the first famous person she'd ever met, her idol even back then, and her seven-year-old brain forced her to freeze up like a statue. All the adults had laughed and insisted her shyness was cute, Nigel included, but Gemma had never gotten over it.

"Come on, Gemma," Carmen said in her silence. "I think you're ready. And it's no secret you want to host. You just have to show Marsha that you can do it."

Gemma considered for a minute. Her boss knew she wanted to host her own show, and Gemma was right on the cusp. She only needed to step up and prove herself—and the opportunity was hanging right in front of her like a big, juicy berry. But of course it had to be Nigel. The *one* artist she couldn't possibly face now stood between her current life in the production booth and the one in front of the mic where she longed to be.

"If Marsha wanted me to do it, she would have said so instead of suggesting canceling it," Gemma said, dismayed and discouraged.

"*I'm* saying so," Carmen said. "Come on. What are you so afraid of? All you have to do is ask him the questions you wrote. Easy."

Easier said than done, Gemma thought. Her fear of Nigel was one thing, but the bigger issue holding her back was one she kept close to her chest. She hadn't told anyone, aside from her therapist, the true reason she held back in her career, and waffling over interviewing her favorite rock star provided a convenient excuse to keep it that way.

"I'm not canceling it," Carmen said. "If you don't want to talk to your old-man crush, it's up to you to pull the plug."

Gemma's face flushed as she thought about the choice before her. Through the whole saga of getting Nigel Black on the show, she had only dealt with his people. She'd planned to merely shake his hand when he arrived at the studio and pray he didn't remember her as a shy seven-year-old before Marsha, seasoned, intriguing Marsha, swept in and monopolized his attention. Though terrifying, she could not deny that getting to talk to him face-to-face and ask him all her questions would be a dream come true.

If she could get any words to come out of her mouth.

At least she had a few hours to figure it out.

Gemma sighed as she passed a slow-moving minivan. "Gotta go, Carmen. See you soon."

"Ten-four. You know where to find us."

She jabbed the screen to end the call and opened a text message to dictate.

"I'm coming over; I hope you're up," she said slowly and clearly to her console. She knew from experience that speaking too fast resulted in jumbled, often comical translations.

She hit send and settled into her seat to slide down the 101 toward Silver Lake. The tight cluster of skyscrapers in downtown L.A. poked up like a crown from the smog in the distance. As the city came to life, she would have to keep an eye on traffic to avoid getting stuck, especially if she was going to be running around when she normally would be at work.

It took twenty minutes to get to Lila's complex from her own, a drive Gemma knew well. She had a slight head start, having left from the coffee shop. She poked her console to turn up the radio's volume, and her favorite song came rushing through the speakers.

She almost swerved into the next lane at the sound of it.

She knew all the lyrics; she and Lila used to sing it in their dorm room. It wasn't a shock to hear the classic pop song on the radio more than a decade after it had come out. The shock was the image of Jack it conjured in her mind. She suddenly saw him softly smiling at her as she told him it was her favorite song. The hazy mental picture blurred around the edges like an old photograph. It triggered the same murky feeling his smile had back in the coffee shop, and that same fold deep in her brain that had sparked faintly when his knee bumped hers beneath the table now lit up like New Year's Eve in Times Square.

It was all familiar, which made no sense at all. Unless, of course, Jack had been telling the truth about everything and she had in fact met him and they'd shared smiles and knee nudges and listened to her favorite song together.

"Impossible," she said, and poked the console to change the station.

She blindly selected a classical music channel and let the innocuous tones of strings and horns score her drive. She tapped her thumbs on the steering wheel and told herself it was all a coincidence. There wasn't an ounce of truth to any of it.

There was also the chance that she was dreaming and would wake to the feeling of Rex's wet nose in her palm any moment. That seemed like a much more likely explanation.

"Wake up, wake up, wake up," she muttered, trying to will herself into consciousness despite being behind the wheel in high-speed traffic. She was pretty sure she was already awake, but it didn't hurt to double-check.

An incoming call cut through the soaring symphony filling her cocoon, and she saw her brother's name on the screen.

She pressed the button on her steering wheel to answer as fast as she could. "Patrick?"

"No, this is your other brother," he said, deadpan.

Her lips twitched into a smile despite her distress. "Any news?"

"Yeah, actually. Things are looking good for this 1:15. They've called Alan Nguyen's name like ten times, and he's a no-show. That seat's as good as mine."

"Good!" she cheered. "Well, not good for Alan Nguyen, but good for you."

"Yep. It'll be a quick stopover in Atlanta, then I'm Cali-bound."

Gemma's heart felt like it sank through the floorboards and bounced down the freeway behind her. "Atlanta?"

"Yeah. It's only, like, an hour to change flights in between, so hopefully everything stays on schedule."

Jack's words came back to her: *He gets stuck in Atlanta, Dallas, or Salt Lake City.* As did the feeling she'd had this conversation with Patrick before.

She didn't want to admit there was a chance Jack had been right, but she also didn't want her brother moving essentially parallel to his current location and no farther west.

"Are there any direct flights?"

"Not with open seats. And they told me I had a better shot with layovers on standby. Or maybe another California airport, and I could rent a car to finish the trip. There's a two p.m. into San Francisco—"

"Don't go to San Francisco!" she blurted. Her heart had picked up speed and was beating somewhere near her tonsils.

"What? Why? What's wrong with San Francisco?"

She didn't know how to explain that a stranger had told her he'd get stuck in any attempt to cross the country, and that the stranger had so far been right. Sounding unhinged over the phone would only make Patrick try harder to get home, and who knew where he'd end up then.

"That's . . . a really long drive."

He sighed. "Well, you're the one who wants me home so badly, Gem."

Guilt roiled inside her. He was right, she was the one making demands.

A silence stretched before he spoke again.

"I've been thinking, and I think you should still go see him if I don't make it in time."

Fear that he would say such a thing had been quietly simmering in the back of her mind since she first got word he was delayed. She hadn't liked the idea then, and she didn't like it now.

"No, Patrick. I'm not going without you."

He paused and came back soft, knowing that her opinion on the matter was tainted by a painful history with their father that he did not share a memory of. "Gem."

She did not want to have the argument, and especially not over the phone. Thankfully, she had arrived at Lila's complex.

"I have to go. Try to find a direct flight," she said with big-sister authority she rarely wielded. She ended the call without giving him the chance to protest.

She parked in one of the guest stalls below Lila's apartment and fought off the negative feelings threatening to cloud her already challenging morning. Patrick meant well, but he did not understand on her same level. He would never understand because his infant brain hadn't been developed enough to grasp the significance of the events that had torn their family apart. But she remembered everything.

She shook herself from the thoughts and remembered why she had come to see Lila.

She needed a reality check.

The small stucco apartment building had emerald trim that set off the palms rustling in the breeze. Lila lived on the second floor, which made for challenges when her sponsors sent large packages that needed hoisting and extra hands. Once, an online bespoke furniture company had been making a play for Millennials, and they wanted shots of Lila lounging in their signature piece. Gemma had helped her carry the blue velvet armchair up the switchback stairs while they giggled and shouted *Pivot!* at each other like that episode of *Friends*.

The things Lila had done to maintain and elevate her status.

People often thought influencers lived easygoing, relaxed lives, simply taking selfies with beautiful things in beautiful places, because that was the image they carefully cultivated online, but Lila hustled nonstop. She filmed and edited almost all her own content. She only slept in because she was up late working every night.

She hadn't responded to Gemma's text, which Gemma hoped didn't mean she was about to wake her with a knock on the front door.

Gemma climbed the outdoor stairs with the sun on her back. The smell of someone's breakfast, bacon in particular, wafted through an open window. She made note to ask Lila for a cup of coffee once she confirmed she was not losing her mind.

She knocked, and the door opened almost immediately.

One of Lila's manicured hands with bright red nails appeared on the doorframe. She pulled the door partway and rested the other hand high on the wood like she was posing inside the slim opening. "Good—" she started with a sultry smile, and stopped. "Oh. Gemma. What are you doing here?"

She wore a silk robe with a loud palm tree print to match the silk scarf tied above her forehead. The ensemble made her look like an old Hollywood siren and set off her green eyes. Her bright face was dewy with a morning acid peel or chemical cleanse or organic moisturizer Gemma was sure she was testing. She smelled like grapefruit.

"Hi," Gemma said. "I texted you that I was coming over. I need to ask you something."

Concern flashed over Lila's face. She let go of the door and folded her arms. "An a.m. house call; this must be important. What's up?"

Gemma took a breath and mustered the courage to say what she had settled on to start things off. "I need you to tell me what day it is today."

Lila laughed. "What are you talking about? *It's my birthday, bitch*," she said in her best Britney Spears impression while jerking her neck side to side.

Gemma normally would have laughed, but she kept quiet.

Lila suddenly grew serious. "What's wrong? You look weird. Why do you look weird?"

Gemma had Lila's undivided attention for all of five more seconds before her eyes flashed at something over her shoulder. Her face lifted, then fell into the same sultry expression she had been wearing when she opened the door.

Quick, focused footsteps pounded up the stairs, and Gemma turned to see a very good-looking man in a delivery uniform appear on the landing. He held a box with big hands attached to big arms that looked like they could carry a blue velvet armchair up the stairs with no fuss. At the sight of him, Gemma noted the sound of a delivery truck idling in the parking lot below.

"Hey, *Tyrell*," Lila sang like his name had ten Ls.

"Morning, Lila. Anything good today?"

Gemma stepped aside and let him hand the box to Lila. She shook it and her face split into a grin. "Always. You can come in for a citrus peel, if you'd like."

A laugh rumbled deep in Tyrell's broad chest. "I'll take a rain check. Have a good one!" He bounded back down the stairs and left Lila gazing after him like a hungry lioness.

Gemma knowingly smiled and watched her friend's face flush under the citrus peel.

"What?" Lila asked.

"So that's what all this is?" Gemma waved a hand over her ensemble. She would have answered her own door barefoot in a hoodie if someone came calling first thing in her day.

"What? No. I wear this every morning," Lila said.

"Yeah, and I bet you see Tyrell every morning too with all the deliveries you get."

Lilah shrugged in surrender. "Okay, yes. But if *that* showed up at your door every day, would you not put on something nice too?" She gestured to the parking lot, and Gemma turned to catch sight of Tyrell pulling himself into the open doorway of his truck in a way that made his arms and back ripple through his polo.

"Okay, fine," Gemma agreed.

"Thank you," Lila said with a smug tilt of her head. She turned to take her package inside, and Gemma followed.

Lila's apartment was a bohemian Instagram ad come to

life. Succulents and pampas grass, glass candle vases, jewel-toned furniture, and shaggy rugs. She did her best to store all her samples in her spare room, but the haul inevitably leaked into the living and dining rooms.

She plunked the new package down on her dining table among a small field of others and returned her attention to Gemma. "Why are you asking me what day it is? I hope you didn't forget my party tonight. You're not talking your way out of it," she said as if the Tyrell interruption had not happened. She found a pair of scissors and whipped open the blades with frightening dexterity.

The reminder of her party shot another memory through Gemma's mind. Jack said they had met at her friend's birthday party—and that they had kissed there. Seeing that the party hadn't happened yet, she didn't know what to make of it.

"I didn't forget your party," Gemma said, and realized the words carried a double meaning. She hadn't forgotten that the party was meant to take place that night, but according to Jack, she had forgotten that it had already happened. "I don't think," she added.

Lila sliced through the tape on her new package. She opened it and tore out a handful of tissue paper, then lifted a squat brown bottle with a simple white label. She unscrewed the cap and sniffed. "Yikes," she said with a grimace big enough to make her flinch. "Not looking good for five stars." She placed the bottle on the table, and Gemma saw the word *shampoo* under a logo she thought she might recognize from an internet ad. "What do you mean, you don't think? And what happened to your shirt?" Lila asked without looking up from her task.

Gemma had all but forgotten about the coffee stains, which were nearly dry. She realized, looking down at the abstract blotch of brown, that she could answer both of Lila's questions with the same piece of information.

"I met this guy."

Gemma worried Lila might have sprained her neck with how quickly she jerked her head up to look at her.

"You *what?*" She set the twin brown bottle of conditioner down without replacing the cap and hurried around to the other side of the table where Gemma stood. She gripped her arms. "When? Who is he? Tell me everything!" Excitement whipped out from her like gusts of wind in a hurricane. Gemma tried to step back but Lila had begun pulling her toward the living room, the offensive-smelling shampoo and conditioner abandoned.

They landed on her dusty rose sofa, also velvet, and Lila squealed in delight. She was so eager for Gemma to date that Gemma suspected she would overlook the senseless elements of the story she was about to hear. But it wasn't like Gemma and Jack had even gone out; one night at a party and a kiss that may or may not have actually happened did not count as a date.

"So, this is going to sound ridiculous, and I don't really believe it myself, but this morning at the coffee shop, I ran into this guy—literally"—she gestured down at her shirt—"and had the strangest feeling that I knew him even though I swear I've never met him before."

Lila studied her shirt and understood. "Accident meet-cutes are the best. Go on," she said, rapt.

"Well, he proceeded to tell me that we *have* met before, and not only that, we've apparently kissed before."

Lila sucked in a playful gasp large enough to pop her lungs. "*Gemma!* Kissing boys you don't remember? I *love* it! You totally deserve that freedom after Nick."

Her ex's name crashed into their conversation like an asteroid. Gemma didn't talk about him, and reminders of him, even a year after the implosion that damaged more than only her heart, still sent her staggering.

"Sorry," Lila said, reading it on her face. "It's the truth, but forget I brought him up. Please, continue telling me about this mystery man lucky enough to get a kiss from you."

Gemma took a breath, ready to get to the truly wild part. "That's the thing. I don't think it actually happened."

Lila's perfectly sculpted brows flattened. "So, what? He spills coffee on you and then gaslights you into thinking you know each other?"

"Pretty much."

She twisted her lips, and Gemma could see her trying to salvage the potential for a happily-ever-after. "Well, is he the kind of guy you would want to kiss? I mean, maybe he confused you for someone else and it's a fortunate misunderstanding, *also* an excellent meet-cute." She reached out and booped her with a finger.

Gemma shook her head. "No, he didn't. I swear I've never seen him, but he knows things about me, Lila."

She recoiled. "Ew. Stalker."

"That's what I thought too, but not only does he know things about me, he . . ."

She paused to consider bailing out at the last second. She hadn't yet mentioned any of the truly unbelievable parts of the story and could still spare herself the look of disbelieving concern about to cross Lila's pretty, grapefruit-scented face.

But telling her best friend the truth was the reason she had come here. If anyone was going to listen to her, it was the woman she shared clothes with and who used to snuggle in her twin bed when she got homesick at college.

She took a breath and dove in headfirst.

"He also knows things about today that haven't happened yet, to me at least, because he says we've been living this day over and over, but only he can remember it, and that I'm the key to breaking the cycle."

She waited for some kind of extreme reaction. Lila was going to gasp, growl like a mama bear concerned for her safety, check her temperature to make sure she wasn't fever dreaming, or maybe even burst out laughing.

But none of that happened.

She narrowed her eyes and then stood, holding out her hand. "Come on."

Gemma slipped hers into it, always willing to trust her. "Where are we going?"

Lila began pulling her toward her bedroom. "We're getting you a clean shirt and then we're going to see Aunt Clara."

Gemma planted her feet firmly in the shaggy white rug that remained white because Lila had no pets. "Oh no, Lila. I'm not going to Clara's."

Her protests did not deter her in the least. "Yes, you are. She has the Sight and will know what to do."

Visions of Lila's eccentric aunt holed up in her cramped Hollywood shop draped in shawls and beads and smelling of eye-watering incense momentarily made Gemma regret involving Lila at all.

"The only thing Clara has the sight for is duping tourists out of fifty bucks."

Lila glared at her over her shoulder as they entered her bedroom, another spread of boho-chic things that the internet loved. The blue velvet *Pivot!* chair sat in the corner beneath a hanging trapeze of rope planters. A tapestry covered one wall. A pile of accent pillows buried her bed. Gemma noted that the décor was only a stone's throw from looking like Aunt Clara's psychic cave, something she would have to monitor closely lest Lila reach a point of no return.

Lila loved her oddball aunt. She had spent summers in high school working in her shop and sometimes leaned into mysticism when other explanations failed. But that did not mean Gemma believed in any of it.

She sat on the bed as Lila went to her stuffed-to-the-gills closet to retrieve a clean shirt.

Lila came back with a tasteful sleeveless purple blouse dotted in tiny black velvet spots. The gold buttons on the low neck gave it a rock-'n'-roll edge. "Well, my dear, you just told me something rather odd, and if there's one person I know who can help explain odd, it's Aunt Clara, so that's where we're going. Here." She shoved the shirt at her and turned for her bathroom. "Give me ten minutes."

Gemma was left changing into the shirt and wondering what she was getting herself into.

"YOU KNOW, YOUR desperation to find me a boyfriend has reached concerning levels. I basically tell you this guy has no grasp on reality, and you drag me to a psychic to convince me otherwise," Gemma said as they approached Clara's shop.

Lila had donned an enormous sunhat and sunglasses that hid the majority of her face. Gemma knew it was not to disguise herself because they were entering an establishment of questionable reputation in one of the seedier parts of Hollywood, but because she hadn't had time to put on the full face of makeup that she always left the house wearing.

"I'm only doing what I would want you to do for me if the situation were reversed," Lila said.

"If the situation were reversed, I'd take you to a head doctor, not a psychic."

"Sorry, fresh out of shrinks on speed dial."

They rounded the corner of the boxy yellow building housing an eclectic strip of businesses: a public notary, a natural medicinal remedies shop, a Chinese restaurant, the remnants of an adult video store that had closed, and Psychic Readings by Clara. An apartment sat on the second floor of each shop. Bits of loose trash and leaves fluttered around the grungy sidewalk spotted with old chewing gum and who knew what else. The whole street was a band of short, flat-roofed buildings with telephone poles and power lines traipsing as far as the eye could see.

They stopped in front of Clara's shop, and the glass door speckled with business hours, a phone number, and the words *Crystal Ball*, which only made Gemma want to do an about-face, swung open before Lila could even reach for it and before Gemma got the chance to bolt.

Clara filled the entrance, her large body a vision in a flowing black dress with a silk shawl printed in noisy palm trees that looked alarmingly like the robe Lila had traded for her cropped denim overalls. A matching turban wrapped her head, and beaded jewelry dripped from every place it could be hung.

"My child!" she gasped, and threw a hand to her ample bosom. Aunt Clara was Lila's mother's sister, and the Thomas women were well-endowed. "I sensed you were on the way to see me. Come in! Quickly!" Clara whipped around in a swirl of robes and a fragrant burst of spicy incense.

Gemma turned and arched a brow at Lila. "Does she say that to everyone?"

Lila smirked, then pushed her toward the door. "You heard the woman. Get in there!"

They entered a dimly lit space where tapestries in bold prints covered every surface, saturating the room with rich colors. A round table with a fringed cloth sat in the center with an honest-to-god crystal ball on it along with a stack of tarot cards. To Gemma's surprise the room was empty.

"Where'd she go?" Gemma whispered, feeling like she needed to be quiet in the colorful cave.

"I don't know," Lila said, and then called, "Aunt Clara?"

Clara suddenly came bursting through the curtain hanging in the doorway at the back of the room, her arms spilling with candles. "Help me with these, Lila."

Lila hurried over and grabbed two of the tall white candles like she knew exactly what to do while Clara set about placing the others around the room. Clara put one atop the chest of drawers in the corner and flicked a lighter to set it flaming. She repeated the process across the room on an end table beside a wingback chair with scrolled arms and feet. Lila put another on the bookshelf down from the chest before she skipped across the room to place the other on a small shelf protruding from the wall. Clara set the final candle at the very back of the room on a table draped in black silk below an antique gold mirror.

Gemma traced the pattern with her eyes and realized they had laid out the five points of a star.

"Sit," Lila told her, and pointed to the round table in the center of it all.

Despite her own overwhelming skepticism, Gemma sensed the urgency in her friend's voice. Not to mention the tense energy pulsing off Clara in waves.

Gemma did what she was told as Clara moved around the room lighting all the other candles. Though Lila had told her many stories about Aunt Clara, and Gemma had met her years ago at Lila's graduation party and been to the shop once or twice, she had never experienced her services. She didn't know what she was supposed to do in the presence of a psychic.

She glanced at Lila sitting quietly beside her, waiting, and decided to do the same.

When Clara finished lighting the candles, she positioned herself in the chair across from them. With one thick arm, she moved the crystal ball and stack of tarot cards out of the way. "Those are for tourists," she said as if Gemma had asked and whatever she was about to do was much more serious. "Give me your hands, child."

Gemma glanced at Lila and got an encouraging nod in response. She slowly lifted her hands from her lap and placed them against Clara's palms waiting atop the table.

Clara sucked in a breath sharp enough to make Gemma jump. The connection between their palms broke for an instant before Clara reached up and gripped both of her hands. "I've never felt energy like this before."

"Energy like what, Aunt Clara?" Lila said, taking the bait.

"Hush! Let me read." Clara closed her eyes. Her lips slightly parted, and she muttered under her breath.

Gemma fought the urge to pull away. Clara had a tight grip, her hands surprisingly strong, but something else unseen kept Gemma in her chair.

"Today is a very important day for you," Clara said. Her voice had drifted off to a breathy whisper. "I see change. Reconciliation." A deafening silence, and then, "Love."

Gemma flinched. On reflex she tried to pull her hands away, but Clara only doubled down.

"But there's more." Clara's eyes had closed. They darted beneath her lids like mice under a rug. "I see a man. An important man." Her head tilted to the side. "He's trying to . . . give you a message . . . but he can't."

The air in Gemma's lungs went rigid. She could not stop herself from speaking. "Why not?" she whispered.

Clara squeezed her hands and gently shook her head. Her words came out like lyrics to a very slow song. "He can't . . . because he seems to be . . . stuck."

Lila's face whipped around. Gemma felt her eyes boring into her cheekbone, but she couldn't look away from Clara. Her heart was suddenly in her throat.

"Stuck where?"

Clara's amethyst earrings the size of quarters swung when she slowly shook her head. "That's the thing. I can't . . . see . . ." She trailed off, and Gemma feared what she would say next. "The path is not . . . straight. It does not go forward or backward. It's as if . . ." Her face scrunched in concentration. "It's as if . . . it's turning in on itself. Like a . . ."

Gemma's heart was about to beat out of her chest. If Clara's next word was what she thought it might be, she was going to lose it.

Clara's grip suddenly tightened. She sat rod straight, making both Lila and Gemma jump. Her eyes flashed open wide enough to see the whites all the way around. And then she said the thing Gemma feared she would.

"Like a loop."

Gemma tore her hands from her grip, and they slipped free, having grown slick with sweat. She stood up fast enough to send her chair tumbling backward to the floor. Before Lila or Clara could say anything, she turned and ran for the door.

She yanked it open and burst onto the sunny sidewalk. The light burned her eyes as she emerged from the dark cave. She threw an arm over her face and blindly ran straight into a wall.

"*Oof!*" the wall grunted. Then it proceeded to grab her arms to steady her.

Gemma blinked away the blinding light and refilled her lungs with the air that had been knocked out by the wall that was in fact not a wall, but a man. A man with shiny blue eyes and soft pouty lips that were bent in concern.

"You," Gemma said.

"Yes, me," Jack responded. "Are you all right?"

She was very much *not* all right, having had a psychic tell her wild, unbelievable stories about her own life, and she hadn't yet gathered herself before she ran smack into the source of those stories.

"I'm fine," she lied.

"Really? You don't look it."

She realized he was still holding her arms. The warmth of his hands made her skin tingle. For a moment, she appreciated it, and then she had a concerning thought.

"Did you follow me here?"

"Yes," he said factually and as if it were no big deal. "Did you just talk to a psychic?"

She moved out of his grip. "As a matter of fact, I did. And shouldn't you have *known* that because I've supposedly done it before?"

"I would have known, if you'd ever done this before," he said as if the whole thing were baffling to him too.

Gemma pulled up short, confused. "I've never come here?"

"No."

Right then, Lila burst through the shop door carrying Gemma's purse, which she had abandoned inside. "Well, you stumped her, Gem. Lucky for you, she said the reading is on the house because she's never seen anything like— Oh. Hello." She stopped yammering and paused, replacing her sunglasses midway up her nose. She eyed Jack up and down and flicked a brow. "Is this the guy?"

How Lila knew that, Gemma didn't know. Perhaps she too possessed some of Clara's Sight, which Gemma was starting to wonder if she did actually believe in.

"Lila," Jack said with the pleasant warmth of a friend. "Happy birthday."

Lila took a dramatic step back with a hand over her chest and suspiciously eyed him. Then her face broke out in a smile. "I see. I'm part of this too. Nice to meet you." She stuck out an arm to shake his hand, and Gemma smacked it away.

"Don't encourage him!"

"Ouch!" Lila cradled her hand, looking affronted, and then she tsked at Gemma and reached out again. "Potentially delusional aside, Gem, you could do a lot worse. Nice to meet you, though I hear we've met before." She said it all right to Jack's face, and he took it in stride.

He shook her hand with a smile. "Indeed we have, but always a pleasure. Jack."

"You can't be serious right now," Gemma muttered, feeling betrayed.

"Oh, stop it, Gem. You heard Aunt Clara. This is *real.*"

"Yeah, about as real as that knockoff Louis Vuitton handbag you bought in the Fashion District."

Lila gasped like she had been punched, far more offended by the suggestion that her favorite buttery yellow purse was fake than the idea that she'd been duped by this stranger. "I will forgive that comment because I know you are under stress right now."

"I wouldn't be under stress if you weren't acting like none of this is *very strange!*"

"Of course it's strange!" she declared, and gripped Gemma's shoulders. She shook her and rattled her brain. "But strange isn't always bad! Maybe you should give it a chance. And by *it*, I mean him." She pivoted Gemma to face Jack, who was watching their exchange like it was very entertaining.

"I think you should listen to Lila," Jack said. "She never steers you wrong."

Lila leaned in close to Gemma's ear. "Oh, he's smart too. I like him."

"Thank you, Lila," he said, beaming at her. "I always appreciate the support."

She clasped her hands together and swayed on the toe of her sandal with the proud energy of a dog who had been told she was a *good girl*. "Of course."

Gemma gave up on them both and started walking back to her car. It took them a few moments to notice she was gone.

"Gemma!" Lila called. "Where are you going?"

"Away from you weirdos," she said over her shoulder.

"Wait, Gemma!" Jack called, and she heard them both hurrying after her. He caught up faster than Lila prancing along in her wedges. He reached for her arm, and when she turned, she saw a look on his face as genuine as when he had told her his theory about her being the key to everything. "I'm sorry I followed you; I didn't mean to scare you. You've never come here before, and I wanted to see what you were doing. This is the first time you've ever tried to understand what's going on, and I think that's a really good sign." His eyes were pleading pools of endless blue. The breeze caught his hair and pushed it from his forehead.

Gemma's knees gave out for a second.

"But what if I still don't believe it?" she asked, her voice part whisper.

"Then let me help you! Please." He half smiled and huffed a laugh. He glanced over his shoulder back toward

Clara's shop and lowered his voice. "Listen, I'm not sure what sent you running out of there, though I think I can guess, but you don't really seem like the type to believe in psychics."

Gemma agreed with a reluctant smile and a roll of her eyes.

"So then come with me. There's someone I want you to meet who can help explain."

Lila caught up, holding her giant hat on with one hand and tiptoeing to a stop in her tall shoes.

"Is it another psychic?" Gemma asked, drawn in by the plea on his face. He wanted her to understand, and despite herself, she wanted that too.

"Far from it. We have to take a drive, though."

"Of course we do; this is L.A." She cautiously smiled, and he smiled back.

"Glad to see you lightening up. I'm happy to chauffeur, if you're willing." He put his hand over his heart and slightly bowed forward in a *you can trust me* motion. He'd changed out of his stained shirt into a soft gray one that seemed to fit him even better.

Gemma weighed the options. Back in the coffee shop when they had only been talking, her *don't get in the car* instinct kicked in hard, and here she was with the chance to actually get in a car with him, and, to her shock, she was considering it.

"Where are we going?"

His face lit with surprise that she was willing. "Only a little east of here. Not far."

There was a lengthy stretch of suburban sprawl east of where they were before a mountain range shot up like a barricade, and Gemma could only imagine who was out there waiting.

The pull she felt toward Jack seemed to hook her behind the belly button. At the same time, her heart rate picked up at the thought of agreeing to his little road trip.

"Will I be back in time for lunch?"

"Definitely."

She dug her keys out of her purse and handed them to Lila, since she had driven them to Clara's. "Leave my car at your complex; I'll come get it later," she told her gaping face.

The smile on Jack's face rivaled the rising sun.

"Where'd you park?" she asked him.

He pointed up the street, and she started walking.

They made it a few steps before Lila called out from behind them.

"Hey! Listen, buddy. I know your name and you better believe I'm going to get your license plate number! I *will* report you if I don't hear from her every fifteen minutes until she's back!"

Gemma whirled around and shot her a teasing glare. "Oh, *now* you're concerned?"

Lila smiled at her, and despite following a man she'd, at least to her memory, only known for half the morning to his car for a ride into the great beyond, she smiled back.

She couldn't say why—maybe it was the psychic reading, maybe it was the sunny day, maybe it was his earnestness, which felt undeniably genuine—but Gemma knew that she could trust Jack.

CHAPTER

5

JACK FOLLOWED THE braided rope of freeways leading out of the thick of Los Angeles. Gemma didn't know much about him other than his name, but she assumed he had a well-paying job based on his car. Other than the coffee incident, which had smelled like coffee, she hadn't yet been close enough to him to realize he smelled like what she could only describe as fresh air in the woods. Something clean and almost absent but distinctly present at the same time. The scent baked into the leather of his SUV made for a heady mix of dark notes with a crisp finish. Despite the alluring smell and the car's smooth interior cupping her like a pair of gentle hands, she sat alert in the passenger seat as they wove their way through traffic.

"You're awfully quiet over there," Jack said over the soft hum of the radio.

Gemma pulled her gaze from the passing billboards and street signs and arched a brow. "Well, it's not every day I take a road trip with someone whose solitary mission is to convince me we've entered the Twilight Zone. Can't say I've got any good conversation starters for that scenario."

He softly laughed.

"And besides, it's kind of unfair that you know all sorts of things about me, and I know nothing about you. I feel like you will have already heard anything I say."

"You know plenty about me."

"Not today I don't."

He changed lanes to loop them through a knot of intersecting freeways that spit them out heading due east. "Fair point. Well, what do you want to know?"

She had been so focused on how she fit into this equation, she hadn't thought much about how he did. She unfolded her arms where she had been keeping them crossed over her chest and placed her hands on the cool leather of the seat beside her thighs. "What do you do for work?"

She expected an answer to roll off his tongue like any single thirtysomething; it was one of the first questions everyone asked each other. But he kept quiet.

"Are you not going to tell me?"

His face pulled into a smile. "You say that a lot."

She stared at him, realizing what he meant. "Do you withhold information a lot?"

"Sometimes, yes. When I want to see if you can remember conversations we've had before and details I've shared."

She kept her eyes on him, studying the straight slope of his nose and the soft swell of his lips. "You've told me what your job is before?"

"Many times."

He grew quiet again. Only the radio filled the space.

"So, are you going to make me guess, then? Because I have no idea."

He took his eyes from the road to look at her for as long as was safe in the rushing traffic. "I think you do, Gemma. Just concentrate for a second."

It was a sincere plea, and although she felt like she was the punch line of a joke that only he knew, she had been growing less skeptical since the scene at Aunt Clara's.

She sat back in her seat and gave her memory a good sweep. Nothing jumped out at her, so she opted for the thought she'd had back in the coffee shop.

"Actor?"

He laughed a funny sound high in his throat before sighing. "No, not an actor. I'm a TV screenwriter."

As soon as he said it, a tiny spark triggered in her brain, but not bright enough to call a memory.

"Interesting. Anything I know?"

He smiled again but there was something reserved about it. Humble. "If you've watched any premium-channel dramas in the past five years, then yes, definitely."

She was impressed at the same time a piece clicked in her head.

"Wait. If you're a writer, you spend a lot of time making up stories. Are you sure you didn't make up this one we're supposedly in? This whole time loop thing?"

He laughed as if she'd said something truly funny. The sound was warm and bright. "Oh no. I'd never write something this cheesy."

"Should I be offended by that?"

"No, not at all. I only mean this is all so riddled with

cliché. I can hardly stand it, and I'm living it. I can't imagine watching this."

"What, you don't like a good time loop story? Everyone likes a time loop story."

"I don't know," he said with a shake of his head and a wry grin. "They are so . . . predictable."

"If that were the case, wouldn't you have found your way out of this one by now?"

He took his eyes off the road, and the way he looked at her, with unabashed wonder in his gaze, warmed her face. "That is an excellent point. This one must be different." He held her gaze for a second longer than felt safe, and Gemma gasped. Not at the vicarious, thrilling rush his driving without looking gave her, but at the song that came on the radio.

"This song!" she blurted, and poked the console to turn up the volume. "It's following me, I swear!" For the second time that day and what felt like the millionth time in her life, her favorite pop song pulsed into her ears.

Jack grinned, eyes back on the road.

Seeing half of his smile and hearing the lyrics, she suddenly remembered the flash of dream-memory she'd gotten when she heard it earlier.

"You know this is my favorite song, don't you?"

He bit his lip as if he was afraid to admit it and nodded.

Gemma paused and thought hard about what she was going to say next. She felt like she was about to cross a line that couldn't be uncrossed, though she might have done that when she got in the car with him back in Hollywood.

"I think . . . I think I remember us listening to it together."

Jack almost swerved the same way she had earlier that morning.

"You *what?*"

"Careful!" she scolded, and reached for the wheel.

"Sorry." He gripped the wheel with both hands until his knuckles turned white. "But, Gemma, what did you say? You *remember* us listening to it?"

"I think so," she said, meekly and reluctant to admit it. "I heard it after I left the coffee shop, and it reminded me of you, of being with you and listening to it in a bar, but it was like remembering a dream, not something that really happened." She turned to him, her quiet voice almost lost in the lyrics. "*Did* that really happen?"

"Yes," Jack said without hesitation. "Last night at Lila's birthday party, I had them put it on because I know it's your favorite song. I was doing everything to put you in a good mood to test my theory."

Gemma felt like her brain exploded. It was the first bit of evidence that seemed real. A warm rush suddenly filled her cheeks as she remembered something else.

"Your theory of kissing me?"

His eyes shifted sideways. He looked a tad guilty, if she wasn't mistaken. "Yes."

She smiled, her face flush with warmth. "Resorting to trickery, I see. Well, it must have worked."

A flash of the kiss came back to her, stronger and with more certainty, perhaps because she was starting to believe it had been real.

"What other tricks did you pull?"

He stroked his chin. "Well, your favorite drink might have played a role. But the whole day was kind of a trick in a sense."

"In what sense?"

He sped around an old pickup truck piled with land-scaping equipment. "As part of my theory, I purposely didn't run into you in the coffee shop yesterday morning. I didn't interact with you at all until Lila's birthday party. I wanted to see if altering the way we met would change anything, and it seems to have worked."

She stared out the windshield, blinking. The idea of him manipulating their interactions suddenly made her feel like a puppet and he was pulling the strings. How many times had he tried to get her to remember him? And in what other ways?

She shifted uncomfortably.

"Have I upset you?" he asked with sincere concern.

"No. It's only that all this is making me feel like I don't have any free will. Like all of it, us, is predetermined."

He shot a coy grin at her. "Oh, you have plenty of free will. Don't worry about that. That's why you never stay, despite my best efforts. Every date we've been on has resulted in you not remembering me the next day."

Gemma stilled in surprise. "We've been out on dates?"

A slightly guilty grimace came over his face, and he nodded. "Yes. I didn't say anything about it before because I know this is all a lot to take in. I know you feel like you've only met me today, so I didn't want to overwhelm you. But we've gone out a few times before."

Gemma silently blinked at him, too stunned to speak. She wondered if he'd waited until she was a captive audience to drop that little bomb. She swept her mind for a memory, an inkling of going on a date with this strange, beautiful man, and came up with nothing. She managed to summon words while her head was still in a whirl. "Why don't . . . Why can't I remember any of them?"

"That is an excellent question and one that I don't think I can answer. Not in detail at least. Though I can say that I've enjoyed them despite the less-than-favorable endings."

Thoughts of Jack trying to woo her into remembering him made her smile, despite her previous thoughts. She wondered if she hadn't met him in the most bizarre of circumstances, perhaps on a day he wasn't claiming was repeating ad nauseam, if she would have given him a chance. Though, according to him, she'd given him several chances. But she had still left after.

A piece of her still-healing heart throbbed in pain as if to remind her of her reasons for being single.

"It's not you. It's . . ." She trailed off, feeling vulnerable and reluctant to open herself up. "My last relationship didn't end well."

He fully turned his head to look at her. Something knowing and hinting at protective flashed in his eyes. "I know. I've blacklisted Azalea from all my devices and audio platforms I subscribe to. I also gave their newest album one star and implored everyone not to buy it in my review."

A small, surprised laugh popped from her mouth. "I've told you about Nick and his band?"

He nodded. "Reluctantly, but yes. Their song came on at the restaurant during one of our lunch dates, and your mood tanked so fast, I thought you had rapid-onset food poisoning or something."

Gemma cringed in embarrassment, though she had no memory of it. "Sorry if that was awkward."

"It wasn't, and it's fine. I'm happy to learn anything about you, especially if it has anything to do with why you're hesitant to get to know me." He shot her a soft, tender smile that felt like it unlocked a closed-off chamber of her heart.

"What did I tell you about him?"

He pursed his lips like he didn't particularly enjoy the memory. "You said you dated for a year and that he was a, and I quote, 'self-absorbed asshole whose insufferable voice I never want to hear again whether it be on the radio or in person.'"

Though she didn't remember it, Gemma could not deny that those words had likely come out of her mouth. She nodded. "Sounds like something I'd say."

"Oh, you definitely said it," Jack said like they were in on a secret. He glanced sideways. "I didn't want to completely derail our lunch that day, so I didn't push, but I sense there's more to the story."

She caught the hopeful, probing, yet still polite look on his face.

She wanted to give him more, but filling in the blank was like firing a gun; she could not put the bullet back inside once it was out. Her and Nick's breakup alone hurt enough, but the reason for it, well, that festered inside an already infected wound that she didn't particularly enjoy poking at.

But she told him anyway.

"You're right. There is more to the story. The missing piece is that my father is Roger Peters."

Jack turned, eyes wide. His voice picked up the reverential inflection she was accustomed to hearing at the mention of her father's name, especially from anyone in the entertainment industry. "Oh shit, really?"

Gemma's lips twitched into a frown. "I take it I've never told you that before, but yes, he is. And Nick used me to get close to him to get a record deal and then broke up with me."

Gemma never thought introducing her boyfriend to her father would have such grave consequences. They'd been dating for several months, and she had brought Nick along on one of Patrick's mandated in-town visits. It turned out that was the opportunity he'd been waiting for, and Gemma was no longer his motivation for sticking around. Even worse, her father had chosen him over her. Nick was undeniably talented, and all her father saw were dollar signs and a new act to nurture to the top of the charts, despite Nick having used his daughter's heart as a stepping-stone to get there.

Jack immediately sensed the bad blood. Instead of asking her about her father's Grammys and all the famous musicians she was sure that he, like everyone else, assumed she had met because of her father's connections as a producer, he sidestepped the shimmery, starstruck trap of suddenly being one degree from a music industry mogul and remembered that Gemma was the person they had been talking about.

"You're not close to your father?"

"That's an understatement." A worn bitterness cut into her words. Over twenty years later, and it still burned deep in her chest.

Her father had always chosen his career over his family— and one time in the most literal sense. The long hours, skipped dinners, missed recitals, and canceled vacations had been one thing, but sleeping with a young, bouncy pop star who Gemma had been a fan of but had since purchased her every album only to light on fire was the final and ultimate act that broke their family.

"I hardly talk to him," Gemma said. "He and my mom split when I was eight and my brother was still in diapers, and I harbor a decades-long, clinical dislike for Summer Hart." She turned to him with her lips pressed tight. "I'm sure you can put those pieces together."

Jack's eyes widened a fraction.

News of the affair had been kept mostly under wraps at the time, and no one really cared a few decades later about the producer who cheated on his wife with a singer better known for her scandalous outfits and dance moves than her voice, but Gemma still hated talking about it. When anyone found out, they either pitied her or asked for salacious details like how long it had gone on for, how they'd been caught, and—her least favorite and the most illogical question if anyone bothered to do the math—if Patrick was the love child of a nineties pop star.

"No Azalea and no Summer Hart. Got it," Jack said with a nod. "She sucks anyway."

A soft, surprising smile tugged at Gemma's lips. She was accustomed only to bitterness and anger when discussing anything related to her father, especially the affair. She'd never once smiled or even come close to laughing over the topic, but Jack had her quietly doing both, even if morbidly, with a lightness that felt oddly freeing.

She caught a small, matching, if not slightly cautious smile on his lips.

"She totally sucks," she agreed, and his smile grew.

She didn't mention that she and her brother were supposed to visit their father that day. It felt too personal, despite everything else she was sharing. People tended to root for reunion, and if Jack found out their father had invited them to meet, he would probably encourage her to go. But he didn't understand. No one ever did.

Anger at the situation drew more words from her mouth.

"He has basically thrown money at Patrick all his life to win his affection, but I was older and saw his attempts for what they were. He couldn't do that with me because I remembered everything. Patrick only ever knew him as the man in the big house in L.A. who sent outlandish gifts and knew famous people. We moved to Phoenix with our mom. We grew up there, then I went to college in the Bay Area."

Jack quietly absorbed her story. He had told her she had not previously mentioned her father, so she was sure she had not shared this information with him, but she could almost guess what his next question would be.

Right on cue, he delivered.

"Why did you move back to L.A.?"

She turned to him with a crooked grin, unable to resist poking fun at the larger situation. "I knew you were going to ask me that."

He grinned back. "Who's making predictions now?"

She playfully rolled her eyes. "I still maintain that we are not in a time loop, and this is all in your overactive writer's imagination. I only knew because everyone who hears this story—there aren't many of you; you've joined an exclusive group—asks me that." She turned sideways in her seat to face him for emphasis. "But the even better question—better

than why did I relocate myself closer to him—is: Why did
I go into a career in radio where I would surely live every
day in the shadow of his industry status?"

He glanced at her leering at him with a slightly crazed
look on her face.

"So?" he asked. "Why did you?"

She held his gaze for a few seconds, building the anticipation and wondering if she might actually tell him, before
she turned and sat back against her seat. She crossed her
arms over her chest. "I'll let you know when my therapist
figures it out."

Jack quietly laughed.

Gemma was suddenly antsy and ready to get out of
the car.

"Are we there yet?"

They had pulled off the freeway shortly before, and now
Jack aimed the car at a collection of buildings Gemma had
seen photos of online, maybe in a movie once.

She sat up straight, curious.

"Are we going to Caltech?"

Jack nodded. "Sure are."

AFTER THEY PARKED, they strode across the university campus sitting squarely in the city of Pasadena. The stone
buildings and shady lawns were a far cry from the parts of
L.A. that Gemma normally frequented, and the break felt
like a breath of fresh air. Though she could not stifle her
curiosity as to why Jack had taken her to the elite private
school made famous by *The Big Bang Theory* and home to
real-life, world-renowned scientists.

"Don't tell me you're a closeted engineer who dropped out of one of the best schools in the country to pursue writing," she joked as they followed a paved pathway alongside a trim lawn that was a startling shade of green.

"Oh no," Jack said with a laugh. "I disappointed my parents with my career choices well before college. We're here to see a friend of mine. A friend of my father's too, actually. They were roommates in school."

"Is your father the engineer, then?"

"He was, yes. He died when I was eighteen."

Gemma almost stumbled, not expecting to hear anything of the sort. The wound was healed over but still sore, she could tell. "I'm sorry, Jack."

"Thanks." He gave her a tight, tired smile that looked like something he had been giving people for many years. "I've actually never told you that before."

The vulnerable trust in his voice put a warmth in her chest. It also made her feel guilty for refusing to see her own living father when they inhabited the same city.

The thought was complicated and messy, and intruding on the scenic campus and sunny day. She shook it off as they turned toward a concrete building with square windows and arches leading through it.

"So, who is this person we're meeting?"

"Dr. Simon Woods. He's a theoretical physicist."

Gemma couldn't help but laugh. "From a psychic to a physicist? I guess we're covering all bases here."

"I told you: leave no stone unturned. And if a chat with a wacky old professor is what it takes to convince you this is all really happening, then so be it." He smiled and stopped to open a door for her.

Her face warmed at the hopeful shine in his eyes as she passed by him, catching a hint of the fresh woodsy smell, to step into the cool building. "Seems like an odd choice to bring me to see a scientist to explain something totally non-sensical."

He grinned at her. "You'd be surprised."

They walked down a long hallway, passing a few closed doors that Gemma could only imagine what was behind. The hard sciences—chemistry, biology, physics—were about as remote from her profession as disciplines could be. She had taken the mandated courses in high school and only scraped by in the general ed classes required in college. Put to a test, she might have been able to remember a few basics but that would have been it.

Halfway to the other end of the hall, Jack stopped and gestured at a door. "Here we are." He held it open for her, and they entered a room that looked like part toy shop and part laboratory. Either way, it was full of expensive, fragile things.

A whiteboard scribbled with equations that might well have been hieroglyphs stretched along one wall. Another wall held a long, black-topped workbench with all manner of mysterious objects balanced on it: spinning globes, tall glass tubes, boxy-looking little robot machines. Against the back wall was a grid of framed degrees from prestigious institutions hanging above a desk teetering with so many stacks of papers, Gemma almost didn't see the man sitting at it.

"Simon?" Jack called into the quiet hum of the room. Gemma couldn't be sure if the sound was coming from the fluorescent lights overhead or the little amusement park of scientific objects spinning and whirling on the workbench, but she found it comforting.

Dr. Woods popped up from behind the stacks of papers quickly enough to make Gemma jump. "Jack, my boy! I was hoping you would visit," he said with a smile. He turned to Gemma and took her in with a bob of his head. He reached for the glasses dangling around his neck from a thin black cord and perched them on his hooked nose. Whether it was a conscious attempt to resemble Doc Brown from *Back to the Future*, Gemma didn't know, but he had nailed the look down to the white lab coat, unruly hair, and excited if not startled look on his face. "Is this the lovely young woman you told me about?"

He swept out from behind the desk in long strides, his body tall and thin but with the look of someone well-preserved for being, Gemma guessed, close to seventy. He probably took laps in a pool every morning.

"Hi, and yes, this is Gemma," Jack said. They had stopped in the middle of the room, halfway along the work-bench. Dr. Woods strode over to meet them with his hand extended.

"Pleasure to meet you, my dear. I've heard wonderful things."

"Nice to meet you," she said with a smile. They shook hands and his grip was cool and comforting when he placed his other hand atop their clasp. The instant warmth Gemma felt toward him made her wonder if they had shaken hands before and she didn't remember.

The thought reminded her that she wasn't only being

introduced to Jack's family friend but was in fact there to meet him for an explanation of a wildly implausible situation.

"Have we met before?" she asked, directing the question at Jack.

Dr. Woods smiled at her before turning to Jack for an answer as well.

"No. This is the first time," Jack said.

"Ah, well then! It is a true pleasure to meet you, Gemma," Dr. Woods said with another squeeze of her hand.

She realized like a kick to the head that Dr. Woods bought into it. Jack hadn't only brought her there for a theoretical explanation; he'd brought her there because Dr. Woods was on his side.

"You believe him, don't you?" she said with no attempt to hide her own disbelief at the fact.

"Completely," he said with as much conviction as Jack.

Gemma looked around the room at all the precise instruments, the stacks of printed research, the intimidating equations. It was entirely incongruent with what she was hearing.

"But you're a scientist."

Dr. Woods chuckled. His bushy brows rose and gave his face an easy, open expression. "But what is science if not studying the unbelievable until we find enough evidence to believe in it?"

The profound statement burst like a little bomb in Gemma's mind. She glanced at Jack.

He shrugged one shoulder and nodded.

"And that's what you think all this is?" Gemma asked Dr. Woods. "Evidence?"

"Indeed." He used his large hands to gently guide her to a stool at the workbench. He moved with such fluid motion, Gemma wondered if he used to be a dancer. "When Jack called me this morning to tell me he had woken in the same day he had been living—how many times is it now, Jack?"

Jack folded his arms and stroked his chin, looking like he might not want to confess the number. "One hundred and forty-seven by my count."

Gemma was glad she had sat down.

One hundred and forty-seven times? She did quick math to know that was almost five months.

Her head spun.

Dr. Woods carried on as if it were no big deal that they had been running in place for so long. "Right. One hundred and forty-seven times. The first thing I asked was how many times we had had the conversation that we were having at that moment." He glanced at Jack. "One hundred and thirty, he told me. One hundred and thirty times he had called me to tell me it was the same day he had lived before."

"It took me about two weeks to realize I needed help," Jack chimed in. He picked up one of the devices on the workbench. Something narrow with spindled arms that looked like a skinny spider.

Gemma was gaping at Dr. Woods. "And you believed him right from the start?"

He held out a hand signaling Jack to answer again because of course he would not remember, given that his memory was erased each time the day started over.

"He did," Jack confirmed. "If only everyone were so easy to convince." He shot her a playful smirk.

Gemma smirked back, if only halfheartedly. She had to admit, an authority like Dr. Woods was a solid point in the win column for Jack. But there was still a chance he was just a kooky old man Jack had put up to the ruse.

Gemma folded her arms and arched a brow. "Okay, then. Explain it to me. Give me evidence to believe."

Dr. Woods's face lit up with a smile. He gently touched her shoulder to spin her stool to face the whiteboard before he purposefully walked across the room, his lab coat billowing out behind him. He used his sleeve to clear a streak in the jumble of equations without thought. Gemma wondered if he had them all memorized. He uncapped a green marker and drew a line across the blank space.

"Time is only linear because that is how we perceive it. And we've built our world around that understanding. We have schedules and routines. We live and die by time, literally. We can't go back, only forward. We think of it like a track that is fixed, in place and unchangeable, and each of us joins it and leaves it when our life, the life we are conscious of, starts and ends." He drew tiny tick marks along the line. Then he turned around and held out his hands like he was about to do a trick. "But time is a convention. We made it up."

He strode back across the room and lifted one of the spinning objects off the workbench. The small purple globe the size of a softball rotated inside a set of gold axes attached to a metal ring surrounding it all. It stood on a small pedestal. "Because our perception is limited by our own invention," he said, and flicked one axis to set it spinning one way, "we cannot say without doubt that 'forward' is the only direction time flows." He flicked the other axis to send it rotating in the opposite direction. The globe inside spun in a third direction, creating a beautiful blur of precise movement. He handed it to her, and she felt the pull of the object spinning in all directions at once but doing so in balanced harmony.

"The universe is a collection of infinite objects in random motion, Gemma. Each with their own path and timeline." He felt his pants pockets, searching, then reached into the breast pocket of his lab coat and pulled out a stylus with a little rubber tip. "In any system with different parts in simultaneous yet variable motion, there is always the chance for disruption." He delicately inserted the stylus into the spinning orb in Gemma's hands, managing to stop one of the axes while the others stayed in motion. "If one piece suddenly becomes stationary, another piece in motion nearby may catch on it. Think of a snag in fabric, or the tiny rough spot on a glacier that carves out an entire valley. For both systems, this small yet mighty disruption can set things on a different course, and in the case of time like you and Jack are experiencing, it can create the perception of a temporal anomaly."

Gemma glanced at Jack at the mention of the words that had caused her to give up on him back in the coffee shop. Holding the orb in her hands and listening to Dr. Woods's explanation, she had to admit the phrase *temporal anomaly* somehow sounded more reasonable.

"So that's what you think I am?" Gemma asked. "The snag?"

"Precisely. When Jack first came to me, I told him to look for the thing that felt like an anchor. The universe has a way of ferreting out irregularities, of sifting meaningful things to the top." He extended his stylus again and this time stopped the other axis, leaving only the globe spinning. "And that's when he told me about you. That *you* are the single thing each day that feels different."

Gemma stared down at the globe, wondering at the outrageous romance of it all. The two golden axes held still while the globe spun on. Was it possible that time, her perception of it at least, had stopped so that she could cross paths with Jack? That might explain the pull she felt toward him, but why now after so many cycles through the same day?

"How come it has taken me so long to realize it, and Jack has known for a hundred and however many days?" she asked.

"That is an excellent question," Dr. Woods said with a smile. "There must have been an event, something powerful, that forced your own perception into perspective."

"We kissed last night," Jack chimed in.

Gemma blushed, and Dr. Woods let out a happy little chuckle.

"Ah, well, yes. That may have done it."

Gemma felt like she was on display in a museum, or perhaps under a microscope, given the setting, with both of them staring at her flaming face.

Dr. Woods flicked the golden axes again, this time to send them spinning in the same direction. "Sometimes all you need is a good jolt to get things back on track."

Gemma watched the purple-gold blur spin by and thought about the bigger picture. The two golden hoops were in harmony, but the globe spun in the other direction still. She pointed at it. "What about everyone else? If we're snagged and stuck in a temporal anomaly, is the rest of the universe spinning on like normal still?"

"That is possible," Dr. Woods said. "You are only aware of your own perception of time. But of course, there is also the chance that the entirety of reality as we know it is stuck as well." He poked his stylus into the blur of motion, the rubber tip against the globe and the stem a barrier for the axes, and instantly stopped the whole thing.

Gemma gazed down and felt the weight, literally, of it all. The thought that she and Jack had collided, gotten snagged on each other, and knocked the universe off kilter was almost comical.

She looked up at Dr. Woods. "That feels wildly egocentric."

He gently laughed. "Perhaps, but a couple's egocentrism is the hallmark of love."

Jack loudly dropped the contraption he had picked up. It clattered on the floor, and he accidentally kicked it when he bent down to reach for it, sending it skidding beneath the workbench. "Sorry, Simon," he muttered, flustered, and sank to his knees to retrieve it. Gemma caught sight of his face flushed a deep shade of red.

Her own face had caught fire. Again. She handed the globe back to Dr. Woods and stood up from her stool, tucking her hair behind her ear.

"Oh dear. Perhaps I have said too much," Dr. Woods said, picking up on the suffocating awkwardness suddenly sucking all the air out of the room. "Forgive me. I know nothing about matters of the heart. No one has discovered any equations for those yet." He uneasily chuckled.

"Gotcha!" Jack said. His voice echoed from beneath the

workbench, where he was stretching to reach what he had dropped. His shirt rode up to show the ravine of his lower back, and Gemma pointedly looked away from the flash of skin and his whole pleasantly tight back end up in the air. Averting her gaze was pointless because when he crawled backward and stood, his shirt stuck around his middle and showed off a panel of flat stomach with a pair of angled muscles at his hips pointing in and down like arrows for her eyes to follow. He saw her staring and quickly smoothed his shirt. He held up the device. A dust bunny clung to one of its spindles. He blew it off and handed it to Dr. Woods with an apologetic smile.

Gemma was embarrassed for staring but she was also suddenly acutely aware of something. Unspoken words crowded the room in a way that was making her dizzy all over again.

"Thank you for the explanation, Dr. Woods. It was very nice to meet you."

"My pleasure, Gemma," he said as she turned to Jack. "Can I speak to you outside for a moment, please?"

"Sure," he said, still flustered and flushed.

She turned for the door and heard them murmuring behind her.

"My apologies, Jack. I didn't realize you hadn't told her—"

"Yeah, hadn't really gotten to that part yet . . ." Jack said. His voice faded as Gemma walked down the hall.

The building hummed in stillness and emitted a smell of burnt rubber that Gemma had not previously noticed. She decided she wanted fresh air to confront Jack about what she had just learned in a roundabout way. By the time she made it to the exit, her mind a scramble of complicated thoughts about Jack's feelings toward her and her own toward him, Jack had caught up.

"Gemma, wait!" he said as she stepped back into the sunlight. He followed her outside and onto the path, which was less empty than it had been when they arrived. Students milled about, some hurrying along, others strolling with their noses glued to phones. Summer session was in swing.

She walked onto the lawn to remove herself from their way and to confront Jack with a burning question.

He almost ran into her when she stopped and turned around.

"Did you tell him you're in love with me?"

His eyes dazzled against the backdrop of sky and the leafy green tree they'd stopped beneath. His lips pressed together as if he were trying to keep the words on the tip of his tongue from spilling out.

Gemma's heart had positioned itself firmly in her throat, and with the force with which it was beating, she was surprised she could speak at all.

"Jack?"

"Okay, so there's a little more to my theory than I let on earlier," he blurted.

She huffed. "Well, please, do share."

He ran his hand through his hair and looked around as if checking that no one would overhear what Gemma was sure was going to sound senseless. "So, I've been thinking about this for a long time. It's not off the cuff, I swear. But I think since the kiss worked—it got you to remember—I think I'm right in that you have to . . . reciprocate my feelings in order for us to get out of this."

"*What?!*" she screeched. Nearby students cast sideways looks at them and rerouted their paths for a wider berth. "So, what are you saying? I have one day to fall in love with you or we're doomed to repeat all of this over and over again?"

"I think so, yes."

"That's the least rational thing you've said so far. I'm going home." She rejoined the busy path and stomped away.

"Wait, Gemma! I know it's hard to believe, but you heard what Simon said. We're stuck! We need a jolt! I know you feel *something*, otherwise you wouldn't have come here with me—and you wouldn't have kissed me last night! *And* you wouldn't have gone out with me all those other times!"

He was right about the feeling something part; she couldn't deny that. And she knew herself well enough to know she wouldn't have kissed him if she hadn't wanted to—even if she had only met him that night. There was some truth to his words. But still.

She stopped and turned around to face him. "Jack, I don't even remember going out with you. How many dates have we been on?"

"Eight."

"*Eight?!*" Gemma blurted in disbelief. Her head spun so fast the scenic campus blurred into a green-blue-beige swirl. "And what have we done on these dates?"

"We've been out to lunch five times and to Lila's birthday party three times, not counting last night since we met there and didn't technically arrive together," he said with a precision to suggest he'd logged each one in a mental journal.

She silently blinked at him.

Reading her skepticism, he gently held up his hands. "Listen, I know this sounds unbelievable, because you feel like we just met today, but I know you're vegetarian and you hate cilantro because it tastes like soap. I know you love mimosas and iced lattes, and order dessert with lunch because you believe ice cream can be eaten any time of day. You started playing the piano when you were three. You love dogs and are mildly allergic to cats. Your birthday is in November and you were always jealous of kids who got to have pool parties in the summer. I now know that you dislike crowded bars and loud parties, and really any activity involving too many other people, but you attend anyway when it's for someone special. I know Lila is your best friend and you met in college and were roommates and you'd do anything for her, and she'd do anything for you." He paused for a breath that sounded both hopeful and exhausted. His eyes shone. "I know enough about you to want to know more, and I know that I'm going to lose my mind if you don't remember me because I've never felt this way about anyone before."

Gemma reeled. Everything he said about her was true—and those were very specific details he couldn't have known unless she told him. She searched her mind again for a memory of when he could have learned so much about her and developed such feelings and found only blips transplanted from imagination rather than true memories.

She admitted to herself that she must have some kind of feelings for him too if she'd agreed to go out with him eight times, plus kissing him last night at the bar. But the fact that she couldn't remember any of those eight dates—nor the previous five months in which they'd occurred—left her lost as to what to make of it all.

There was also the fact that she wasn't ready to put her heart any place vulnerable again. Not even in the hands of a man who was looking at her like he was collecting trivial, personal facts about her as if they were precious gems. Like perhaps getting to kiss her was his calling in life.

Even more, it was also nearing noon and she had to get to work. And she needed to check if Patrick got on a flight. And she needed to go back to Lila's and get her car.

"I have to go, Jack," she said, and turned to go.

He grumbled in frustration that she was leaving yet again. "At least let me give you a ride back!"

Gemma kept walking. She had already pulled out her phone to summon a ride. She saw no new messages from her brother but had a few emails from work.

With the sun beating down on her, always hotter a bit inland than in the city, she felt foolish for abandoning such important responsibilities to chase down a wild theory with a complete stranger. Although it sounded like science fiction, Dr. Woods's explanation of the snagged realities was plausibly credible. He was a scientist, after all. Who was to say what could or couldn't be possible in the great expanse of a universe humans barely knew a sliver of? But Jack's proposed solution for unsnagging reality—the thought of falling in love in a single day—*that* was the part that Gemma couldn't believe. And she didn't have the time to start trying.

chapter 6

As it turned out, a rideshare from Pasadena back to Silver Lake was not cheap. Gemma considered invoicing Jack for the inconvenience.

She had texted Carmen to tell her she was on her way to the studio after a quick stop to pick up her car, then spent the rest of the ride sorting out her thoughts about the morning. By the time she was knocking on Lila's front door, she felt ready for a nap.

"Oh good, you're alive," Lila greeted her. She had changed out of her overalls and into a sundress. Her hair was twirled up in a towel and she wore a pair of half-moon stickers beneath her eyes. Gemma had always assumed they helped with puffiness, but she really had no idea what they did. "How did it go?"

Gemma pushed in the door and words came spilling out of her mouth as if someone had turned on a fire hose.

"That was a mistake. He took me to see a professor out at Caltech, this old theoretical physicist who was a friend of his dad's, and he basically gave me a private lecture on our perception of time and reality and how everything in the universe is random and moving in different directions all at once, and sometimes things crash into each other and get stuck, and then you need some kind of jolt to unstick it all, and Jack thinks the jolt is that I have to reciprocate his feelings and fall in love with him! Today!"

Lila stood still and blinked at her as she paced the living room breathing hard and fast. "And you thought what Clara said was senseless?"

"Lila!" Gemma snapped, and stomped her foot.

"Okay! Okay, calm down. Here, have a seat. I'll get you something to drink." She gently pushed her onto the couch with her cool, well-moisturized hands.

Gemma obeyed and tried for a deep breath. She had been stewing in the car the whole way, but apparently her thoughts were not as organized as she had believed.

Lila returned with a brand of seltzer Gemma had never heard of with a straw bobbing in it. She held it to Gemma's lips like a mother giving her kid ginger ale for a stomach-ache.

"Thank you."

Lila patted her back. "Now, tell me again what happened?"

Gemma took a gulp of the bubbles and another deep breath. She started over, much more slowly. "Basically, he had a really smart scientist explain to me how a time loop might actually be possible, and said that we've relived this day, today, one hundred and forty-seven times. The scientist said I've started to remember Jack now, as of last night, because he kissed me, which was a jolt that made me tune in to what's going on. Jack thinks that's further evidence that . . ." She took another sip of her drink to buy herself some time because she knew Lila's reaction to the next part was going to be nothing short of overdone. "He thinks that me falling in love with him, today, is what will break the cycle."

Lila blinked big green eyes at her and, to Gemma's surprise, did not jump up off the couch to sing in celebration. "That's the most romantic thing I've ever heard."

Gemma grumbled despite Lila's relatively tame response. She'd had the same thought in the coffee shop, but now that she was experiencing the fallout, her opinion had changed regarding where this situation fell along the sanity-romance spectrum. "It's the most *irrational* thing I've ever heard! Fall in love in a single day? That's impossible!"

Lila reached for her flailing arms and removed the seltzer so that it didn't spritz her sofa. "Gem, listen to yourself right now. This gorgeous, sweet, maybe-a-little-bit-weird-but-so-what guy tells you this wild, fantastic, impossibly romantic story about the two of you essentially stopping time, and the part you can't believe is that you have to fall in love with him?"

Gemma scoffed and looked away. "You make it sound like I'm some heartless monster."

"You're not heartless." Lila gently reached for her chin and turned her face back. She looked into her eyes with a level of understanding that only a best friend could possess. "You've had your heart broken, badly, and I know that has made it hard for you to open it up again."

In true Lila fashion, she had gone straight for the truth.

A warm rush of pain surged up Gemma's throat. Her

eyes involuntarily washed over with tears. She sighed, embarrassed that the wound was still so vulnerable. "Sorry," she said, and wiped her eyes. "I should be over this by now."

Lila reached behind her for a tissue out of the box on her end table. "Don't apologize. You can cry all you want in front of me. I just hate to see you so jaded."

Gemma breathed a soggy laugh and dabbed her eyes. "I'm not *that* jaded."

"No?" Lila asked as she wiped a tear off Gemma's cheek. "Here you are in this real-life fairy tale where you have to rescue someone—and maybe even save the whole universe, who knows—with true love, and your response is to run away screaming?"

Gemma rolled her eyes and laughed. "Again, you're making me sound like a monster."

Lila smiled and then grew serious. "Gemma, the reason I always push you toward dating is because I saw how much you loved Nick, and what that did for you, how it opened you up. I know the thought of doing that again is scary, given how badly that turned out, but doing it with the *right* person, Gem? Someone who deserves you and will put you first? Just imagine."

Gemma had imagined. Long before Nick, she imagined falling in love with the perfect guy and watching her world blossom into something new and beautiful. When she met Nick, she had felt that. She had even broken her *no musicians* rule because she had fallen so hard for him. He was charming and talented, not to mention hot as hell. He had Kurt Cobain hair and played the guitar, for heaven's sake. And that's what he was in one go: heaven and hell. Hot and cold. A man who made her feel more than she ever had, and also the kind of man who could take it all away without a look back. When it turned out that nothing in their relationship was sincere and he had been using her as a means to get to an end—her father and a record deal—she stopped imagining love was so great.

But now Jack had crashed into her world like a wrecking ball, spilled coffee all over her, confessed he loved her in so many words, and was making her start to imagine again.

She wiped her nose with an inelegant sniffle she would only perform in front of Lila, Patrick, or her mother. "And you think this nutty guy chasing after me is the right person?"

Lila shrugged. "He could be! He seems pretty stuck on you if he's lived this day—what did you say? A hundred and forty-seven times?"

Gemma nodded, and Lila's eyes bulged.

"If he's spent that much time trying to get you to remember him, then I'd say he's worth a shot."

Gemma shook her head, feeling herself sway but still skeptical. "We've also apparently been on eight dates, three of which have been attending your birthday party together."

Lila pulled one of those frown-smiles where her mouth turned down, but she nodded in approval. "I like it."

Gemma narrowed her eyes. "You don't remember that at all?"

"I do not," she said, like it was no bother it made zero sense whatsoever.

"This is all so strange, Lila."

Lila reached up for the towel on her head to undo it. Her hair tumbled around her shoulders in damp, dark waves. "I told you, strange doesn't have to mean bad. And think of it from his perspective: he spends every day chasing the woman of his dreams, and every day she can't remember who he is. Maybe he's the man of your dreams, and you just haven't realized it yet."

Lila's hopeless romantic optimism was contagious, Gemma had to admit. It made her realize that not only was Jack trapped in a day, but he was also trapped in a *bad* day for him. According to his math, he'd had about five months to develop feelings for her, and she had to wonder whether if she had been aware of those five months as well, she would have been as desperately chasing after him. Based on the pull she felt toward him, the dizzying flashes of their kiss— the fact that she had kissed him at all—she could not definitively say that she would not be doing the same thing.

Lila pinched a hunk of her hair and sniffed the ends. "*Oof.* This stuff stinks. Please tell me you're going to give this guy a chance and not leave me stuck here to wash my hair with this horrible shampoo for a one-hundred-and-forty-eighth time."

Gemma laughed, and Lila joined her, leaning over so their shoulders bounced together.

"Smell it! I'm serious! Don't doom me to this fate, I beg you!" She shoved her wet hair at Gemma's nose, and they fell over giggling.

GEMMA LEFT LILA'S to head to work, finally. She might have been living in the most warped fairy tale she'd ever heard of, but she still had a life to attend to. Not to mention, she had no contact information for Jack, even if she wanted to reach out. But she had the feeling they'd find their way back to each other eventually, especially since he'd already admitted to following her once.

She was driving toward the radio studio, a humble suite inside a corporate building in Hollywood, when her brother called again.

She pressed the button on her steering wheel to answer. "Hello?"

"Hey, Gem." He sounded weary. Any flight he got on by now would have put him on the West Coast well into the evening.

Still, Gemma had hope.

"How's it looking?"

"Not good. All the direct flights are full. I had another standby look promising, but people keep showing up at the last second. It's like I'm not destined to make it home today." He huffed a defeated-sounding laugh, and Gemma swallowed hard.

"Don't say that. You can still get on a plane."

"I'm not betting on it."

Gemma gazed out at the busy street around her, traffic and pedestrians moving through another L.A. day. She wondered what Dr. Woods would say about Patrick being stuck on the East Coast. Was he snagged on something of his own? Or was his experience a consequence of Gemma being stuck?

"Patrick, has today seemed strange to you? Have you had any sense of déjà vu at all?"

She held her breath while she waited for him to answer.

"Well, I've walked about fifty laps around this terminal

and can't tell you which gate is which anymore, and I've seen the same people waiting for flights over and over, but other than that, no. Why?"

She mulled over his answer and felt guilty for condemning him to a crowded airport as prison. It seemed a lot worse than Lila's smelly shampoo situation. And yet, she didn't want to worry him from so far away. *We're stuck in a temporal anomaly* seemed more like a face-to-face conversation.

"It's been a weird day, that's all."

"You're telling me. I woke up on a different continent, remember? Well, I think technically that was yesterday. Or was that tomorrow for you? I have no idea; I've lost track of time."

"You and me both," Gemma muttered, wondering if she and her brother had had the exact same conversation one hundred and forty-six times before.

"What's that?" Patrick asked.

"Hmm? Oh, nothing."

A pause passed, and Gemma took comfort in being on the phone with him. A tiny moment of peace in an otherwise overwhelming day.

The PA system came to life in the background on his end. "Paging passenger Tiffany Sanders. Tiffany Sanders to gate eight."

"That's one of my standbys," Patrick said, an ounce of hope in his voice. "Annnd, there she is."

Gemma's heart sank, and Patrick let out an enormous sigh that made it sound like he had in fact witnessed Tiffany Sanders take his shot at a seat one hundred and forty-six times before.

"Listen, Gem. I want to talk to you about Dad." He changed topic and caught her off guard.

Gemma was nearing her building and did not have time to get into an argument over the topic of visiting her father by herself, and she was sure, time loop or not, that Patrick was about to bring it up. She decided to nip it in the bud.

"Patrick, I already told you, I'm not going alone. I'll wait until you get here."

As she said it, she remembered what Jack had told her that morning hours before. *Your brother doesn't make it.* If they were stuck inside the day, and Patrick never came, did that mean she would never see her father ever again? For that matter, would she never see Patrick ever again either?

Both thoughts put a sudden ache in her chest. About Patrick, of course, but she was surprised to feel any kind of pain over missing her father.

She scoffed, uncomfortable with her own emotions, and continued blabbering before Patrick could say anything.

"Why does he even want to meet? I mean, he better not be dying or something dramatic."

"Jeez, Gem."

"Sorry, but why else would he call? He never wants to see both of us."

"He *always* wants to see both of us, you just refuse to go."

"I—"

Gemma started and stopped because he was completely right. She only visited her father when Patrick forced her to, which meant the opportunity only arose during the six months when Patrick was in L.A., and even then, she found an excuse not to join them almost every time. She hadn't seen him for nearly a year.

Patrick took a patient breath. "Gem, listen. I have something to tell you. I was going to wait to do it in person, but that's not looking like it's going to happen anytime soon. You have to promise me you won't freak out, okay?"

Gemma had arrived at the studio. She was glad she had parked because whatever Patrick was about to say was surely not something to take in while operating a motor vehicle. They had had this conversation before; she could sense the emotion of it. But there was nothing there to grab hold of, no flash of a memory. As nerves shot through her body, for the first time that day, she wished she knew what was about to happen.

"You know it only freaks me out more when you say that, Patrick."

"Sorry, but I know how you get." He took another breath. "Look, the truth is, *I* asked to meet with Dad. I have news to tell you. They offered me a full-time position at the institute as a program director, and I'm going to take it. It's an incredible opportunity, Gem. I can't say no. But that means I'll be moving to Lagos. Permanently. I'm only coming to L.A. on this trip for two weeks before I head back. I can't leave knowing you and Dad aren't on good terms. I know you'll never see him if I'm not there to be the glue, so I wanted to, I don't know . . . try and *fix* you guys before I'm gone."

Gemma was completely speechless. She could hardly even breathe. Somewhere deep in her mind, she reasoned that if she and Patrick had had the conversation before, she must have blocked it out as an act of self-preservation.

The words *Lagos* and *permanently* echoed around her head like a deafening explosion. She hardly heard Patrick through the car's speakers.

"Gem? You there?"

"I have to go," she said numbly.

"Gemma, wait—"

Patrick could not finish his plea before she ended the call.

She walked in a daze across the hot parking lot, the concrete baking in the midday sun. She couldn't process the news that her beloved brother was leaving the country for good. She'd thought she would have half a year with him, but they only had two weeks. And then he would be gone.

She couldn't remember entering the building, crossing the lobby, and taking the elevator, but she was suddenly standing outside the studio. She thought it might all be a bad dream until she entered and saw Carmen and Hugo crowded around a table of Chinese takeout. Their studio looked like most others in the business: cramped, decorated in posters and signed memorabilia, electronic equipment scattered about. Her coworkers sat in the open space they used as a lobby, kitchen, and green room all at once. Carmen leaned back in her chair on two legs, as was her habit, and Hugo hunched over the table, looking like a linebacker ready to tackle someone for food.

"'Bout time," Carmen said with chow mein noodles dangling from her mouth. Hugo used chopsticks to pick up a pot sticker. "I ordered extra in case you need to eat."

Gemma dropped her purse on the bench against the wall and realized she hadn't thought about lunch. She sank down into one of the empty chairs at the small round table.

"Thanks."

"What's up with you?" Hugo asked. His voice rumbled deep in his barrel chest. He took up most of the space in their small production booth when the three of them crammed in together.

"Um . . ." Gemma wasn't sure what to say, still reeling. "Busy morning."

Carmen slammed her chair's front legs onto the floor and dropped her box of noodles. "Well, snap out of it, sister. Marsha's kid is still puking his guts out, and we didn't cancel Nigel Black. I told her you'd cover. That means you're on in"—she glanced at the wall clock hanging above the booth window—"twenty minutes."

At that moment, Gemma was thankful her stomach was in fact empty. She had not recovered from her phone call with Patrick, and news that she had to interview one of her idols live on air surely might have otherwise made her hurl.

CHAPTER

7

AT THE NEWS that she would be interviewing Nigel Black in a matter of minutes, Gemma did an about-face and ran back outside.

She was pacing the sidewalk in front of the studio, breathing like she was going into labor, trying not to throw up, and wondering when her life had diverted into madness when she heard a familiar voice.

"Gemma?"

It was Jack. And the rush of relief that surged through her felt like a warm blanket in a snowstorm.

"You," she said.

He approached slowly with his hands half raised as if he was afraid she would run. "Yes, me."

Obviously, he had followed her again, and she realized she was thankful. After the past fifteen minutes, she needed a familiar face, and even if Jack was only familiar by some inexplicable cosmic accident, she would take it.

"Are you all right?" He had asked her that question before, and she was pretty sure she had lied to him.

"Not really, no."

"Do you want to talk about it?"

"Don't you already know?"

He shrugged and gave her a kind smile. "Let's pretend I don't." He pointed at the bench up against the building's outer wall, thankfully shaded by an overhang.

Gemma didn't have much time, if she was going to do the interview at all, but at least an attempt to process everything that had happened was a welcome invitation.

She turned for the bench and he followed to sit beside her.

"I just got off the phone with Patrick. He's still stuck in New York, but he told me he's moving to Africa, permanently, because the institute he works for offered him a job that he can't turn down. He was only coming to L.A. for a few weeks and turns out he was the one who set up a meeting with my father today, because he wants to play some kind of peacemaker before he's gone for good. If this has already happened, I must have blocked it out."

Jack let out a long breath. "That's heavy.

A swell of emotion jammed Gemma's voice in her throat. Her words came out high and desperate. "I only get to see him six months out of the year already! What's going to happen if he moves to Africa for good? Then I'll *never* see him. And then he'll meet someone there and fall in love— maybe he already has!—and then I'll never, *never* see him, and it'll only be me and my mom having sad Christmases in Phoenix for the rest of my life!"

Gemma sniffled, and Jack's face lifted into a soft, sympathetic smile.

"That spiraled quickly."

She grumbled and rolled her eyes at him. "Shut up. You don't know me."

He pressed his hands into the bench and leaned forward, slightly lifting his body and scooting closer to her. His heady, breezy woods smell came with him. "Actually, I do, remember? And sorry if what I said outside Simon's lab came on a little strong, but it's probably best that you know. I know how hard this is for you. I know Patrick is one of your best friends."

His words struck Gemma like a blow to the temple. She had never thought of her brother as her friend, but hearing Jack say it made it so obvious, she blinked in realization.

"You're super lucky too," he went on. "I've never met the guy, but the way you talk about him, and how hard he's trying to get here for you today, he seems like an amazing person."

"He is. He's pretty much the only reliable man in my life. Well, him and my dog Rex."

Jack leaned back and nodded. "Ah, yes, Rex. You know, I was extremely jealous the first few times you said you had to go home because someone was waiting for you. When I found out the someone had four legs and a tail, I felt much better about my chances."

Gemma's face flushed. She tucked her hair behind her ear. She'd had Rex for so long, she had used him as an excuse to bail out on many social events. Depending on who the person was inaccurately assuming he was a human, she often didn't correct the mistake. The fact that Jack knew the truth about him must have meant she'd trusted him enough to have been honest and had been willing to give him a chance at some point.

"He's a really good dog."

Jack smiled. "I'm sure he is."

"You've never met him?"

"No, I haven't had the pleasure."

Gemma thought silently about what that meant. She at least knew that in one hundred and forty-six days and eight dates, Jack had never made it as far as her apartment—which would have been a lot after knowing him for only one day. The thought that he had never pushed hard enough for that earned him several bonus points.

She smiled at him. "He'd like you."

"Who, your brother or your dog?"

Her smile widened. "Both of them."

Jack's eyes shone brightly as he grinned at her. "I would be honored to meet them."

"Well, we can work something out for Rex, but unless you want to hop a flight to New York, I don't think Patrick is in the cards. Not today at least." She let out a big sigh and felt the sting of their phone call all over again.

"You know," Jack said, "based on what I've seen, I can't really see him living on another continent changing anything about your relationship. You guys seem like the kind of siblings who nothing can break apart. You're lucky to have each other."

A warmth washed over her. "Well, we were all each other really had as kids. He was a baby when our parents split. I was his babysitter basically from the time we moved to Arizona, and having left all my friends in L.A., he was who I had to play with. Then we just kind of stuck." She thought fondly of sun-drenched days in their Phoenix backyard, she and Patrick splashing in their pool while their mother read a magazine in a lawn chair.

Jack smiled at her. "See, I don't think a few thousand miles has any chance of damaging that. And besides, you can always visit him since planes fly east too."

She studied his face, noting the sincere kindness. "Are you always so optimistic?"

He laughed a curious sound that went layers deep. Gemma couldn't decipher it but found herself wanting to dive in. "Today I am. I learned when my dad died that you have to hold on to people. Don't let anger or distance or whatever else seems so important at the time get in the way, because in the end, it's not worth it."

Having never lost a family member, Gemma knew he spoke from a perspective she could not share. The wisdom in his voice was as painful as it was profound.

"Were you close to your dad?"

Jack let out a heavy breath. "Not as close as I wish I had been."

A silence settled between them, and despite feeling closer to him, given the conversation they were having, Gemma stirred uneasily.

"I suppose this is the part where you lecture me about wasting precious time and tell me I should go visit my father."

Jack clucked his tongue with a shake of his head. "No. That decision is on you, I'm afraid, though I'm sure you can guess what I would do in your shoes."

Although surprised, Gemma was pleased to see him refrain from meddling in that particular matter.

"Thanks."

He nodded as her phone rang from her pocket.

She grabbed it to see Carmen calling. The reminder of the other issue—the primary one—that had sent her running outside came galloping back like a band of wild horses.

Her stomach flipped and her heart lodged in her throat again.

"Hello?" she almost squeaked when she answered.

"You coming in, or am I going to have to talk to this old hack?" Carmen greeted her.

Gemma scoffed. "Don't call him that. He's a legend."

"Yeah, a legend about to roll up to an empty studio full of leftover chow mein unless you get your butt in here, missy. You have two minutes or I'm calling it, and then *you* get to explain to Marsha and Nigel Black's people why we canceled at the last second." She hung up and left Gemma swearing at her phone.

"Problem?" Jack asked.

The nerves screaming through Gemma's body felt like electric cables in a thunderstorm. Her voice shook when she spoke.

"Um, only that a very famous musician who I happen to be a very big fan of is due here any minute for a live interview, and since my boss is out, I'm going to have to do it." She had stood up at some point, and she was clutching her phone like her hands were a sweaty vise.

The memory of that day she met Nigel as a child lived in vivid color in her brain, seared like a feature film of shame. Her father had taken her with him to the recording studio, and Nigel had been there with his whole band. Cool and tall and ruggedly handsome, he smelled like leather and spice and a refreshing burst of mint. He was everything Gemma had imagined and more. Larger than life in the best way possible. Her father shook his hand and nudged Gemma forward to do the same, but she had gone catatonic. She'd had the chance to claim her industry birthright as a miniature mogul who casually rubbed elbows with rock stars, and she blanked. Everyone thought it was cute, but she thought it was a failure. Her chance to be who she was born to be, and she'd blown it. The brief interaction that probably didn't register as relevant to anyone else in the room still haunted her.

If it were anyone else at her studio today. *Anyone* else.

"I want a job in radio, like, actually on the air someday," she told Jack, still breathing too hard. "It's my dream, but I can't—Nigel is—I think I'm going to throw up." She threw a hand over her mouth.

Jack popped up from the bench and gently gripped her shoulders. "Hey, don't throw up. Having to interview a rock star is a pretty awesome problem to have as far as problems go, right? I mean, look at the rest of the day in comparison."

Gemma tried for a smile, but she had broken out in a clammy sweat. She glanced around for a trash bin and hoped she wasn't about to ruin Jack's shirt for the second time that day. If she couldn't pull it together for one interview, she had no hope of hosting her own show someday. She would never prove herself to Marsha. Perhaps she was not cut out for her dream job after all.

"You don't understand," she told Jack. "I met Nigel as a kid, and I totally froze. I couldn't even speak. I don't know how I'm supposed to interview him now. This is going to be a disaster."

"Hey hey hey, you're fine, Gemma. You're fine." He squeezed her shoulders and took a deep breath, nodding his head in an effort to get her to do the same. "You were a kid when that happened. You're an adult now. A professional. And I talk to famous people all the time at work. They're just people. So what if Nigel is the front man of one of the biggest bands of all time—*okay*, that was the wrong thing to say! Forget I said it!" Jack jumped sideways when she dry-heaved.

She tried to focus. Earlier, she had momentarily thought it would be a thrill to talk to Nigel Black, but facing the situation head-on, she didn't know if she had it in her, and the clock was ticking. There on the hot sidewalk, her body a rigid ball of nerves and sweat, she couldn't decide what would be worse: canceling the interview and enduring Marsha's and Nigel's people's wrath or going through with it and throwing up on a famous rock star she had idolized since she was a child.

"Hey, Gemma, listen, listen." Jack gripped her shoulders again and met her eyes as she took deep pulls of air through her nose. His brow bent in concern, but he kept focused. "I know you don't like me telling you about things before they happen, but I think this situation calls for breaking the rules."

She sucked in two tight breaths. "What are you talking about?"

"What if I told you that you get this nervous every time, but you do the interview, and you totally nail it?"

It might have been the lack of oxygen to her brain, but she couldn't believe what she was hearing. "Really?"

"Yes," Jack said with a sure nod. "I've heard it a million times, well, about a hundred and forty-six times, actually." His face split into a crooked grin that summoned a vision of him in the bar from the night before. It put a flutter in her chest that dampened the panic.

"And it goes well?"

"Yes. I know you can do it because you've done it before. Over and over."

Gemma stood up straight and fought for a deep, full breath. He could have been right, she thought. She had not remembered the conversation she'd just had with Patrick and she had reasoned it was because it was too overwhelming. Perhaps her mind was protecting her.

Jack smiled at her. "When I say you got this, I really mean, *you got this*. Trust me."

Hearing him say it gave her an undeniable confidence boost. Though she had to admit she could not imagine pulling herself together from a state of sidewalk panic to being composed enough to go on air in a matter of minutes.

Right then, a black SUV with tinted windows pulled to the curb with a low, imposing purr. Gemma could not see inside it, but she knew who it was. She knew there was no turning back.

"There's your cue," Jack said with a reassuring nod.

Her heart was about to beat out of her chest for all kinds of reasons. He released her arms, and as his hands dropped to his sides, she reached out and gripped one.

"Will you come in and watch?"

Jack almost stumbled, suddenly looking like he was the one who needed support. He looked down at their hands clasped together and his smile broke out. "I wouldn't miss it for anything."

GEMMA SAT ACROSS from Nigel Black in the recording booth. They both wore enormous headphones. She had positioned herself at an angle so that she could see his face rather than the microphone hanging in front of him.

After a round of introductions—Gemma having managed to both maintain consciousness and not throw up on a famous rock star—they had entered the booth. Now, from the inside, Gemma discreetly eyed Carmen, Hugo, and much to her unexpected pleasure, Jack on the other side of the glass. He gave her a silent thumbs-up. Nigel had brought two people: one a burly man in all black who looked like he'd give Hugo a run for his money in a brawl, and a woman with flaming red hair who'd had enough plastic surgery to preserve her face at least twenty years younger than her age. She introduced herself as Nigel's publicist, Bridget, and reminded everyone they had thirty minutes for the interview and not a second longer.

Those thirty minutes had cost the radio station an exorbitant amount of money and several favors that Gemma proudly did *not* drop her father's name to get. She had the music industry at her fingertips, given her heritage, but she refused to take advantage. She had always been determined to make it on her own.

Nigel watched her from across the table. His famous ice blue eyes twinkled. He had the face of a rock legend, a man who had seen decades of tours and adoring fans, and it went perfectly with the gravelly sound of his voice. And the British accent, well, that didn't hurt either.

The truth was, he reminded Gemma of her father. Not in appearance, but because she and her dad used to listen to his songs together, singing all the lyrics, back before their family had fallen apart. It was the one sweet memory she allowed herself to hold on to.

She glanced up at the red *On Air* light shining like a beacon. Then she took a breath and spoke into her microphone.

"This is Gemma Peters in the studio today with Nigel Black. I have to say, what a tremendous honor it is to have you with us."

"Thanks, love."

Gemma tried not to swoon.

"You're in L.A. for one night as part of this comeback tour. How did you select your tour stops for this once-in-a-lifetime event?"

"Ah, well, I love Los Angeles. She's a tough old broad, but one of my favorite places on earth. Always sunny, everyone running around trying to be famous. Never a dull moment."

Gemma found herself under his spell, and at the same time she was totally in a groove. The interview flowed seamlessly. She hardly had to look at her script because conversation with Nigel Black was everything she hoped it would be.

He told a scandalous story about the first time he played the Hollywood Bowl back in the eighties, the same location of his show that night, that left everyone in the studio laughing. He spoke of his favorite songs from his most recent album, and hinted that he was writing something new. He swore he would retire only when he was dead, and Gemma hoped he wasn't exaggerating.

"Who are your favorite artists today? Is there anyone you're excited about for the future?" Gemma asked.

Nigel stroked his scruffy chin. He wore a black tee shirt and tattered leather bands around his wrist. He'd clipped his sunglasses to his collar. The question was one of her favorites that she'd written because she knew whoever he named would feel like they'd received a blessing from on high. "Oh, there are plenty of acts out there today doing really exciting things. Our openers on this tour are all excellent. In fact, we just added a new one tonight. Bridge, what are they called?" He leaned away from his mic and waved at his publicist through the glass.

Gemma glanced at their rapt audience through the window. Carmen and Hugo were all business, and Jack watched with wide eyes and a smile. Bridget mouthed something they of course couldn't hear.

At the sound of it, Hugo jerked his neck back and glanced at Carmen. The two of them had a silent argument resulting in a thrown elbow and Carmen swatting Hugo's big hand, which he'd braced over the switch that would allow Gemma and Nigel to hear them.

Bridget's voice came through, straight into Gemma's ears in a sharp, nasally tone that made her heart dive off a cliff. "Azalea."

"Right, that's it," Nigel said. "Azalea. They were a last-minute add for this stop; not sure it's even been announced yet, but they rip. I can't wait to see what they do next."

Gemma suddenly understood what the silent argument had been about. Her tongue glued itself to the roof of her mouth. She pried it loose with a clucking sound she hoped didn't deafen her listeners. "Yep. Definitely heard of them."

"Yeah, yeah. I'm real excited about them. They're local too, right?"

Too local, Gemma thought.

She wanted to scream. How dare Nick come anywhere near Nigel Black. She knew she had no claim over a global superstar, but damn it, the *one thing* she cherished, and he had to come stomping in and tarnish it too.

She took a breath and kept her composure. "They sure are. So, what's next after this tour? Back in the studio?"

Nigel didn't miss a beat. He shared more about his new project and the different direction he was taking with his next album. He name-dropped some serious talent he'd be collaborating with, and even mentioned he was meeting with a famous director while he was in town to talk about a small part in an upcoming film.

By the end of it, Gemma's spirits had been restored. He was back on her favorite pedestal. She was staring at him with stars in her eyes like she was still seven years old. She gave her outro on air and waited for Carmen to signal that they were off before she slipped her headphones from her ears.

"That was excellent. Thank you so much," she said.

They both stood, and he shook her hand. "My pleasure, Gemma. Hey, you're Roger's kid, aren't you? I remember you from when you were this big," he said, and held his hand near his hip. She thought for a mortifying second that he was going to recall her freeze-up of shame, but he softly smiled instead. "All grown up now. How's that old shit doing these days?"

Gemma's face flushed at what she knew was not a slight aimed at her father. Nigel probably had scandalous stories about him too. She did not want to get into the details of their relationship and ruin the high she was riding.

"I assume he's well. I don't see him that much."

He gave her a knowing nod like she didn't need to explain any more. Gemma knew he had two ex-wives and three kids with any number of grandkids by now; perhaps he had his own share of strained relationships.

"Tough break, love. But you've got a knack for this. The industry is in your blood."

She forgave him for bestowing his blessing on Azalea in that moment. She beamed brighter than the sun.

"Thank you."

"You'll be in the audience then tonight?"

Her sunbeam snapped out.

"Oh, actually no. I couldn't get tickets, and it's my best friend's birthday party tonight."

It was part lie. She *could* have gotten tickets, of course, even though the show sold out in twenty minutes. All she would have had to do was ask her father. But.

"Well, that's an easy fix. And I can do even better. Bridge!" he yelled at the glass wall.

"Oh, she can't hear—"

"Get this lot backstage passes for tonight! However many they need!"

Gemma flinched at his voice booming off the sound-proof glass. She saw Bridget nod like she understood and reach for her phone.

Nigel turned to Gemma with a smile. "Fixed. Bring your friend for her birthday."

She was back to beaming like the sun. "Wow. Thank you!"

"Of course, love. Thanks for the chat. I have to run." He reached for her and kissed her cheek.

She almost fainted on the spot.

"Bye, Nigel Black," she said as if she were in a dream and not actually watching her idol walk away.

He replaced his sunglasses and marched out the door. Carmen and Hugo stood to shake his hand, and Jack slipped inside the booth.

He came at her with a huge grin. "You were amazing."

Gemma mimicked a curtsy. "Thank you!" She was still riding the high of having been kissed on the cheek by Nigel Black. She reached out and pressed her palm to Jack's chest. "And thank you for the pep talk. Seriously."

He put his hand over hers. "Of course. But do you want to know a secret?"

The feel of her hand sandwiched between his heartbeat and the warmth of his palm made her dizzy. His eyes were suddenly dazzling.

"What?"

He squeezed her hand and smiled. "That was the first time you've ever done that."

Gemma stopped swooning as she followed what he had said. "Wait, what? I've never done the interview before?"

He shook his head. "You always cancel it instead. This is the first time you've gone through with it."

She blinked at him. "So, you lied to me?"

"Yes. Sorry, but I knew you could do it, so I wanted to give you a little—"

Gemma, suddenly swooning for a different reason, closed

her fist around a handful of his shirt and pulled him into a kiss. She had been out-of-her-mind terrified on the sidewalk, and he'd given her the boost she needed. Without him, she never would have had the guts to talk to Nigel.

He sucked in a sharp breath and almost lost his balance.

Gemma had been caught up in the moment, yes, but kissing Jack felt both new and like returning home from a long journey. Once he recovered from the shock, he kissed her back like his life depended on it. His lips molded around hers like complementary shapes cut out for each other. The soft pout was everything she'd imagined, and his tongue tasted like something she could get drunk on. She leaned into him, a dizzying warmth spreading over her, and felt his arms hook around her back. Flashes of their kiss in the bar came back but they were no longer dreamlike blips. She felt the familiarity of his lips and his arms. She couldn't make sense of what any of it meant, but she knew it meant something big.

She pulled back, and he followed for a second, almost unconsciously, like he wanted to hold on longer. She softly smiled at him and pressed her fingers to his lips. "Thank you for lying to me."

He looked positively stunned. A dazed shine filled his blue eyes. He softly kissed the pads of her fingers in a way that made Gemma tingle before she dropped her hand. "I'll lie to you all day if this is the consequence."

Gemma laughed as she heard the audio system click on.

"Uh, Gem? Who is this guy again?" Carmen's voice came through the speakers in the ceiling.

Gemma flushed a shade of scarlet, she was sure. She had forgotten they were on display behind the glass.

"This is Jack."

"Uh-huh. So, Jack, you're not a musician, are you?" Carmen said protectively. She leaned over Hugo where he sat at the soundboard with his arms crossed like a father waiting for his daughter to come home from prom.

"No," Jack said. "I'm a writer."

Carmen exchanged a glance with Hugo. "Not sure if that's better or worse in this town."

"I vote better," Hugo said.

Jack gave them a puzzled look. "Thank you?"

Gemma quietly laughed.

"Well, whatever you did to get our girl out of her shell, thank you. She totally nailed it," Carmen said.

"Nailed it," Hugo echoed like a parrot. They tended to get in a rhythm when they spoke.

Gemma proudly smiled that her work family was cheering her on.

"Way to handle that curve ball, by the way," Carmen said. "We heard Azalea, and I had to put it through to keep the interview flowing. Sorry about that."

"It's fine," Gemma said, thankful she'd been able to handle it well.

"Her ex is the front man," Carmen tacked on for Jack's benefit since her romantic history was no secret to anyone else in earshot. "Guy's a dick."

"Total dick," Hugo said.

"He used her to get a record deal because her dad knows everyone in the industry," Carmen added like a sprinkle of salt on a wound.

"Every—"

"Thanks, guys! He already knows!" Gemma shouted over whatever Hugo tried to add.

Jack still had his arms around her. He gave her a sympathetic squeeze.

She shot him a sad half smile and shrugged. "So, now what?" she asked. "If I just did something I've never done before, is that going to set the whole day on a different path?"

Jack paused in thought. "I don't know. You'd never visited Dr. Woods before, nor had you visited the psychic, and we still ended up here. And for that matter, I'd never explained what was going on in the coffee shop back at the start of it all. And you've *definitely* never kissed me during the day, so who knows what we've set in motion."

Warmth filled her cheeks. She had been bold on several counts, and she liked the turn of events. She also liked the feel of Jack's arms around her and the memory—a real one she was sure about this time—of his kiss.

The shine in his eye felt like a promise.

She smiled at him. "Do you want to find out what we've set in motion?"

He smiled back and nodded. "Definitely."

CHAPTER
8

THE FIRST THING they decided to set in motion was lunch. Neither of them had eaten anything since breakfast, and with all the running around and Gemma's career-changing interview, she was starving.

They ended up in Koreatown at a restaurant inside a rooftop greenhouse with marble tables and all manner of plants suspended from the slatted ceiling. Natural light poured in from every angle. They sat in upholstered bucket chairs at a small, square table among a softly murmuring crowd of lunchgoers. Gemma had strategically let Jack sit with his back to the window filled with blue sky the same color as his brilliant eyes. She ordered a mimosa because the orange juice was fresh-squeezed and because Marsha had called to commend her on the interview and give her the rest of the day off.

Jack squeezed a lemon over his iced tea and sent a squirt of mist zesting the air between them.

"Have we ever been here together before?" she asked, eagerly awaiting her avocado toast.

Jack shook his head. "No. I've intentionally taken you someplace new each time we've gone out in hopes it makes a difference."

"Where else have we gone?" she asked, simply curious. She wondered if they'd dined at restaurants that she'd never been to before and had no memory of.

"Well, before I knew you were vegetarian, we went to a barbecue place. That didn't work out too well," he said with a soft laugh. "In fact, that's how I found out."

She smiled at him. "So, do you have like a list of places to go in case I agree to a date on any given day?"

A flush curled into his face and he gave her a cheeky, boyish grin. "Mm-hmm."

Gemma burst out laughing. "Well, I can't fault your determination."

"Tenacity is my middle name."

"That is certified fact," Gemma said, and sipped her drink as a thought struck her. "If I've never done the interview before, am I usually in a bad mood at lunch?"

Jack tried to hide a grimace and lightly hunched his shoulders. "You're usually pretty bummed out, but I always enjoy your company no matter what."

Something warm and soft spilled out inside her chest at the thought that he didn't give up, even on her bad days. "That's generous of you."

He shrugged like any time with her was a gift.

"So," Gemma said, "what do we usually talk about?"

"Let's see." He gazed up at the jungle hanging from the ceiling in potted planters. Vines and mosses reached down like spindly green arms. "You usually tell me about Patrick coming home, you mention Nigel Black and your radio show, and you say it's your best friend's birthday."

Gemma groaned at the banality. To her, that all would have been exciting for the first time, as it had been that morning, but she couldn't imagine Jack feigning interest in the same details day in and out. "You must be so bored of me."

He smiled at her and shook his head. His eyes turned soft and warm. "I don't think that's possible."

Her face flushed as their server appeared balancing their lunch on her long, elegant arms. She was abundantly symmetrical and the requisite amount of gorgeous to be an L.A. waitress.

"Anything else?" she asked with a sweet smile aimed directly at Jack.

"No," he said without taking his eyes off Gemma.

The waitress turned away and Gemma picked up her fork to distract from the flush burning her face.

"It's not fair," she said, and stabbed a tiny cherry tomato lounging on her toast.

"What's not?" Jack asked, and poked a fork into a sweet potato wedge.

"For you to look at me like that. Like you've had a hundred-and-whatever days when I've only had one." She waved her fork over her plate and did not meet his eyes while she spoke. Her lunch was thankfully distractingly delicious.

He stayed silent long enough to make her look up.

"Well, if it's any consolation, I looked at you like this the first time I saw you too."

A piece of seedy whole-grain toast tried to wedge in her throat. She gulped her mimosa to wash it down.

The bald flattery was not something she was used to. Nor was the feeling of someone so intently gazing at her like she was the only person in the room. It filled her with warmth and insecurity at the same time.

"Well, you should dial it back a few notches unless you want me to combust from embarrassment," she said with a half smile and eyes back on her toast.

Jack quietly laughed. "You've never combusted, don't worry."

Gemma chewed a bite and thought of a question she had been wondering about. "How does it vary so much within any given day? You said sometimes I do certain things, little things, and other times I don't. How does that work if it's all the same day over and over?"

"That's a great question. Truthfully, I don't know. I guess it's little changes in your mood or experiences that slightly alter your behavior."

Gemma considered it. In normal circumstances, her life did follow a pretty standard routine. There were no wild variations in walking Rex, going to work, coming home, walking Rex again, and then reading a book or streaming something before bed so she could get up and do it all over again. But even within that routine, on any given day a slight shift in her mood could lead her to make different decisions and change up the repetition while keeping it along the same general track. Like someone switching their customary coffee order because they felt like it. It made sense then that she would sometimes do certain things and other times not while living the same day on repeat.

"What would Dr. Woods have to say about it?"

"Oh, he'd probably draw you a diagram and try to explain it with one of his gadgets," Jack said, and warmly smiled.

Gemma thought of the purple spinning globe with golden axes. She couldn't help but wonder about all the different ways she had behaved within the same day.

"How am I different every day? What's, like, the meanest I've been to you?"

Jack laughed. "I don't think you're capable of being truly mean, but there was one day where you didn't apologize after the coffee incident. You scowled at me and stomped away. I didn't try to chase after you that day."

"Yikes. Sorry." She wondered what else had happened that morning to make her so impolite. "What's the nicest?"

Jack sipped his tea and smiled. "Well, that kiss at the bar was pretty great, but you're always nice. Like, unduly nice to some idiot who crashed into you because he was texting."

Their collision already felt like months ago.

"Aside from yesterday when you were testing your theory, have you ever *not* crashed into me to see what happens?"

He nodded. "Several times. Your favorite shirt does make it through the day every once in a while, believe it or not."

"Good to know she is spared. What else happens?"

"It's pretty uneventful. You go to work free of coffee stains, the interview gets canceled, Patrick never makes it home, you don't go see your father, then you go to Lila's birthday party in a pretty sour mood from it all."

She frowned at him. "That sounds like a terrible day."

"Yeah, not too hot for you all in all."

Gemma took another bite of toast and mulled it over.

"So, then it seems like I'm better off on the days we crash because then I at least get to meet you, even if all that other stuff still happens."

Jack softly smiled, crinkling the corners of his eyes. "That's kind of you. If only you could remember me from day to day."

Gemma thought about what it would be like to remember Jack. How she would undeniably wake up looking forward to seeing his smile and the shine in his eyes. She would probably have a budding addiction to kissing him and think about their lips touching all day, perhaps even count down the hours until she could make it happen. She would know his voice and his laugh and miss him when he wasn't there. She would want to be near him and make memories together.

The warmth bubbling in her chest reminded her of a feeling she hadn't had in a long time. At the same time that her heart was cartwheeling, her head was reminding her to be cautious. She had fallen head-over-heels for Nick, and it had left her broken and alone.

But she hadn't met Nick on a day cosmically designed to bring them together, so she told her head to shut up since there was no logic to be had about whatever was blossoming between her and Jack.

"How did you first notice you were stuck?" she asked him, realizing they hadn't yet broached the topic.

"As soon as I crashed into you for a second time," he said with certainty. "I told you: it feels like the earth tilts, so when it happened twice in a row, it was a serious wake-up call."

Gemma's face warmed at the thought that she had that

kind of effect on him, and she couldn't deny there had been a little earth-tilting for her too. "And what, you'd been asleep for the morning up until that point?"

He shrugged. "I mean yeah. My day is pretty routine, so nothing jumped out as *this is exactly what happened yesterday* for the first hour until I found myself slamming into the best person who I could possibly hope to spill coffee on."

"You're doing the flattery thing again," she said, and poked her food.

"Sorry. I can't help it. But you'd be the same if you spent every day with you too."

Gemma laughed. "I do spend every day with me. I'm not that exciting."

"I beg to differ."

She was nearing the end of her mimosa and wondered if a second would be permissible since she was off work for the rest of the day. The juicy bubbles had her head feeling light and curiously accepting of her whole situation. "What about yesterday?" she asked Jack. "And I don't mean yesterday as in the previous iteration of this day, I mean the *real* yesterday, as in the day before all this started."

Jack was halfway done with his sandwich. He looked up at her with an interested tilt of his head. "What do you mean?"

"I mean, what's the last thing you remember before you got stuck in a spiral of spilling coffee on me every day?"

"You're never going to let that go, are you?"

"Not until you buy me a new shirt, or we make it out of this day."

He smiled and picked up his tea. "Let's hope for the latter so the former isn't necessary."

She lifted her mimosa and clinked her glass to his.

"So?" she asked. "What happened to you yesterday?"

He stared down at his plate like he was concentrating. "Yesterday . . ." He blinked a few times, clearly struggling, and shook his head with a laugh. "That's funny. I've never really thought about it. I must have . . . I mean, today is Thursday, so it would have been a normal Wednesday, but I'm not sure what . . ."

An odd feeling washed over Gemma. It felt very significant in an unsettling way.

"Can you not remember, Jack?"

His eyes snapped up to hers. He blinked a few more times and narrowed his gaze. "I mean, I must have gone to work. We're midseason on the show, and I've been on set most days, but I can't . . ." He let out an uncomfortable laugh, and a look of true concern filled his face.

Gemma reached for his hand, not wanting to see him upset.

He squeezed her hand with a tight, warm grip. "Gemma, have I been stuck too long to remember what came before?" The edge of worry in his voice grew sharp. He looked at her, desperately, like she would have the answer. "Can you remember yesterday?"

Gemma scanned her mind and didn't have to look far. She had taken Rex to the groomer and talked to her mother on the phone about Patrick returning home. They had planned a trip to Phoenix to visit.

"Yes," she told Jack. "But it's only been one day in here for me from my perspective. You've been here much longer, so maybe that's why?" She threw out the suggestion having no idea if it made any sense.

Jack held on to her hand, and for the first time, the bright optimism faded from his face. He looked frightened. "Gemma, what does this mean? I can't remember what came before."

She didn't have an answer for him, but she was spared by his phone ringing.

He let go of her hand to reach for it and frowned. He let out a big sigh.

"What is it?"

He scrubbed his face with a hand. "The worst part of the day, other than when you leave me. Damn it. I lost track of time." He switched his phone to silent and left it buzzing on the tabletop. Gemma recognized the upside-down name of the caller not because she knew Jack's personal contacts, but because she had seen it on TV.

"You're not going to answer that?"

"She'll call back," Jack said wearily. "Again and again and again . . ." He repeated the word with a swinging tempo and sighed.

They hadn't discussed too much about his job, but she put the pieces together easily enough to know he was screening calls from an Emmy-winning director who was for all intents and purposes his boss like she was a persistent tele-marketer.

"Sorry," Gemma said, "but what's going on?"

He rested his elbows on the table and held his face with a grumble. Gemma had only seen the charming, optimistic side of him, other than a moment before when he seemed fearful. This weary exasperation was new.

"She's calling to tell me that Duncan Miles is refusing to come out of his trailer and shoot the new scene I wrote because he hates it. He's holding up production, and she wants me to come talk with him because, '*I swear to god, Jack, I'm going to murder him.*'" He changed the pitch of his voice to a rather spot-on impersonation of Erica Bennet, the director in question. He met Gemma's gaze with an exhausted look in his eyes. "It happens every day, and I'm so sick of dealing with it."

Gemma quickly digested everything he said. He had told her when he was trying to calm her down for her interview that he talked to famous people for work all the time, but she hadn't registered in what capacity or the caliber of fame he had meant.

Duncan Miles had a shelf of golden statues, had been named Sexiest Man Alive twice, and was currently starring in one of the most popular shows on television, which Gemma now knew Jack wrote for.

Jack's phone stopped buzzing before starting up again like a diver coming up for air between descents. He grumbled at it.

"You mean to tell me that Duncan Miles is a diva?" Gemma asked in an effort to lighten his mood.

His lips bent into a tiny grin. "Oh, the biggest. But no one knows it because he has an excellent publicist. Her name is Lucy Green. I've met her on days she comes to clean up his messes. I've been through this with him so many times, I've gotten to the point where I let him quit."

"He quits?" Gemma gaped at him. "The star of the show?"

"Yep. On some of his finer days he rips up the script in my face and storms off set. It's really a good time for everyone." His voice dripped with sarcasm that made Gemma feel bad for him. She didn't know what she could do, but she felt the need to help.

"Want me to talk to him?"

Jack perked up, interested. "You would do that?"

Gemma shrugged, feeling a bit brazen after her face-to-face with Nigel Black. Jack had intervened in that situation in a way he hadn't before, and it turned out for the best. "What have we got to lose?"

Jack laughed a cynical sound. "Only our patience and a multimillion-dollar contract with an actor who'd be impossible to replace midseason. I mean, I'd happily write his character's death, but fans would riot, and I think the studio would actually kill me."

"Does someone have to die in this scenario?"

"Let's hope not," he said, and lifted his phone. "I appreciate the offer, Gemma, but he's not the guy you see on TV. Are you sure you want to do this?"

She gave him a nod. "Yes. You helped me with the interview, so let me help you with this."

He let out a big breath. "Okay, if you're sure." He answered his phone, which had never stopped ringing. "Hey, Erica."

"Jack! I need you down here right now. Duncan has lost his goddamned mind over that new scene. No one can get him out of his trailer. *Please* come fix this." Gemma heard her sharp, clear voice coming through the phone. She had a vision of the short blond woman she'd seen on TV at awards shows currently wearing headphones looped around her neck and holding a clipboard under her arm.

"Okay," Jack said. "I'm across town, but I can be there in a little bit."

"I swear to god, Jack, I'm going to murder him."

"Don't do that. You're running out of places to bury bodies, Erica. Hang tight. I'll be there soon."

"Thank you."

He ended the call and replaced his phone on the table. His smile briefly returned. "Well, let's go see what kind of trouble we can cause."

GEMMA HAD LEFT her car at the radio studio before lunch, so Jack drove them up over the Hollywood Hills to get to the set where Duncan was causing problems. At the studio lot's gate, he flashed a badge at the security guard, and they passed through.

He parked, and Gemma tried to reel in her overwhelming giddiness of being behind the scenes on a studio lot. He led her through like it was another day at the office while she ogled the exterior sets and famous logos. When they arrived at a row of trailers and walked to the farthest one, she remembered what she had volunteered to do.

A wave of nerves hit her when she saw the small cluster of people standing outside the king-sized trailer looking impatient. They all wore lanyards and headphones and carried tablets or clipboards.

"Jack! Thank god." Erica Bennet greeted him with a hand on her hip. She was tiny and every bit as formidable as Gemma had imagined. She tapped her phone with one hand and muttered something to the production assistant standing at her side. "We've lost an hour to this nonsense.

Please go in there and do whatever it takes to get us back on schedule."

"Hi, Erica. This is Gemma. She's here to help."

Erica shot Gemma a glance as her phone rang. "Great. If she can fix this, we'll give her a PA credit on the episode. I'll be on set. Hello?" She said the last word into her phone and marched off.

Gemma didn't really have a plan, but she suddenly felt the weight of the production resting on her shoulders. The small crowd of important-looking TV people expectantly, and perhaps dubiously, eyed her before they dispersed to follow Erica.

She turned to Jack and whispered, "What do I say to him?"

"Whatever you want. Nothing I've ever said has worked, so I don't know what it'll take, if it's even possible."

Gemma swallowed her nerves and reminded herself that she had recently talked to Nigel Black, so some snooty actor would be nothing. She stepped up to the trailer door and knocked.

"Go away!" Duncan shouted from inside like a child who'd locked himself in his bedroom.

Gemma looked at Jack, and he shrugged.

She knocked again, firmer this time. "Duncan? My name is Gemma. Can I come in?"

"Gemma? I don't know any Gemma." The closed door and nearby generator powering the trailers muffled his voice.

"I'm a friend of Jack's."

"Jack? I don't want to talk to Jack. He's ruining everything."

Gemma took the cue and gently pushed Jack to the side. "Jack's not here. That's why he sent me."

A long pause passed, and Gemma eventually heard footsteps approaching the door. The trailer slightly swayed as if someone large were moving around inside. The door swung open.

Duncan Miles filled the small doorway, all six-foot-something of his sculpture-like stature and Sexiest Man Alive face. He was in costume, the open suit jacket and dark jeans he wore to portray the titular character in the gritty crime drama *Mac Drake*. Gemma's knees wobbled at the sight of him. He arched a dark brow. "Who are you?"

Finding her voice took an embarrassing amount of effort. "Gemma. I'm here to talk to you about getting back on set."

He sighed and eyed the empty space behind her. Jack had slipped out of Duncan's line of sight, but Gemma could see him lingering in the corner of her eye. She made a conscious effort not to look at him. "Did Jack send you as some kind of peace ambassador?" he said. He left the door open and turned inside. She took that as permission to follow.

She shot a quick glance at Jack, and he gave her an impressed thumbs-up.

Duncan Miles's trailer was fit for a king, with a full-sized fridge, bed, sofa, and dining area. A European soccer game that must have been beamed in via satellite was muted on the giant TV. A half-eaten tray of fresh sushi sat on the dining table beside a brand of bottled water Gemma knew Duncan was a spokesperson for. A small bowl of all red Starburst candies sat beside a tattered script that looked like it had been rolled up and used to hit something. The edges curved on either side, and Gemma recognized character names in the lines of Courier font. She tried not to retain any information and, as a fan of the show, she hoped she could make it out of the interaction without spoiling the new season for herself.

"So," she said, unsure where to start. "I hear there are some issues with this new scene that Jack added."

He picked up the water bottle and took a swig. "Who are you?"

"I'm Gemma."

He dipped his long fingers into the candy bowl and pinched a Starburst. Gemma wondered if some poor assistant had to open sleeve after sleeve to pick out all the red ones, or if they special-ordered them in bulk. He unwrapped the candy and popped it in his mouth. He noisily chewed. "And why are you here?"

She suddenly understood what Jack had meant about losing their patience. "To talk about the scene. Jack told me you're upset with him for writing it."

He frowned at her, which really only made him more brooding and attractive. "That's what he thinks I'm upset about?"

Gemma pulled out a chair at the table because she felt like this was a sit-down conversation. "Isn't it? I thought that's why you're refusing to shoot it."

He rolled his dark eyes. "I'm not *refusing* to do anything. I'm taking a moment to express my discontent."

Gemma had heard Erica say they'd lost an hour, and she could only imagine what that hour had cost in dollars. Reminding Duncan of the time he was wasting did not seem like the right tactic, so she took another.

"Can you tell me what you're discontent about? Something with the new scene?" She spoke to him gently, like she was trying to run interference on a toddler threatening a tantrum.

By some miracle, it seemed to work.

He heaved a sigh and sat down in the chair opposite her. He reached for another Starburst. "It's not the scene. The scene is great." He bit down on the candy, and Gemma wondered if red Starbursts were his preferred stress food.

"Then what is it?"

He looked side to side although they were alone and leaned in. "Look, people talk, and I'm not supposed to know this, but I assume you already know if you work for Jack."

"Oh, I don't—"

"But I heard that he's leaving the show."

"He's what?" Gemma said at the same time the trailer door swung open.

"I'm *what*?!" Jack blurted from the doorway.

Duncan suddenly stood up, his height swallowing up all the space inside. "Jack! Were you listening to us?"

"Yes," Jack said without hesitation. He climbed the short steps inside, wearing a look of confusion. "What did you say, Duncan? I'm *leaving* the show?"

Duncan stood back and crossed his arms with an indignant scowl. Gemma was going to scold Jack for interrupting what she thought had been a decent attempt at intervention on his behalf, but based on the look on his face, she needed to let him resume control of the situation.

"First," Duncan said, pointing a finger at him, "rude. Second, more rude that you sent Gina to spy on me."

"It's Gemma," she chirped.

"*Third*," Duncan continued, "how dare you abandon

me. Were you going to go without telling me? No one writes this character like you can, Jack. I don't want him in anyone else's hands. You're really going to leave me—*me*—to go write a show about dragons and made-up kings? That's not you. *This* is you. *Mac Drake* is you. I don't want to do this without you." Duncan sat back down with a forceful huff, crossed his arms, and stubbornly turned his head.

Jack stared at him with his mouth hanging open. Gemma was at a complete loss.

"Duncan," Jack finally said, "I have no idea what you are talking about."

Duncan scoffed. "Oh, don't lie to me. My agent told me she heard the news this morning. At least I can trust *someone* to be honest with me."

Jack ran a hand through his hair and stroked his chin. For all the certainty he'd had over being stuck in a time loop, Gemma could tell he was genuinely reeling. "Wh-what news?"

Duncan cast him a brutal glare. "Now you're just insulting me." He reached for another Starburst. "You're going to make me break out from all this stress candy; my esthetician bill will be outrageous. I won't be abandoned midseason, Jack."

Jack pulled out a chair and sat opposite him. He spread his hands on the table in the same way that he had when he first explained to Gemma that they were in a time loop. His voice carried every bit of the same sincerity. "Duncan, I'm not sure what you've heard, but I swear to you, I'm not leaving the show."

Duncan stopped chewing and turned to him. "You're not?"

"No. I thought you were refusing to shoot today because you hated the new scene. You've never said anything before about—" He stopped himself from saying anything about all the times they had lived the day before because that would only make matters worse. He cleared his throat and started over. "I didn't know you thought I was leaving, and that's what you were upset about. I promise you, that's not the case."

Duncan eyed him suspiciously before his face broke out in a relieved grin and he threw a big hand to his chest. "Oh, thank god, man," he said with a charming laugh as if his mood had done a one-eighty. "I knew you wouldn't do that to me, especially with no warning like that."

Jack joined him in smiling, and Gemma knew he was burying his confusion and putting on a performance for Duncan's sake. "Of course not. I would never do that to you—or Mac."

Duncan stood and grabbed his script. "Of course you wouldn't. We're like family, all of us." He rolled up the script and excitedly whacked it against his palm. "Then let's get back to it. This new scene is sick."

"Thanks," Jack said, and stood up too.

Duncan reached out and pulled him into a back-slapping half hug. "You're the best, man. Mac Drake still has the best in front of him. Watch out!" He pointed his fingers like guns and pushed open the door with a laugh. "Nice to meet you, Greta."

"You too, and it's Gemma!" she called after him.

She heard him jump down onto the concrete and shout, "We're back, baby!" to a round of cheers. She felt like she had whiplash from it all.

"Well, that was . . . dramatic."

Jack snorted. "Welcome to Hollywood." He stared at the floor with a pale, concerned look on his face.

"What's wrong?"

He shook his head and met her eyes. "Gemma, I seriously have *no idea* what he was talking about. Me leaving the show? Kings and dragons? I mean, that sounds like a pretty specific rumor if someone's trying to harm me."

She hated to see him so distressed. She couldn't easily imagine what benefit there was to be gained over a rumor like that, but she knew Hollywood was cutthroat. She was sure there were stealth forms of sabotage beyond her imagination.

"Would someone do that to you?"

"No one who I can think of," he said with a shake of his head.

Gemma didn't know what to make of that. "Then maybe it's somehow true?"

"It can't be. I think I'd remember if I agreed to walk away from the show that I've been with for five seasons and completely change genre."

The word *remember* rang like a gong in Gemma's head. The conversation they'd had at lunch came back to her in a rush.

"Jack, what if you *don't* remember? What if it happened yesterday?"

CHAPTER
9

"OKAY, NEW THEORY," Gemma said as they climbed back into Jack's car. "You made some life-changing decision yesterday—the real yesterday—that somehow set today in motion."

Jack punched the gas hard enough to make the tires squeal and rock Gemma against her seat. They had swapped positions, and now he was the one spiraling in a panic with her trying to calm him down. Given the change in roles, she wondered if she should have been the one driving.

"Where are we going?" she asked as he hit a speed bump hard enough to bounce her off her seat.

"I need to go home." He jabbed his finger into the console screen. A wavy line appeared, waiting for a command. "Call Charlie," he ordered.

"Who's Charlie?" Gemma whispered as they whipped out of the studio lot. She grabbed the handle above her door.

"My agent."

The outgoing call rang loudly inside the car. It put Gemma's nerves on even higher alert.

A few rings passed before a deep voice answered.

"Jack, what's up?"

"Tell me I didn't quit *Mac Drake.*"

A pause passed. Gemma held her breath.

"What?" Charlie asked.

"Duncan Miles just had a meltdown on set, and he said it was because he heard a rumor that I was quitting to go write for some fantasy show. Tell me that's not true."

They made it away from stoplights and surface streets and Jack directed them toward a freeway. Gemma really wondered if she should have been driving, given the speed he was going.

"Jack, man, what are you talking about?" Charlie said.

Jack exhaled a mighty breath that Gemma mimicked. "Thank you."

"The deal is done," Charlie came back and said. "We made it official yesterday. I figured you were giving everyone at *Mac Drake* notice today."

Jack paled and gripped the steering wheel hard enough to pop one of his knuckles. "What?"

Charlie nervously laughed. "Is this some kind of reverse buyer's remorse? Because I'm lost."

Jack took a hand off the wheel and scrubbed his face. Gemma could tell he was struggling to decide what he could say and not complicate matters.

"Yeah, sorry," he said. "It's been a wild day. Can you remind me of the details?"

"Did you party too hard last night or something? Because you're kinda freaking me out."

"Charlie, just tell me!"

"Okay! Paramount bought out your *Mac Drake* contract

on top of offering you seven figures to join their new fantasy series. It shoots in Scotland starting this summer. I'm having my real estate agent send you all those listings in Glasgow you asked for."

Jack stared out the windshield blinking and looking pale enough to vomit.

An ache filled Gemma's chest. Even after a day, the thought of losing him hurt.

"But I don't write fantasy," Jack said.

"Hey, buddy, listen," Charlie said. His voice picked up a soothing, familiar tone. "I know this is a big change, but that's what you wanted."

"I did?"

"I mean, you came to me and said, 'Charlie, I need something different in my life. I want a change,' so yeah. I told you to get a dog or take up a new hobby, thinking we had a great thing going with *Mac Drake*, but you told me to shop for other opportunities, and then boom! Found one we couldn't say no to. You're a hot commodity, Jack."

Jack was speechless. Gemma knew he was trying to reconcile the present with things he couldn't remember his past self doing, because she had spent the day doing the same thing herself.

"Jack?" Charlie said. "You still there?"

"Yeah," Jack said numbly. "I gotta go, though. Thanks, Charlie."

"Anytime. Let me know if you need anything."

The call disconnected, and Gemma didn't know what to say in the silence.

Jack steered them onto a windy road at the top of Laurel Canyon. Downtown L.A. hovered like a gold-dusted mirage far below. Given what she had just learned about his personal finances, she was not surprised he lived in the Hollywood Hills.

"Have you ever talked to Charlie today?" she asked, already knowing the answer.

Jack shook his head. She got the sense he was too stunned to speak.

"He seems like a good agent," she offered. It felt frail and insufficient. Jack had just had his world turned upside down.

"Yeah," he finally said. "Yeah, Charlie is the best."

Gemma watched the hillsides rise and fall out her window as they wound down the canyon. They passed mansions wedged into the earth like fallen glass-and-stone meteors, private driveways, a few normal-looking houses, and a small shopping center with a cluster of old, local businesses. She knew the area well despite avoiding it to the best of her ability. Jack turned them onto a street with more modest homes shrouded in bushy trees. When he pulled into the shallow driveway of a white house crawling in ivy, the fit felt right for him. The house sat above a two-car garage, and a stone staircase wrapped the side, disappearing into the lush greenery. A small balcony hung out over the driveway, and Gemma could bet it had a stunning view.

The setting was familiar, but the house was not.

"Have I ever been here before?" she asked as they climbed out of the car and headed for the staircase.

"No. Nothing since we met at your radio studio today has ever happened before, minus lunch and Duncan's meltdown. I've never come home at this point in the day."

Jack led the way across his driveway to the stone staircase

spun with green vines. Gemma's feet scraped against the steps as they climbed a rounded bend up to a small court-yard crowded with leafy trees. Over the top of a short gate, she could see the white stucco house with large rectangles of glass bookending the front door. Jack opened the gate, and she followed him along a pathway made of flat stones spaced like river rocks with tiny gravel in between. Jack unlocked the front door, and where Gemma had been trained to ex-pect the patter of paws, she heard silence. It was so quiet, in fact, that she felt the need to speak just to make noise.

"This is beautiful."

The interior was austere, mostly white, and wide open. Small accents of color—pillows, vases, the occasional splashy painting—gave it a little life. His furniture was low and clean, and he kept neat stacks of books on his shelves and end tables: novels, screenwriting guides, biographies. Every window showed some shade of green since they had climbed up into the trees. Aside from the stunning view of the city out the living room balcony, she felt remarkably as if they had left L.A.

"Thanks," Jack said. She could tell by the sound of his voice that he was still reeling from the phone call in the car. "Make yourself at home; I just need a minute."

"Sure."

He nodded and headed for a hallway.

Gemma found herself alone and felt an urgent need to explore. This man who knew all sorts of things about her had just left her to her own devices inside his home. Obvi-ously, he trusted her. Or perhaps he was too distracted to worry that she might give in to her temptation to snoop in the revealing crevices of his house like the pantry or a medicine cabinet. She did neither and instead looked for pieces of him subtly scattered around the orderly space.

A pair of worn running shoes spilling untied laces sat by the front door. A coatrack held a raincoat and gray hoodie that she imagined him pulling on to take out the trash or walk downstairs to get the mail on a cool morning. She smelled his breezy scent on the soft sleeve when she pressed it to her nose.

When she stepped down into his sunken living room, the first thing she noticed was the upright piano in the corner. She imagined it sounded lovely echoing into the enclave of his vaulted ceiling and wondered how movers had managed to get it up the stairs into the house. Perhaps a crew of burly men had shouted *Pivot!* at one another until they made it, sweat-drenched and straining, to his living room. Or maybe they used a crane and lifted it through the balcony doors.

The second thing she noted was a thick paperback crime thriller on his coffee table with a spine that had clearly been bent back. She smiled to herself at the thought of him lounged on his plush couch, maybe in his gray hoodie, with it folded over in one hand and a concentrated look on his face as he read it for research for his show, or perhaps for pleasure. Jack, the spine breaker.

Next to the book sat a stack of tattered scripts much like the one she'd seen in Duncan's trailer, except these were marked up in a violent shade of red ink. Slashes crossed out sections and slanted, thin lettering crawled up the margins. Gemma lifted the top stack from the pile, avoiding reading the actual script, and ran her fingers over the indents made by Jack's pen. His notes to himself were half cryptic and wholly harsh. He was ruthless about finding the right word, the right tone, and Gemma found seeing his handwritten thoughts as intimate as if she'd opened his underwear drawer. She smiled at an aggressive circle around a line of dialogue with an all-caps note to *MAKE THIS BETTER* in deep red strokes. Jack, the perfectionist.

She replaced the script and wandered to the mantel above a gas fireplace. It held a single photo of Jack and who had to be his parents. He was clearly a teenager in the picture, which made sense, given he'd told her his father had died when he was eighteen and there he was, standing beside Jack in the picture. Jack looked like his dad, with the same dark hair and blue eyes. He had his mom's smile and seeing it on both their faces put a soft, warm feeling in Gemma's chest that made her smile as well. Jack, the beloved son. She was about to pick up the photo and touch her fingers to his young face, compelled to feel the image of his smooth skin, when the doorbell rang.

The ringing chimed into the house only to be followed by insistent knocking.

"Um, Jack?" Gemma called out, not sure where he had disappeared to or if she should answer the door. She stepped forward to look around the corner but didn't see him approaching. "Jack? There's someone at the door!" she called.

Before her words even made it down the hall, the front door burst open.

"Oh!" Gemma gasped, reassuring herself they'd left it unlocked. Whoever was entering must have been friendly enough with Jack to invite themselves inside.

To her complete and utter shock, she saw a startlingly familiar and completely out-of-context face. A dark-haired woman wearing wedges to rival Lila's most daring heels hurtled in through the door. An oversized tee hung off one of her bronzed shoulders and she wore cutoff denim shorts. With her hair twirled up in a bun and enormous hoop earrings, she managed to look glamorous and like she had just rolled from bed all at once.

"Jack!" she blurted, and yanked off her sunglasses. Her thick lashes fanned like a Cover Girl ad.

Gemma simply gaped at her, confounded as to why Angelica Reyes, movie star and red-carpet darling, had just burst through Jack's front door.

Angelica paused her dramatic entrance and noticed Gemma. "Who are you?" she asked with a tilt of her head. Her dark, perfect brow furrowed like she didn't know what she was looking at and wasn't sure if she liked it.

Gemma was partially starstruck but mostly just confused. "I'm, um . . ."

Jack chose that moment to reappear from down the hall.

Angelica burst back to life at the sight of him. "Jack! Oh, thank god you're home!" She threw herself at him. "I couldn't leave without seeing you."

The emotion on Jack's face ran the gamut from shocked to confused to downright scared. Gemma still didn't know why this woman had appeared in the first place, nor why she was flailing in Jack's reluctant embrace like they were in a soap opera.

"Uh, Angelica," Jack eventually said. "What are you doing here?"

Still baffled by the whole scene, Gemma wondered the same thing. When Angelica squeezed Jack's shoulders and buried her face in his chest, Gemma got the sense it was not just another dramatic Hollywood meltdown. The way she touched him said it wasn't only an actress wailing at a writer. It was more intimate than that.

Gemma took a step back, suddenly uncomfortable and feeling like she was intruding.

"I'm here to see you!" Angelica gushed. She pressed her hands to his face and stood on her toes to lean into him. She draped her arms around his neck and dangled from him like a little A-list accessory. "I hate the way we left things, and I couldn't leave without seeing you."

Jack stood rigid with his arms out and elbows bent like a scarecrow doing jazz hands. He was clearly trying not to touch her while she was grabbing at him like he was the antidote to a poison she'd swallowed. "Leave where?"

Angelica giggled and nuzzled his chest again. "For Milan, silly. My new movie starts shooting next week! But I had to see you first. I was on my way to the airport and thought I'd stop by. It was only a little hiccup what happened the other day, right? We can still fix everything. I'm so glad I caught you because I can't stand the thought of leaving without saying goodbye!" Her voice rose an octave into a squeak. She cupped his face and pressed a loud kiss to his mouth.

Gemma loudly cleared her throat.

Angelica turned and shot her a cold, dismissive look. "Sorry, but who are you?" She eyed Gemma up and down. "Are you Jack's new assistant or something?"

An odd feeling settled itself in Gemma's chest. It felt at once like she was being smashed and like she might explode.

"Um, *no*?" She directed the upward inflection at Jack,

the man who had spent all morning trying to convince her not only that they were inexplicably bound together in a time loop but also that he was in love with her, and that her falling for him was the way out—and damn it, if she hadn't started to fall—all the while failing to mention he had a famous actress in his life who made house calls and kissed him on her tippy-toes.

"Gemma," he said.

The pained look on his face could not rival the pain suddenly filling Gemma's chest. It was more than a flashback of what Nick had done to her. It was betrayal fresh and new, and so what if she'd only known him for half a day. It hurt like hell.

"What's going on, Jack?" she asked, fearing the answer.

He tried to pry Angelica off himself but only succeeded in moving her backward a few inches. "Gemma, this is not what it looks like."

"Oh?" she said, the pain in her chest uncomfortably radiating out into her limbs. "It looks like you forgot to tell me you have a girlfriend." She hated the tearful pinch in her voice almost as much as she hated the sight of Angelica Reyes clinging to him like plastic wrap.

Angelica's mouth popped open. She still had her arms looped around his neck. She looked back and forth between Jack and Gemma. "Wait, are you guys like . . . ?" Her brow furrowed and she scoffed at Jack. "Oh, this is rich. You lose your shit over me sleeping with someone else, and here you are days later with some doe-eyed assistant? Nice, Jack."

Gemma reeled at everything she'd said. She felt as if she'd stepped in a hornet's nest and was being stung all over. She obviously didn't know Jack like she thought she did, and the need not to have her heart trampled in front of a stranger—*two* strangers, apparently—overcame her.

"I need to go," she said, and headed for the door.

"Gemma, wait!" Jack blurted.

Angelica folded her arms and glared at her. "Yeah, probably best for you to leave, sweetie. Girls with your brand of ambition don't usually fare well in this town."

The mean words felt like a taunt verging on a threat. Gemma pushed past them and out the door back into the sunny day.

"Angelica, stop it," she heard Jack say behind her. "She's not my assistant. I don't even have an assistant."

Gemma made it to the gate and hurried down the stairs. The warm, tender feelings she'd had moments before from seeing bits of Jack's life on display felt like they were tumbling from her grasp and shattering on the stones. She made it back to his driveway to find a shiny red convertible parked sideways and blocking in Jack's car. Of course Angelica Reyes drove a sports car fit for a villain. Gemma skirted around it and set off into the street.

The narrow avenues of the hills had no sidewalks. Traffic was minimal and cars and pedestrians and bikes all shared the same cracked concrete space. The sun beat down on her from above as she started in the opposite direction from which they had driven in. She made it two houses down before she heard Jack.

"Gemma, wait! Please."

He had said the same words so many times that day; what was once more?

She kept walking until he caught up and reached for her arm.

"Leave me alone, Jack."

He held on to her so that she turned to face him. His eyes were as blue as ever under the soaring sky. Remnants of the shock she'd seen inside his house lingered on his face. "Please, let me explain."

Embarrassment at her foolishness for letting herself trust him prickled her whole body. "You didn't tell me you have a girlfriend. Convenient detail to leave out of this little fantasy of yours."

"She's not my girlfriend!"

Gemma looked over his shoulder to make sure Angelica hadn't followed him. "No? Then why did she show up desperate to see you and make amends before she flies off to Europe? You sure you didn't plan to meet up over there and start your new life together?" Gemma felt the bite in her tone growing harsher. Her defenses were up, and she'd had enough experience getting hurt to sharpen her blades.

Jack ran his hands through his hair, exasperated. "Look, I'm sorry she's here, but I don't know what's going on. She's never shown up today before. I haven't seen her in essentially five months!"

He sounded sincere, but she found it hard to care.

"Well, she's here now, so." Gemma turned to leave again, feeling a hot ache at the back of her throat that felt embarrassingly like tears. She was not willing to listen to any more far-fetched explanations of things that had or had not happened before, and she was not willing to cry in front of him.

"Gemma, wait!"

"Goodbye, Jack!"

"Where are you even going?" His voice faded behind her. She did not turn around but pictured him standing in the middle of the sunny street with his arms out in question.

She continued up the road and around the bend. A slight incline forced her breath to come out harder. By the time she made it to an intersection and turned downhill, a layer of sweat had sprung up on her skin. She continued walking, angry at Jack and at herself for entertaining the idea of something possibly blossoming between them and doing her best not to imagine Angelica Reyes feeling him up in his house. Perhaps they had gone to his bedroom, and she was giving him a proper goodbye before she jetted off to star in another blockbuster.

"Argh!" Gemma grumbled, and swiped at a nearby lilac blossom innocently dangling in someone's yard like a bunch of fragrant grapes. The familiar smell hit her like a smack in the face. She noted that the bush hung over a sandstone wall made of mismatched bricks of all sizes. Some were skinny, some were wide, some were little squares, and others long bars. The striking pattern stood out as familiar not because she had walked the street on a previous iteration of the day, but because she had walked it as a child.

She'd been ignoring the coincidence, pretending it wasn't some bizarre and possibly cruel twist of fate from the moment Jack had turned them into the hills, but she knew exactly where she was. She knew the lilacs, the stone wall, the latticework wound in wisteria across the street. If she looked a few houses down, she'd see a distinctively tall palm tree rising into the sky like a beacon.

And there it was.

She hadn't walked far from Jack's, only up the street and around the corner, and she knew that if she continued walking, she'd end up someplace she definitively did not want to be.

She pulled out her phone, realizing she could use some advice, and that there was only one person who knew the extent of what was going on. She stepped out of plain view in case Jack came looking for her and shoved herself uncomfortably close to someone's hedges to sit on the short stone wall.

Lila answered after four rings. "Hey, Gem. I'm kinda busy. What's up?"

Gemma heard the distinctive sounds of camera equipment being loaded into a car. A *thump*, a scoot, and a trunk closing. Lila must have been off to film something.

"He has a girlfriend, Lila."

The packing sounds stopped.

"He what?"

"You heard me. A *girlfriend*. And not just anyone, Angelica freaking Reyes."

Lila sucked in one of her huge, signature gasps. *"The Bond Girl?"*

Until that moment, Gemma had forgotten Angelica had in fact played the most recent in the storied line of superspy love interests.

"Yeah," she said like a deflated balloon, if a deflated balloon could speak.

"Oh, Gem."

The ache in her chest compounded at the sound of Lila's sympathy.

"I knew this was too good to be true."

Lila mulled her response. "How did you find out?"

"Believe it or not, I went to his house with him. We were

at lunch, and then he had to deal with something at work, so I went with him. He's a screenwriter, and we found out he quit the show he works for and signed a new contract to move to Scotland. That was news to him, so he came home to deal with it, and Angelica showed up. She's kind of awful. She thought I was his assistant."

Lila scoffed. "Obviously, she's misguided and not that bright." Gemma softly smiled at her immediate offense on her behalf. Lila was quiet for a thoughtful beat. "That's a lot to learn in one go, Gem. And you're at his house now?" The surprise in her voice was obvious. Gemma had to admit, it was a surprising turn of events.

"I was, but I left. And get this: he's my dad's neighbor."

"Shut up."

Gemma could hear her gape over the phone.

"I know. I didn't say anything as he drove us here, and after the Angelica bomb went off, I started walking up the street because I don't have my car. It feels—"

"Like a big fat sign?"

Gemma didn't want to admit that she'd had the same thought. She sighed. "So, here I am hiding in someone's hedges with a guy I don't want to talk to up one end of the street, and a guy I *really* don't want to talk to up the other. Can you come get me?"

There was a pause, and then the packing sounds resumed.

"I would, but I have to catch the light for this live shoot. You know how it goes: when it's gone, it's gone. I'd hate to miss out on the opportunity right in front of me . . ."

Her message was not subtle. Lila would drop anything to come to her rescue no matter what, and the fact that she was leaving her to hide in someone's hedges in the Hollywood Hills said very clearly that she did not think Gemma needed to be rescued.

"When I said earlier your efforts to find me a boyfriend were reaching concerning levels, I hadn't considered actual abandonment."

"I'm not abandoning you; I'm *encouraging* you," she said over her car door closing. "And the prospective boyfriend is not the direction I'm figuratively pushing you, in case it's not obvious."

Gemma glanced toward her father's house. Lila was one of the root-for-reunion people in her life. Her intentions were pure, but with two adoring parents who loved each other as much as they loved her, she would never fully understand Gemma's strained relationship and the reasons she avoided it.

Lila's car started in the background. "And besides, you can call a ride if you don't want to see him. Gotta go."

She ended the call and left Gemma frowning at her phone. Although it felt like it, she knew her best friend was not abandoning her but instead trying to help her. And she really could not deny that it felt like fate. The day had brought her and Jack together in a way that led them to his house, which happened to be right down the street from her father's house. She feared that calling it a coincidence might crack the snagged universe in half.

But the thought of visiting her father without her brother there as a buffer still did not sit well.

"Oh my god, Patrick!" she suddenly said out loud. In all the mayhem of her interview, lunch, visiting the studio, and then Angelica, she hadn't checked in with him for a few hours.

She pressed his name in her phone and returned it to her ear.

Patrick answered on the first ring. "Gemma?"

The worry in his tired voice reminded her that their last conversation consisted of her all but hanging up on him when he told her he was permanently moving to Africa.

"Hi, Patrick. How are you?"

"I'm fine. All good. How are you?"

She smiled in appreciation of his propensity to put everyone before himself, always. He really was a wonderful person.

"I'm fine. Just checking on you. Have you found a flight yet?"

He sighed. "And here I was thinking you were calling to set me free. No, still on standby."

"Damn."

"What are you doing?"

"You're not going to believe this, but I'm actually outside Dad's house."

Patrick paused. "You're what? Why?"

The thought of explaining it all to him was not only exhausting, but she also knew it would only lead to more questions, most of which she did not have answers to.

"Long story."

"Well, I've got nothing but time."

Gemma thought about what she could tell him without causing him to panic from three thousand miles away.

"I've had a really interesting day," she said. "I met someone, and he turned out to live up the street from Dad."

"Met someone? He's not a musician, is he?"

The protective bite in Patrick's tone made her smile. The only time he had ever come home during one of his six-month stints in Lagos was when the Nick situation imploded. He had crashed on her couch for a week, eating junk food and bingeing sad TV with her and Lila. He talked Lila out of slashing Nick's tires, though he offered to do it himself.

"No, he's not a musician," she said, and wondered if telling her brother the truth about the current situation would result in another offer of criminal mischief on her behalf. She hated to think Jack could fall into the same category as Nick.

"Good. Who is he, then?"

"He's . . ."

Gemma thought about how she could describe Jack. In the span of half a day, he had gone from stranger to potential soul mate to heartbreaker. She realized they had covered a lot of ground in the short time they'd known each other. It usually took a few months for a guy to disappoint her, and Jack pulled it off in the same time she could have binged half a season of *Mac Drake*.

"He's not who I thought he was," Gemma told her brother.

"But you like him."

"What? That's not—I don't—How can you even tell?"

He laughed like he used to when he'd prank her as a little kid. "Well, first of all, your reaction just told me."

Embarrassment warmed her already hot face. It always drove her nuts when he tricked her.

"I don't want to talk about him."

"Well, then what *do* you want to talk about, Gem?" She heard a knowing smile in his voice. "I mean, you find yourself randomly in front of Dad's house—the place you refuse to visit without me—and you give me a call. I can't imagine you really think I'm going to talk you *out* of going inside."

Gemma grumbled at his intuitiveness, but she had to admit, the situation was pretty transparent. Even if it had been subconscious, she'd called her brother for a reason.

"Gem, remember that time when I was in sixth grade and I had to do that book report, and I was so terrified to stand up in front of the class and speak?"

She remembered it well. She was in college and had helped him make his required visual aid on a weekend she was home visiting from school. She also gave him a pep talk and helped him practice.

"I see where you're going with this, but I don't see how presenting *Percy Jackson* to a room full of twelve-year-olds has anything to do with me talking to Dad. It's not the same."

"It's exactly the same! I was afraid, and you told me that everything would be all right, and that even if you couldn't be there, you would be supporting me from far away."

Gemma blinked in surprise that he remembered something from so long ago. The thought that it had such a profound impact on him made her wonder what other casual interactions in their youth he had taken to heart.

"Well, I'm glad you found that helpful."

"I did. And I got an A on that project." She could hear him proudly beaming through the phone. "The point is, Gem, you don't need me. Yes, you might be uncomfortable at first, but isn't that better than all this avoidance and anger?"

He had a point, and she remembered what Jack had said earlier about losing his father and unimportant things not being worth it in the end.

She looked at her surroundings and realized that the immediate alternative of waiting for a ride was unfavorably uncomfortable. She was hot and thirsty, and rideshares weren't readily cruising the hills waiting for orders. Most people tucked away behind their private gates probably had their own drivers on call. She was *not* going back to Jack's, and if she was going to call a ride, at least she could wait for it from the air-conditioned comfort of her father's house.

"Fine. I'll do it. But mostly because it's hot and I don't want to get caught in these people's hedges."

Patrick quietly laughed. "I love you, Gem. Call me if you need anything."

"Love you too."

She ended the call and cursed *Percy Jackson* for being the reason she was about to go visit a man she hadn't spent time alone with for over twenty years.

CHAPTER
10

GEMMA STOPPED OUTSIDE the black gate guarding her father's stone driveway. Her heart trilled somewhere near the base of her throat, and she found her hands sweating from more than only the heat.

She stood in a wonderland of memory. An alternate reality of what her life could have been had the adults in it made different decisions. Had her parents not split, she would have been raised in the hills. She would have been gifted a brand-new car at sixteen; gone to beautiful, superficial parties; danced on the periphery of fame—she might have even become famous, who knew. She did know that had they stayed, she would have grown up with a warped sense of reality. Certainty that she was better off having escaped that life filled her as she gazed at the mansion in front of her with its circular driveway, fountain, and jacaranda tree dripping purple petals like confetti, and saw it for what it was.

There had been a time she resented her mother for taking her and Patrick away from the life the house in the hills promised. She had felt deprived of a privilege she hadn't even known the full extent of back then. It wasn't until she was older that she realized her father was the one she should have been disappointed in, and her mother had had all the courage to stand up for herself and her children. She had protected them in a way that took Gemma many years to recognize.

She took a breath and pressed the call button at the gate. The video screen mounted into the gray bricks came to life, and a familiar face filled the panel.

"Yes?"

Gemma's tongue had grown heavy and dry. "H-Hi, Elena. It's Gemma," she said to her father's housekeeper. The woman was in her sixties and had been taking care of Roger Peters for most of Gemma's life. Of course he didn't marry Summer Hart and live happily ever after. He lived alone, and Gemma chose not to keep track of his love life.

Elena gasped a sharp sound and leaned toward the camera, enlarging her face on the screen. "Gemma? What a lovely surprise! Is your brother along with you?"

She couldn't fault Elena her surprise; she usually lurked in the background while Patrick did all the talking. Her heart took a tumble at the reminder that she was alone. "No. Only me."

A dog barked on Elena's end, and Gemma heard the *click-clack* of nails on marble flooring. A second, much deeper imposing bark followed, and she couldn't help the upward twitch in her lips. One thing she and her father had in common was their love for dogs.

"Duke, Cash, shush!" Elena called. "Sorry, dear. I'll open the gate. I'll let your father know you're here."

"Thank you," she said, but the video had cut off over sounds of excited barking.

The gate swung open, and before Gemma even made it halfway up the driveway, the two dogs barking came barreling out the wide front door.

Duke, her father's Great Dane, who was nearly the same size as Gemma, led the charge, with Cash, a French bulldog comically tiny in comparison, close behind. Duke greeted her with deep, resounding barks while Cash scampered around yipping. They pranced and slobbered, giving her the customary warm welcome that some people might expect from their human relatives. Duke landed a full-tongue streak from her jaw to her temple before she managed to wrangle him with a pet on the head. Cash spun donuts around her feet like a wind-up toy.

"Forgive me, Gemma!" Elena called as she ran out the front door, arms waving with a leash in each hand. "You know they love it when you visit!" She approached and snapped her fingers. Her voice took on a tone as formidable as Duke's bark. "Boys, *sit!*"

Both dogs instantly stopped and sat back on their haunches. Gemma kept stroking Duke's ears. He leaned his massive head into her hand with a loving whimper. As much as she disliked visiting, seeing her canine siblings always warmed her heart.

"It's time for their walk anyway," Elena said as she clipped a leash to Duke's collar.

A feeling of dread sank Gemma's warm heart like a stone. She almost considered begging Elena not to take away the only remaining barrier between her and her fa-

ther. Without Patrick, the best she could hope for was dis-
traction from two slobbering show dogs.

"Oh, you don't have to take them out on account of me,"
she said, trying to keep the plea in her voice from being too
obvious.

"Don't worry, dear. They are about to tear the house
down demanding their afternoon walk anyway," Elena said
with a laugh as she clipped on Cash's leash. "And besides, it
will give you some peace and quiet with your father. I know
it's been a while for you two. He's in his office in a meeting,
but make yourself at home while you wait!" She lurched off
when Duke pulled her toward the gate. Gemma wondered
if she had any chance of controlling him at all, given his
size, or if the leash was only for show. "We'll be back!" she
called over her shoulder.

And just like that, Gemma was alone.

Her father was busy in a meeting. Shocking. Whatever
part of her thought her surprise arrival would prompt him
to drop everything to come greet her shriveled up inside the
permanent ache in her chest.

At Elena's instruction, she decided to make herself at
home while she waited. After all, the sprawling mansion
had been her home once upon a time.

Gemma walked up the shallow steps onto the stone
porch. Elena had left the front doors wide open, and she
passed into a gaping foyer that could easily fit her apartment inside it. She closed the doors behind her and the
sound reverberated up the sweeping staircase like a tomb
sealing shut. She trained her eyes on the yawning glass wall
at the back of the house where an infinity pool disappeared

off the hillside into the L.A. Basin below. In another life she would sunbathe in one of the lounge chairs on the deck instead of battling for poolside real estate with neighbors at her apartment complex. Although frequenting her father's backyard oasis would mean losing opportunities to see Hot Guy in 202 in his finest swimwear.

A blast of breeze ruffled her hair as she realized one of the giant glass panels was open to the day. The room ached with memory. A grand piano she used to play, furniture arranged to allow the people who sat in it to have close and meaningful conversations, custom art pieces she never appreciated as a child for their strange, shapeless patterns. A sculpture Patrick dubbed *Willy* once she confessed to him that it had always reminded her of a whale. The corner that held an obscenely large Douglas fir tree each Christmas when her father's house bustled with inebriated industry titans currently held a giant palm in a pot large enough to sit in.

Holidays put a special kind of ache in Gemma's heart, for it had been that time of year when her family fell apart. She had sensed it brewing long before, in her parents' harshly hushed conversations and the fact that she saw her father's closed office door more than she saw him, but the Summer Hart implosion had happened on Christmas Eve. There had been shouting and crying and her mother's voice repeating *that girl* as if she couldn't bring herself to say her name. Gemma hadn't learned the truth until she found all her Summer Hart CDs in the trash one day at their new house. That night, they had abandoned their holiday dinner on the table like they were going to return to eat it. Gemma held a crying Patrick, trying not to cry herself, while their mother stuffed clothes into suitcases and gifts into the trunk. They drove half the night to her mother's sister's house in Phoenix, and Gemma opened gifts the next morning with cousins she hardly knew. Her father hadn't come after them. There had been no waving out windows or sad snow softly falling. Only leaving the dry gray of winter in L.A. for the desert heat.

Gemma pulled her eyes from the empty living room and wandered toward a hallway. Platinum and gold records from some of the biggest artists of the past few decades lined the walls with the importance and prominence with which some might display family photos. Where there might have been smiling faces and cherished memories, instead there were cold, round discs and sales numbers. A source of pride, sure, but also a reminder of her father's priorities.

She kept walking past a guest bathroom and came to the door of the room that was once her and Patrick's playroom. Mostly hers while they'd lived there, since Patrick had hardly been big enough to walk when their parents split, but their father had kept it for them when they visited as they grew up.

Gemma had dreaded those visits. Every summer, their mother would pack her and Patrick up and drive them to L.A. for a week. In her younger years she had thrown full-blown tantrums in protest, but they had simmered down to angsty silence in her teen years, and as soon as she turned eighteen, she stopped going altogether. The mandate of shared custody with visitation ran out when she became an adult, and she stopped visiting until Patrick was old enough to guilt-trip her into starting again. By that point, her father was little more than a stranger who shared her last name.

She pushed open the playroom door, wondering for a

brief but hopeful moment if she was going to find it un-
touched from her youth like a nineties time capsule. The
glow-in-the-dark stars would still be stuck to the ceiling
and the fuzzy mats with city maps she and Patrick used to
push toy cars around would still line the floor. The little
easel where they used to pretend to paint the backyard view
like landscape artists would still stand in the corner, and the
old upright piano they would bang away at with sticky fingers would sit beneath the window.

Part of her liked to think that this pocket of her childhood remained safely preserved in time and space. When
she visited with Patrick now, if they met their father at this
house instead of on neutral territory like at a restaurant or
an event, she rarely ventured beyond the living and dining
rooms. What tempted her to walk into her old playroom,
she wasn't sure, but when she found a neatly appointed guest
room void of childhood, memory, and toys, her heart ached
with a specific kind of loss.

At least the old upright piano was still there. It had been
moved from its window seat to the wall opposite the bed,
where it sat with a collection of framed photos on top of it.
Gemma recognized her own face from across the room. She
stepped over the fancy rug that had replaced the map mats
and felt a lump rise in her throat at the sight she found.

Above the ivory keys aged to yellow where she used to
place Patrick's pudgy hands sat framed photos of the both
of them. She smiled out from her high school graduation
photo, mortarboard hat with tassel dangling. Patrick's sat
right beside it, looking sharper and more advanced with
some eight more years of digital photography technology
behind it. Then came a slew of old snapshots from their

summer visits. Dodgers games, Disneyland, that trip to the San Diego Zoo when Patrick saw an elephant for the first time. Gemma remembered being particularly surly on that trip until she saw the wonder on Patrick's face. A friendly stranger had snapped a photo for them outside the elephant habitat, and it captured gangly Gemma with braces and a baggy tee shirt over pink shorts standing beside her father with four-year-old Patrick on his shoulders. Patrick was twisted sideways, beaming, and pointing at the elephants behind them. Their father held his legs and smiled with his eyes upward and forehead crinkled as if he was trying to see his son. Gemma had all her braces on display and a look of joy on her face simply from the look of joy on Patrick's. She could almost hear his excited shriek just looking at the picture.

Beside it sat a more recent photo of Patrick, all grown up and standing with an elephant at the wildlife institute sanctuary in Nigeria. He had one hand on the enormous animal's leathery leg and the same wonder on his face as in the photo from the zoo. Gemma couldn't help smiling at it.

She scanned the rest of the pictures and realized all the recent ones were only of Patrick: more from the institute, one with an icy white background and him in a parka from his days in Greenland, a selfie with an ink-and-gold nighttime skyline Gemma didn't recognize, one with their father on a golf course somewhere. Her most recent photo was from high school. It was as if she had stopped aging. Or maybe even disappeared.

When she came to the end of the collection, she saw two things that surprised her. The first, a newspaper clipping a few years old that she knew had been buried deep enough in

the *L.A. Times* that someone had to have been looking for it
to find it. *Industry Mogul Roger Peters's Daughter to Pro-
duce Radio Show*, the headline read. The brief article was
short enough to fit printed into a picture frame. Gemma
remembered when it came out and how ambivalent she'd
been about the announcement. The article centered her
identity on her father, and it was hardly a blip buried deep
in the Arts & Entertainment section. Not that she'd wanted
a big, flashy headline about herself—and she should have
been grateful she was getting mentioned in the *L.A. Times*
at all—but the whole situation felt symbolic of her struggle
to carve out her own space in an industry that already knew
her name.

Her personal conflicted feelings aside, the fact that her
father had cut out the article and framed it gave her a timid
feeling of pride. And hope.

The other item on the piano that surprised her was a
framed photo of her whole family—her and Patrick, their
father, and their mother.

Gemma picked it up and felt the ache inside her soar like
it had wings. She and Patrick had gotten their dark eyes
from their mother, but while their mother's hair flowed a
rich chestnut, their father's coloring had diluted them with
a beachy shade of blond. Lynn smiled in the photo, but
Gemma could see the strain in it. Perhaps she was imagining it because she knew the outcome of the happy family
posing in front of sunny palm trees. Anyone else looking on
would only have seen proud parents, a grinning seven-year-
old with a missing front tooth, and a baby with chubby
cheeks. Little did they know what was coming; what Gemma

knew had already taken root and begun to spread based on her age in the photo. She couldn't remember it being taken, but she knew it had to have been only months before everything fell apart. Perhaps it was their last happy moment together.

The thought filled her with immeasurable sadness that was offset only by the thought that they had once been whole. That an element of stability, of reliability, had existed at the start of her life.

The fact that her father had the photo in his collection of all the others gave her hope that perhaps a piece of that stability still existed.

"Gemma?" She heard him call her name from somewhere in the cavernous house.

Startled, she jumped hard enough that she dropped the photo. It fell face first into the music desk on the piano, the glass front hitting the hard wooden edge and splintering a large crack.

"Oh!" she said as an enormous rush of guilt hit her. Not to mention, an acidic sting at the symbolism of what she'd accidentally done. And also, an actual sting from the glass slicing her finger when she tried to catch the frame and stop it from falling all the way to the floor. "Ouch!" She gasped and looked at the damage she'd done. The jagged crack cut across the smiling family like a lightning bolt, and a bead of blood sprouted on the tip of her index finger.

"Gemma? Are you here?" her father called again.

She stuck her finger in her mouth to suck the blood, hoping there wasn't a shard of glass in it that would cut her tongue too. As the coppery taste of pennies filled her mouth, she considered shoving the broken photo under the bed and hiding the evidence. Instead, she froze in a panic and heard her father approaching.

"Gemma? Are you in here?"

He found her at the piano, bloody finger in her mouth and possibly the only photo that existed of their family broken in her hand.

"Hi," she said as if she had been caught doing something illegal.

Roger Peters looked the part of industry mogul comfortably at home in his linen shirt, khaki pants, and loafers. He otherwise looked a lot like Patrick with his height, slim build, and fair hair, which Gemma had a hard time reconciling since she loved her brother and felt conflicted about her father at the very best. The last time she had seen him was nearly a year before at a soiree he hosted that happened to line up with Patrick's homecoming—a coincidence Gemma realized was likely his own attempt at buffering their reunion.

He stayed in the doorway and his brow furrowed at the sight. "What happened?"

Shame for snooping flushed her face. His eyes traveled to the broken picture frame, and worry that he thought she'd smashed it on purpose hit her with another helping of guilt. "I accidentally dropped this, and it cut my finger."

His eyes went wide, and he entered the room. He reached out, she thought for the broken photo and to perhaps scold her, but instead took her hand. He tenderly rested it palm-up in his own palm and frowned at her bleeding finger. A little red droplet had reappeared with gusto. "Let me get you a Band-Aid," he said like she was a child, and in that odd moment, she found herself not jerking away but instead letting him take care of her.

"Okay."

They walked across the hall to the guest bathroom, and she didn't realize she still had the photo in her other hand until she needed to set it on the counter to wash out her wound.

"Why do you have this?" she asked as her father opened the medicine cabinet. The mirror swung out into the clean, tiled room decorated in hues of soft blue and seashell. Gemma saw neat rows of toiletries lined up inside and wondered if her father had enough guests to warrant stocking the bathroom for regular use.

He pulled out a box of bandages and eyed the broken photo. He seemed to mull his answer; she saw his jaw working like Patrick's when he was deep in thought. "To remind me of things I should have done differently."

His response struck her like a blow to the chest. She heard layers of pain and regret in it that she didn't know he harbored. He looked at her with a sadness in his eyes and a soft curve of his mouth like he wanted to say more but didn't know how.

"I'm sorry I broke it."

He peeled the wrapper off the little Band-Aid. "I'll get it fixed, don't worry," he said with a certainty that made Gemma wonder where that dedication had been when their actual family broke.

She held out her finger and let him wrap the bandage around it. She'd had plenty of scraped knees and skinned elbows as a kid, but she couldn't remember her dad ever being the one to patch her up. It was always her mom wiping her tears and planting whisper-soft kisses on her injuries. Having him do it now felt equally out of place and welcome.

"There you go," he said once he finished. He crinkled up the wrapper and tossed it in the trash.

"Thanks."

"Might make playing the piano tough for a little while, but it didn't look too deep."

Gemma scoffed, feeling the familiar distance settle between them. "Dad, I don't have a piano in my apartment. I hardly play anymore."

The soft smile that had been lighting his face dipped into a frown. "Ah. Well, I have two here if you ever want to come by and use one."

"Thanks," she said, rote and noncommittally as she did to all his thinly veiled pleas to win her affection and invite her company.

An awkward beat filled the space, and her father looked around as if he just realized they were standing in his bathroom.

"Where's Patrick?"

"In New York."

"Oh."

Another pause passed.

"It's only you?" He stated the obvious. Gemma noticed his voice carried no disappointment, and she relaxed slightly.

"Only me."

He gave her a soft smile that looked surprised and pleased all at once. "Well, I'm happy to have you. Sorry about your finger. Why don't we go somewhere more comfortable?"

"Sure."

Sometimes she hated feeling like a guest in her father's house, but she knew most of it was her own doing. Had she been at her mom's, she would already have her shoes off and the fridge open for snacks. Here, she was trailing her dad through his glass castle feeling like a visitor from space.

"Were you in the area?" he asked as they returned to the living room at the back of the house.

Thoughts of why she was in the area and what she had run away from fizzled in Gemma's brain like an angry bumblebee. "Yes."

He paused like she might add something more. "Would you like something to drink?" he asked to fill the silence and perhaps curtail the discomfort filling the big, airy room like gas.

She knew top-shelf liquor was in no short supply in his house, and the thought of a drink serving as a last-ditch buffer tempted her. But it could also make things worse, she decided.

"Water is fine."

He left her alone, and she considered punching a ride-share order into her phone so that she had an out at the ready, but instead she found herself gravitating to the piano. She loved to play, and she did miss it dearly without a piano of her own. She'd considered an electronic keyboard with headphones for her apartment but couldn't bring herself to buy one when she knew the sound quality, the weight of the keys, of a real piano. She and Patrick had played the old upright in the playroom for fun, Gemma teaching him "Chopsticks" because that was all he had the patience for. But when she wanted to play for real, to pretend she was onstage at the Bowl or the Forum or Walt Disney Concert Hall, she sat at the full grand piano in the living room, dark and elegant as a black tuxedo.

She stood at it now and gently pressed her fingers into a few keys. The soft tinkle made her smile.

"Here you are," her father said when he returned with a glass of sparkling water. "In the mood for a performance?"

Gemma found creating music too intimate to do in front of someone she felt so distant from. She stopped touching the piano and took her glass and sipped. "Not today." She let the tiny bubbles soothe the uncomfortable burn in her throat.

Another awkward beat passed.

Her father cleared his throat. "I wasn't expecting you and your brother until later this evening. Did Patrick decide to stay in New York?"

"No. His flight out of Lagos was delayed, and he missed his connection. He's on standby still trying to get here. He's having bad luck." She sipped again, thinking the *luck* might have been less luck and more fallout from her bizarre and exhausting day.

"I see. Well, I could make a call and have him on a plane in an hour."

Gemma casually turned away so he wouldn't see her roll her eyes. Money and ridiculous resources were his solution to every problem. The thought of asking her father for help hadn't even entered her mind, honestly, because she had chosen not to live in a world where every issue had a remedy for the right price. And the fact that Patrick hadn't mentioned it either put a tiny, proud smile on her lips. She had to wonder what Jack would make of factoring a private flight into the equation. Would Patrick have gotten home that way? Or would he still have gotten stuck midcountry?

The thought that Jack was the only person, aside from Lila, she could talk to about such a thing filled her with a sense of anxious sadness. If she never got out of the day, and she didn't want to talk to Jack, what was going to happen?

An expansive, lonely future unfolded in her mind and made her gulp at the water she suddenly wished were something stronger.

"It will be quite the change having Patrick permanently in Africa, won't it," her father said. He had opted for something other than water. He swirled the amber liquid in a crystal glass. His comment made Gemma wonder if he'd somehow picked up on her sense of impending loneliness.

"Patrick told you he's moving?" she asked, surprised.

He hesitated before sipping his drink, looking like he wasn't sure if he'd misspoken. "Yes. He told me last month."

Gemma's eyes bulged.

A month? Patrick had known for a month that he was moving and hadn't said anything to her?

Don't freak out, Gem. She heard his voice in her head, remembering what he'd said when he told her over the phone. She certainly had freaked out, and she was still recovering, but that was beside the point. She suddenly realized, if he hadn't gotten stuck at the airport, when would he have told her he was permanently leaving? Was he going to drop that little bomb on her in front of their father?

Anger at her brother, who wasn't even there to defend himself, made her set her glass on the coffee table and march toward the back wall. She needed some air. She sucked in a deep breath and noticed it was void of the gritty smog that settled over the city below. The urban mass sprawled like a tumorous growth in an unapologetic tangle of concrete and asphalt that had taken over what was once desert. The city held four million people, and any number of their hearts were broken daily, so many dreams crushed. People in the hills fancied themselves above it all, but Gemma knew it was all a charade. The façade of a big glass house and private gate was nothing more than a cage filled with loneliness. Her father was no exception, and with Patrick leaving, she wondered if she was destined to the same fate, minus the big glass house.

The delicate scratch of a needle dropping onto a record caught her attention. When the acoustic chords of one of her favorite Nigel Black songs floated into the air, she snapped her head around.

Her father stood at the record player behind the piano. The enormous box speakers of her childhood had evolved into sleeker, more modern versions of themselves, but they still filled the room with the same rich, resonant sound Gemma could feel in her bones. The purest form of recorded music, her father always said. Nigel's gravelly voice poured into the room like a grainy syrup.

Gemma's heart surged up into her throat and felt like it was about to burst out of her mouth. "What is that? What are you doing?"

Her father turned to look at her over his shoulder, a hopeful smile on his lips. "We used to sing this song together, remember?"

Of course she remembered. It was one of her favorite memories. She kept it safe in a chamber of her heart and mind that she only visited when she was feeling strong enough. Having it yanked out into the open of her father's vacuous, terrarium house made her feel exposed. Like a vulnerable baby bird with no feathers.

He was obviously trying to extend whatever bonding moment they'd had in the bathroom with the Band-Aid, but it felt like too far of a leap for her.

"Can you turn it off, please?" She fought to keep the wobble out of her voice.

He smiled at her. "Come on. You love this song! I was listening to it earlier because I heard Nigel on your show. That was an excellent interview, by the way. How did you book him? I know he's in town tonight. If you had called me, I—"

She knew he was about to launch into a story of privileged access riddled with celebrity names, but her mind snagged on one thing he'd said and the memory of the framed newspaper article in the bedroom.

"You listened to the show?"

He cut off his story and gave her a sincere look that she wasn't sure she had ever seen before. His eyes softened into something both warm and repentant. "Gemma, I always listen to your show. Even if it's not your voice on the waves, I know you're there in the background. It's the only way I can be near you."

A sensation bloomed in her chest that felt at once delicate and beautiful and like she was being stood upon by a very large foot. Learning that her father listened to her show fed some deep-seated desire for approval and a longing for connection and explained the proud little news clipping in a picture frame, but his ending comment felt more like a guilt trip than anything endearing.

"That's not entirely my fault, you know. You're a busy

man." The bitterness in her tone, along with the accusation, couldn't have been missed.

He gave her a look that said he was well aware she was referring to his elective absence in her childhood. He squared himself with a breath and looked, perhaps, like he wanted to remind her she was the one who never returned his calls and messages and only visited when her brother who lived on the other side of the world dragged her along when she lived close enough to stop by for dinner whenever, but he resisted. His leverage in any argument was minimal, if it existed at all.

Nigel continued singing in the background. Her father attempted to change the subject and pointed to the record player with his drink in his hand. "His show at the Bowl tonight, I pulled some strings and got Azalea added to the opening lineup, but you probably already know that. How's Nick?"

At first, Gemma wasn't sure she had heard him correctly. But by the way he smiled at her like he had performed some enormous favor, she knew that she had. The earth felt like it fell out from beneath her feet. Whatever fate had twisted to land her on his doorstep suddenly felt like a giant middle finger.

Of course he had played a hand in making Nick a part of Nigel's show. Only her father had the clout to do something so blind and fantastically inconsiderate. And only *her father* would casually ask about the relationship that had imploded and left her broken as if it had never ended.

In that moment, she realized the man she was staring at was a total stranger.

"Are you serious?" she said with a bite that dulled his smile. "Nick and I broke up over a year ago."

He frowned at her, confused. "You what? He told me you were still together."

The earth that had disappeared beneath her felt like it returned only to disappear again. She was falling standing straight up. "He what?"

Her father nodded as if convincing both of them he hadn't been the one to make a mistake. "Yes, he said you were still dating."

Gemma blinked at him several times, trying to process this. She was both shocked and not at all surprised that Nick would stoop low enough to lie to her father to get ahead—to use her. *Again.* She had trouble forming words around the half scream lodged in her throat, but she needed to set the record straight.

"Nick and I are not together, Dad. He used me to get to you and then broke up with me."

He flinched in surprise, and his ignorance felt as thick and wide as the distance between them. "He what?"

She scoffed again, feeling her anger that always simmered begin to boil with more force. "You don't remember that the night I introduced Nick to you, it changed everything, do you? How he suddenly became more interested in *you* than me? How you fell for him even harder than I did and didn't even realize that he dumped me as soon as you got him a record deal?"

He took a step back, startled. "Gemma, I didn't know any of that."

She had to fight not to roll her eyes. "Of course you

didn't. You are so deep into your career and the business and all *this*"—she held out her arms and gestured at their surroundings—"that you can't see anything else."

His face folded into defensive lines. "Now, that's not fair. You hardly talk to me, Gemma. How was I to know—"

"Fair?" She cut him off. "Do you really want to talk to me about fair, Dad?" She could feel something unlocking inside her. The vault where she kept all the things that she wanted to say to her father was dangerously close to spilling open. "Was it fair that you always put us second? Me and Mom and Patrick? You *never* chose us first. I don't fit into your life now because you pushed me out of it back then. Patrick only comes around because he was too young to remember it. He doesn't know what it felt like to always be second place, but I do, and god knows Mom does."

He paled and looked as if she had slapped him. He gathered himself after a breath. "Gemma, I know I made mistakes, and believe me, I've suffered the consequences. But I can't make amends if you won't talk to me."

"Why would I want to talk to you when you're still doing it?"

"Doing what?"

"Putting me second!"

He blinked at her as if he still didn't understand.

"Nick broke my heart, Dad! He *used* me, and you let him. All you saw was his future and how it played into your own. You're too selfish to think about how your actions affect *your own family* that you don't even see that you've chosen Nick over me at every step. Your own daughter!"

She could not describe the dam bursting inside her as a sudden event. More like an unstable wall riddled with holes she had been plugging for years finally gave way from too much damage. The pressure behind it nearly knocked her down.

He took a breath in an effort to calm himself and regain control of the conversation, but Gemma was not going to let him have it. "Gemma, I didn't know that he mistreated you—"

"Well, now you do, so what are you going to do about it?"

"I—" he started, and stopped.

In truth, Gemma wasn't sure what punishment was fit for Nick's transgressions, but she wanted her father to do something, *anything*, to stand up for her. Just once.

Roger Peters rarely got flustered. Decades of making and breaking careers in a cutthroat industry had hardened him like a stone. He knew his footing and was ruthlessly sure of himself. But he currently looked as if Gemma had punched him in the stomach.

He took a step back, his face pale and awash with what might very well have been guilt.

Gemma had never seen him wear the expression, so she wasn't sure how to categorize it. She hardly had time to name it before it shifted into a soft, yielding look that made her think that she was going to get a long-overdue apology. Her mind flitted to the possibility that perhaps arriving on her father's doorstep *had* been an opportunity after all. Aunt Clara—whose visit felt like eons before by then—had mentioned seeing reconciliation during her reading. Was it possible she had been right?

Her father cleared his throat with a shake of his head. He drained his glass with a large gulp and set it on the speaker still playing Gemma's favorite Nigel Black song. He wiped his hands together and folded his arms, looking resolute. "I'm sorry to hear your relationship with Nick is over. He is an incredibly talented artist, and it would have been a mistake for me to pass him up."

Gemma's heart shattered. The delicate hope she had held in her hands moments before died on a single breath. She thought she would have been used to it by then, the disappointment like acid in her chest, but it was no less painful at thirty-two than it had been as a child.

The bitter, dark laugh that popped from her lips surprised her. But maybe her emotional reservoir for her father had finally run dry and cynicism was all she had left. "Is it worth it? Is all this worth it? I mean, I can't fault you for wanting to be successful, but at what cost? You've driven away the people who loved you and what do you have to show for it? A big, empty house and a few million records?" She undershot the number on purpose and didn't miss his flinch.

His jaw clenched like he wanted to correct her, but he kept his mouth shut.

"You know," Gemma went on, trusting her anger to keep her voice from breaking, "what hurts the most in all this is how I keep hoping you'll change. Patrick told me he wanted to meet today so he could try and fix us, whatever that means, before he moves to Africa. But I don't see how that's ever going to happen if you can't learn to think of anyone but yourself."

She gave him a chance to say something, but he silently gave her a look that was more stubborn than sorry, so she turned to show herself out.

The cut on her finger smarted like a physical reminder

of the damage to her heart. She felt each pulse ache all the way to the core of her as she walked to the front door.

She didn't know where she was going, but she knew she needed to get out. The tears boiling behind her eyes threatened to fall. She had to leave before they could.

The day felt unfairly bright, the chipper hills showing off in shades of green with pops of fuchsia bougainvillea against the clear sky. Though she knew she hadn't been inside long enough for the weather to change, she felt like she should have walked back out to storm clouds and rain, given her mood.

She opened the rideshare app to request a ride back to her car at the radio station and saw that she would have to wait fifteen minutes. She had time to kill and nowhere to do it. Jack probably had a movie star wrapped around some part of his body or another. She didn't want to see him anyway, even if she had spent half the day falling for him and he was the nearest person who could possibly give her a hug in that moment. She both needed to be alone and could not bear the thought of it.

She decided to call the one person more learned in being disappointed in Roger Peters than she was. She exited her father's gate and leaned against the stone wall. She pressed her phone to her ear and waited for an answer.

"Hello?"

"Hi, Mom."

"Gemma, sweetheart. How are you?"

"I'm—" Her voice cut off in a tearful choke, as if the presence of her mother even from 350 miles away was enough to let her guard down.

"What's wrong?" Lynn immediately picked up on it. Her tone slipped into one that was soft and concerned.

Gemma took a steadying breath and tried to funnel all the emotion from inside into an intelligible summary. "I just had a pointless and frustrating conversation with Dad."

"I'm sorry to hear that. Does that mean your brother made it home?" She heard her mother's voice shrink away like she'd lowered her phone to check for a missed text announcing Patrick's arrival.

"No. Patrick is stuck on standby in New York still. I went by myself."

"Oh?" Her surprise was nearly tangible. Gemma's dislike of visiting her father alone was no secret. "What prompted that?"

Temptation to spill the whole sordid story to her mother, one of her confidantes, rose inside Gemma like a pressure that needed releasing. But she knew in the same way that if she told Patrick about the time loop, he'd try to hitchhike home out of concern, that her mother would get in her car and drive straight to her from Phoenix. She didn't want anyone worrying more than they needed to, or perhaps taking her in for an involuntary psych evaluation.

"I was in the area and it seemed like the right thing to do," she told her mom. "It didn't turn out how I'd hoped."

Lynn paused for a moment, and Gemma wondered if she was censoring her response. Though in her defense, her mother had never been one to verbally bash their father in front of her children. Her methods were subtler. Like burning pop albums and clipping him out of old photos. "Unfortunately, not surprising with your father," she eventually said.

The resignation in her voice hurt Gemma's heart. "Did you ever forgive him, Mom?"

"For what?"

Gemma shrugged, though she couldn't see her. "All of it. Any of it."

Lynn released a mighty sigh that sounded decades deep. "Gemma, I loved your father once upon a time, but I was able to find happiness with someone else that I never would have found if I had stayed married to him. I had to let go of what was between us, the good and the bad, in order to find it. So in a way, yes."

Gemma knew she was referring to Steven, her partner of fifteen years, who was for all intents and purposes Gemma's stepfather, though they'd never married. Divorce was one scar Roger Peters left on Lynn that she wouldn't risk repeating.

"Do you think he deserves it? To be forgiven?"

Her mother sighed again. "The ways your father hurt me are not the same as what his actions did to you and your brother. I had the choice to leave, to find a different partner. You, unfortunately, can't choose a different father. What you decide to forgive him for is entirely up to you."

The answer annoyed Gemma, and it seemed to be everyone's go-to response. But the truth was, as much as he angered her, she wanted to forgive her father. Patrick was right, of course. It would be better than living with all the anger and resentment. But letting it all go was so much easier said than done. Every time she got close to even starting to forgive, he'd go and do something wildly selfish that pushed her back ten steps and reminded her why neither of them were ready—her to give and him to receive. She honestly wondered if it would ever be possible.

"When do you expect your brother?" her mom asked in a change of subject. The topic of her father was unpleasant for both of them.

This time Gemma sighed, sounding just like her mother. "I don't know. No time before this evening by now if he's even able to get on a plane." She tried not to hit the *if* with any emphasis.

Her mother hummed in consideration, oblivious to the fact that Patrick might never make it on a plane and spend the rest of eternity playing gate roulette in New York. "Well, hopefully he makes it soon since it'll be a short trip."

Gemma's phone buzzed with an alert that her rideshare was approaching. "What?" she asked her mother, half distracted but suddenly aware of something important. "What did you say?"

"What?" Lynn asked in a contrived innocent tone as if she'd realized her mistake and wanted to cover it up.

"You said it would be a quick trip," Gemma said, not giving her an inch and feeling her annoyance with her brother return. "Mom, did you know that Patrick is moving?"

"What's that?" Lynn said, but not directed at Gemma. She'd leaned away from the phone and called to someone out of earshot. "Okay, just a second, Steve!" she sang. Her voice came back louder. "I have to go, honey. Steve needs me. I'll see you guys next week. Let me know when your brother lands!"

Gemma rolled her eyes at her mother's obvious attempt at avoidance. Clearly, Patrick had told everyone he was moving but her. She silently vowed to put him in a headlock when she saw him and hold him there until he apologized for making her the last to know.

"Bye, Mom," she said, and ended the call.

Although it had felt good to talk with her mother, all the family drama left her not wanting to be alone. She would not go back to Jack's, her father was as disappointing as ever, a six-hour drive to Phoenix didn't sound like a pleasant way to spend the afternoon, and her brat of a little brother was still stuck on the other side of the country.

That left her with one person to lean on.

GEMMA CLIMBED INTO her rideshare and pulled out her phone and texted Lila.

Total disaster with my dad. Where are you?

She sat back against her seat and stared out the window. She could only imagine the theories running through her driver's mind as to why a distraught young woman had left a Hollywood mansion and climbed into his car. At least he had the decency not to ask her about it.

Lila responded with a sad face and a location.

Shooting at Urban Light.

Gemma entered the new location into her app, noting the garbled pain in her voice when she spoke. "I changed the destination to LACMA."

Her driver nodded and poked his phone mounted on the dash. He didn't ask any questions, and again, Gemma was grateful.

They wound their way out of the hills, thankfully driving in the direction opposite Jack's house so she did not have to see confirmation that Angelica's car was still parked outside. She could not sort out if her feeling of betrayal was reflex left over from Nick or if she really, truly cared about Jack enough to be hurting so much. Probably the latter, she assumed after the day they'd had, though she couldn't discount the former since Nick had driven quite the spear into her heart. And apparently, he wasn't above driving it in even deeper by lying to her father.

She huffed a dark laugh at the thought of the situation with Jack. *Too good to be true.* She should have trusted her preliminary conclusion back in the coffee shop that a good guy wouldn't just fall into her lap. Of course there was a catch. There was always a catch. Unfortunately, the catch in this case was an unreasonably gorgeous and talented, albeit eccentric actress who she could never compete with, with or without cosmic forces working in her favor. Not to mention the fact that Jack had accepted a job on a different continent.

Another man to disappoint her.

They had been disappointing her all her life, as evidenced by her father's resilient inability to see beyond his own nose. She wondered, as they came down out of the hills, if she was attracted to a certain kind of man, one prone to shortsighted self-indulgence, because of her upbringing. Perhaps she was trying to fill the void her father had created and subconsciously sought out men who were exactly like him, only to remain perpetually disappointed. At least the fact that Jack wasn't a musician seemed to be a step in the right direction.

This train of thought was too heavy for the back seat of

her rideshare, she decided, and much better suited for her therapist's couch.

When they arrived at the Los Angeles County Museum of Art, Gemma climbed out onto the sidewalk directly in front of the Urban Light sculpture. The two hundred and two antique streetlamps stood in a neat grid framed by palm trees and blue sky. Visitors wandered in and out of the cast-iron poles topped with ornate glass bulbs, craning their necks for a glimpse into the past.

Gemma did not know what Lila was livestreaming, but part of her brand was iconic L.A. landmarks. She had lugged her camera equipment everywhere from the Santa Monica Pier to the Griffith Observatory for the perfect shot. Whatever she was plugging likely had nothing to do with Prohibition-era urban architecture, but the famed streetlamps in the background would give her audience the extra flair they knew and loved.

Gemma spotted her positioning a tripod near the corner of the lamps. She held a second, smaller tripod in her hand, and each tripod held a phone. Lila kept poking the screens of each as she shifted her body back and forth, angling in and out of the shadows. A black duffel bag sat near the base of the big tripod. She held a wide, taupe-colored hat to her head as she looked up at the sky. When she looked back down to reposition, she saw Gemma approaching. With a loud gasp, her customary greeting, she trotted over on her wedges. She threw her arms around Gemma and wrapped her in a hug scented with traces of the smelly shampoo.

"I'm so sorry, Gem," she said with a warm breath into Gemma's hair. "I was hoping things would work out with your dad, but I guess . . ."

Gemma knew there was no good ending to that sentence, so she didn't wait for Lila to provide one.

"Thanks," she said, and savored the feel of comforting arms. She melted in the warmth of the embrace and the afternoon sun.

Lila gently rubbed her back before she pulled away. Gemma wished the hug had lasted longer, but she couldn't blame Lila for getting back to her equipment. They were, after all, on a street in the middle of Los Angeles. Anyone could easily run off with it if they weren't careful, and Gemma knew Lila had invested in high-quality goods.

Gemma let out a big sigh. "Can I help with anything?"

Lila flapped her hands with a casual shake of her head. "No. I've got it."

Gemma knew she didn't need help. She was a one-woman operation. "I'll get out of your shot, then," she said, and stepped aside. She was restless and had come all the way into the city to be near someone who cared about her, but now she only felt like she was in the way.

"Oh, please stay," Lila said with a smile. "Walk around in the background like everyone else; it adds to the authenticity."

Gemma felt her face lift with a smile for the first time in what felt like hours. "Thanks, but I'm not sure I want to be broadcasted to your two hundred thousand Lila in L.A. followers."

"But you didn't seem to mind when the airwaves of L.A. heard you talking to Nigel Black earlier," she said as she angled her camera one last time.

Gemma's heart lifted again. "A, that's different because radio is invisible, and B, you listened?"

"Of course I did. You killed it. Now, if you're going to be in the shot, you can't be talking to me. That would be weird. Act natural or get out." She waved a hand over her shoulder and positioned herself in front of her cameras. Gemma had seen the trick before: she recorded with the standing tripod and livestreamed with the handheld. That way, she had a record of her video even after it evaporated into the ether of the internet.

She softly smiled to herself at the thought of being anonymously present for countless viewers to see. A face in the crowd. She looped her hands behind her back and tried to look casual as she wandered into the lamps. Lila's bubbly voice appeared and then faded as she stepped deeper into the grid.

"Hey! It's Lila in L.A. . . ."

Gemma pressed her hand into one of the poles as she walked by, searching for the story in its history. She wondered which street corner it had lit once upon a time and what old Hollywood stars might have strolled beneath it.

She saw a sudden movement out of the corner of her eye. Other patrons wandered in and out of the lights, she wasn't alone, but this movement was quick and deliberate, not someone casually strolling an outdoor exhibit. On second look, she didn't see anything out of the ordinary.

She kept walking deeper into the structure, passing a few more lamps, and noticed the same quick movement each time she passed another pole. A tingle spread over her scalp at the thought that someone was following her, but she convinced herself it was no more than a visitor who happened to be walking at a slightly faster pace and disappearing behind each pole she passed before she could see them all the way. It was nothing.

Until she saw it again.

She was in wide-open public, and Lila was a shout away if she needed her—with a live video feed to thousands of potential witnesses at that—but she got the sense she was not in danger. Not physically at least.

Deliberately, she sped up and walked two lamps, heading for a third at the same speed, but stopped before she came out the other side of the second lamp.

A man in a gray tee shirt and jeans appeared, and Gemma stopped in her tracks.

"You!"

Jack turned and saw her out in the open. His face flushed at having been caught. He recovered and calmly held up his hands. "Yes, me."

He approached, and she immediately turned away.

"Gemma!"

Gemma realized she had lost count of how many times he had chased after her that day. Clearly, he was not going to give up.

She stopped walking and turned around to confront him right in time for him to crash into her. The heat of his body sent a shock wave through her. She remembered her frustration and shook it away.

"What are you doing here, Jack? How did you know where to find me?" She folded her arms and glared at him. Unless he had waited outside her father's house to see where she'd gone, he had no way of knowing, and since he didn't even know who her father was until that morning—and it was an even slimmer chance that he knew they were neighbors—Gemma suspected something else was at play.

Jack's eyes softened. He reached for her but closed his hand into a fist and dropped his arm instead. Gemma wondered at how she could miss the feel of his touch already. "I knew you were upset with me, and Lila would be the only person you have to talk to. I know she livestreams at this time every day because I've seen it, so I knew where to find you." The sadness in his eyes suddenly made Gemma feel like he was pitying her.

She grumbled at him and turned away. "Stop acting like you know me!"

He reached for her shoulder and made contact this time. He quickly stepped around her so that they faced each other. "I *do* know you, Gemma! And I love—" He stopped himself and cleared his throat with a shake of his head. "I care about you a lot, Gemma, and I'm really sorry for what happened at my house. Let me explain, please. You have to trust me."

Gemma chewed her lip and felt warmth at the backs of her eyes. She didn't know if the tears were happiness from the words that he had almost said or anger that he'd reminded her of what happened at his house, but she would not cry in front of him. She swallowed it all down and took a breath.

"How can I trust you if I don't even know you?"

Pain washed over Jack's face. He closed his eyes for a second, and Gemma took the opportunity to slip away.

She made it two lamps down before he caught back up. She kept walking straight ahead, refusing to look at him. He skipped to the next aisle over and walked sideways, touching each pole between them as they passed so he didn't crash into one while not looking.

"Okay, I realize how unfair this is to you. In testing my theory, I've been trying to gauge what you remember all day. I've been withholding information, and I see how one-sided that is now." He expectantly cut off as they kept walking. Gemma took a sharp turn to the left.

"So, what? That's supposed to make everything better?" she asked, and started a new path through the poles.

"No! Of course not. I just want to say that I'm sorry, and that you can ask me anything. Get to know everything you want about me. Right now."

Gemma glanced sideways at him, still upset but unable to deny that it was a tempting offer. She had spent most of the day with him, but most of that time had focused on her. She had only begun to learn about him before everything derailed. But she wasn't in the mood for twenty questions. She turned her head forward and kept walking.

"Fine, if you don't want to ask, then I'll start listing random facts," he said. He kept disappearing behind the lampposts and reappearing as they walked like the strangest game of peekaboo. "I'm an only child. I grew up in Vermont. My mom's name is Pamela and I talk to her every Sunday. My dad died in a car crash when I was eighteen, and I still think about him every day." He held out his arm and kept walking. "This is his watch. I know today is real because this watch is never wrong, and the date hasn't changed for one hundred and forty-seven days now."

Gemma risked another glance before taking a right turn.

Jack didn't miss a beat. He reappeared the next aisle over, popping in and out of view again. "I majored in creative writing in college. I wanted to be a novelist. I even moved to New York after school to live out the cliché. Turns out writing books is not my strong suit, so I took up screenwriting and moved to L.A. for the West Coast version of the cliché. I've lived here for ten years and have never been to Disneyland. I think In-N-Out is overrated, but I would fight someone for a California burrito. Hockey is my favorite sport, though I can't play it worth a damn. I met Tom Hanks once and he's every bit as nice as you'd hope. I love classic films more than anything contemporary but would rather read a book than watch anything at all. Given the chance, I think I would visit outer space. I can't read music, but I own a piano. My first pet was a beagle named Barney. I don't think I can ever live in the snow again after L.A., but I still miss it each winter. I've never seen a whale, I'm terrified of heights, I know every word of 'Bohemian Rhapsody,' I secretly love romantic comedies despite what I said earlier about classic films, and I think I was a miserably unhappy person until I met you."

He grabbed a lamppost and swung around it to stop in front of Gemma. She bounced on her toes to prevent herself from running into him just in time. They had zigzagged their way through the grid and ended up back where they started. Gemma could see Lila's back only a few lamps away.

They stood inches apart, him gazing down and her gazing up. His eyes matched the sky coloring in the gaps between lamps. She felt like the two of them were tiny bugs in a grove made of iron trees. He reached out and gently tucked her hair behind her ear. He looked like he wanted to kiss her, and Gemma was about to let him, but she realized that in everything he'd said, he hadn't answered one very important question.

"What happened between you and Angelica?"

His soft smile went slack. The light in his eyes faded. "She cheated on me, and we broke up."

The words were cold and harsh, and Gemma knew they were true by the way he said it.

"It happened a few days before the time loop started." He sighed and swiped a hand through his hair. "I actually caught her with someone else, and it all imploded. That's why she said what she said at my house. But the truth is, we were terrible together. We should have broken up ages ago, but she's really persistent, as you saw today."

The memory of Angelica dangling from his neck put a sour taste in Gemma's mouth.

"She's vain and self-obsessed, and it was all a mistake. I had forgotten about the breakup and the reason for it until I saw her today and she told me because I've been in here for so long." He frowned at his explanation, and Gemma narrowed her eyes.

"That seems like a really convenient thing to forget, Jack."

He held up his hands and blew out a breath. "I know. I know it looks bad, especially for her to show up like that, but I swear, I had forgotten. It was like I hadn't seen her in five months until today, because she's never shown up before."

He'd said the same thing in the street by his house, and Gemma had been too angry to really think about it.

"How is that possible? You've never crossed paths with her until today?"

"Yes! That's exactly it. I've been thinking about it, and I

think it's because you and I set different things in motion. *We* are the anomaly now. Angelica has probably shown up at my house at that exact time every day for the past five months, but I've never been there before. I was there today because you and I went there on purpose. I think we were meant to run into her."

Gemma frowned and crossed her arms again. "We were *meant to run into her*? To what end?"

"So I could finally end things with her! Again!" He explained it like it all made perfect sense, like he had explained the temporal anomaly back in the coffee shop. And like then, he read the skepticism on her face. "Look, Gemma, I think we've set things in motion by diverging from the normal path. Things are happening now that have never happened before, and I think it's a good thing."

The temptation to believe him flitted near the center of Gemma's brain like a hopeful little butterfly, but the reminder of the past few hours smashed it dead. She was, quite honestly, losing faith in some cosmic justification for the day's events. If she had been *meant to* meet Jack and *meant to* visit her father, why was it all going up in flames?

Her tone came out sharp. "How is me seeing you make out with your girlfriend a good thing?"

He closed his eyes and released a frustrated breath. By the time he opened his eyes, Gemma was gone again.

She moved closer to Lila, ready to leave the towering light maze and go home to Rex.

Jack reappeared and reached for her arm. His hand was warm and urgent against her skin. It sent a rush to her head that made her turn and look at him.

Sincerity painted his eyes the purest blue. "Gemma,

Angelica and I are done. As soon as you left, I went and told her that. I'm never going to see her again. I swear to you, it's over between us."

She hadn't been so emotionally vulnerable, so raw, in a long time. Allowing herself to believe him, to trust him, opened her back up in a way she wasn't sure she was ready for.

Jack could see it on her face.

"Gemma, please. She doesn't matter to me. Isn't it a sign that I literally forgot about her? What happened between us isn't important. It's *you*, Gemma. *You* are the center of everything. My whole universe has shifted to revolve around you. I'm literally stuck on you and only you. I need you. For more than one reason."

His lips pulled into a soft smile that reminded Gemma with a jolt of the bar from the night before. The best kiss of her life.

She was tempted to kiss him again. Her heart was pounding out a rhythmic *Yes*, but her head was screaming *Danger*. And there were things besides a persistent Bond Girl ex-girlfriend to consider.

"What about your job, Jack? You uprooted your whole life the day before you met me, and based on what your agent said on the phone, it sounds like a big deal."

Jack let out a tense breath and squeezed his hands. "Yes, I know. That's complicated and I still need to sort it out, but if Charlie got me out of one contract, he will get me out of another."

The conversation she'd overheard between Jack and his agent was looping through her head when the gravity of what he had said suddenly hit her.

"Wait, what?"

He looked at her without much expression on his face other than the honesty in his eyes.

Gemma couldn't believe what he was silently saying. "Jack, you're going to give all that up? You're going to have your agent undo the deal?"

He blinked once like it wasn't even a question.

"That's ridiculous."

At the sight that she was about to turn to leave again, he suddenly sprang back to life. He reached out for her. "Is it, Gemma?"

"Completely, Jack," she said without hesitation. The thought that he would even consider changing his life like that . . . And for her?

A rush of self-preservation overtook her, accompanied by what felt like pity for him.

"This whole thing is ridiculous, Jack." She pointed at the ground as if to signify the moment they were standing in and all her frustration because of it. "Every single thing that has happened since you spilled coffee on me has been absurd."

He took a steadying breath for the both of them. "I know, okay? *Believe me*, I know." He swiped a hand through his hair and gave her a pained, pressing look. "But I still think I'm right. I think we need each other, Gemma." He glanced over his shoulder and then stepped closer to her. "Listen, it might not feel like my place to say anything, but I've known you for five months now, and I think . . . I think you're unhappy too." His eyes searched hers, pleading and sincere. Gemma swallowed a lump in her throat. "I think you feel stuck in your job. I think you're lonely. I think what that asshole ex-boyfriend did to you that I didn't even know about until today is still hurting you. And I think your dad—"

"Stop!" she blurted, and held up her hands. The lump in her throat was threatening to boil up into her eyes and spill over. She felt like he'd pushed every painful button she kept hidden at the same time. All at once she wanted to shove him away and fold herself into his arms. No one had seen her vulnerabilities in a long time—she hadn't let anyone. And there he was, stripping her down in broad daylight.

"I'm sorry," he said. "I just think there might be things that are keeping you stuck—keeping *us* stuck—in this day, and I want to—"

She recoiled, and he stopped talking. "You think this is my fault?"

"No! That's not what I meant. I only meant that I think we have to help each other."

She folded her arms and glared at him. "I thought I was the key. Now I'm partially responsible?"

"Yes, I think so! But not in a bad way. Everything is different now. We changed it." His eyes were bright and hopeful again, and temptation to believe him thudded in her chest.

But there were too many obstacles for her to throw her heart into the unknown and hope a stranger would catch it.

"I don't think so, Jack. What if it's been you and only you all along? Maybe a plane to Europe, to your new life, will fix this whole mess, and you don't need me for anything."

His face crumpled into hurt as if she had truly wounded him. "Gemma, you can't say that."

"Why not? How do you know it's not the solution? Have you tried leaving?"

As soon as the words were out, part of her wished she could suck them back in.

Jack paused. The answer was obviously *no,* and the

contemplative look on his face made her feel as if her stomach had been thrown off a very high cliff. She'd just told him to leave, and despite her uncertainty, the thought frightened her.

But she couldn't unring the bell.

Lila cleared her throat from beside them. They both turned to see her watching them, having finished her video. She held her smaller tripod down at her side and gave them a look that Gemma hoped didn't mean she was about to provide an unsolicited romantic mediation service to mend their spat. Thankfully, she gave Gemma a cautious but encouraging smile and left the next move up to them.

Gemma decided to listen to the logic in her head saying that the day and her belief in something magical happening to her had been a mistake. Plus, she'd given Jack the green light to run away from it all. It was over. Maybe it was all for the better.

She turned to him and removed her arm from his grip. "Bye, Jack."

She left him standing there amid the lights and the sunny day and went to help Lila pack up her equipment. To her relief, or maybe disappointment, he didn't follow her.

GEMMA WAS STILL without a car, so she found herself in Lila's passenger seat as they battled traffic back to Silver Lake. Lila tapped her thumbs on the steering wheel and hummed along to the radio rather than pressing her about her conversation with Jack. She might not have heard it, but given the fact that Gemma had walked away at the end, it obviously had not gone favorably.

She sat lost in her thoughts, gazing out the window as they inched their way across the city.

First her father and then Jack. Actually, first Jack, and then her father, and then Jack again. What an unpleasant little emotional sandwich of an afternoon she'd had.

But at least she had severed the tie.

As she sat in traffic, Jack was probably realizing that moving to Europe was in fact the way out of the loop and he had wasted five months chasing after her for no reason. Forget the snag, forget the earth tilt. Forget their kiss. None of it mattered. All that mattered was his new life five thousand miles away, where he would write fantasy stories in the misty Highlands and wear thick sweaters and drink espresso in tiny cafés and never think of her again.

She angrily stewed at the same time she felt as if a rope were suddenly slipping from her hands and the end was going to disappear and take Jack with it before she could get a grip.

It was unfair, really. All of it. The guy showed up out of nowhere and she was supposed to let him turn his entire life on its head for her after a single day? And what about him telling her she was unhappy? How presumptuous.

She had to admit, though, the truth of what he'd said felt like it had slapped her in the face. To some extent, she *was* stuck at work. She'd been wanting to move up but never took the opportunity.

Until he had encouraged her to do the interview.

She hated to admit it, but aside from hanging out with Lila and calling her mom, she buried her loneliness in books and TV and caring for Rex and the six months of the year she spent planning for her brother's return.

Until Jack came along.

When he had told her things about himself at the lamps, it made her want to know more. Learning about him somehow made her feel like she missed him. How that was at all possible, she couldn't explain other than by accepting the fact that they really had known each other for five months, and something deep in her brain, or perhaps her heart, longed for his presence.

And he was right about Nick. It did still hurt. It hurt enough that she'd closed off her feelings out of self-preservation, which had left her alone.

Until Jack.

She'd cut Jack off before he said anything about her father, but that one was a no-brainer. One of the greatest sources of her unhappiness was her troubled relationship with her dad. Too bad it appeared it would be permanent because of her father's undying commitment to his own ego. She couldn't imagine he'd ever do anything to repair it, even if part of her wished he would try.

So then in those ways, Jack was right about her unhappiness—and he'd even helped her fix some of it. But what did that prove? Only that he was nice and caring and more observant than most. Certainly not that they were each other's solution to breaking out of a day skipping like a broken record.

Lila turned onto a street in her neighborhood, and the song that had been haunting Gemma all day came on the radio.

She snapped out her hand and turned it off.

Lila scoffed in surprise and turned it back on. "What are you doing? I love that song. And so do you!"

The poppy melody pulsed through the speakers, as joyful as ever. Lila instantly started singing along to it. Gemma knew resistance was futile.

She looked back out the window and tried to ignore that the song might have been a sign. Even though she had decided the "signs" today had been random coincidences that conveniently aligned, a nagging sense that it did all mean something bounced around her head like an incessant little insect.

With the song insisting it be heard and nothing to do but stare at taillights, she surrendered to a feeling she'd been fighting since she first heard the song that morning—of when it had reminded her of being in the bar with Jack. Instead of denying the surge of familiarity and chalking it up to something impossible, she welcomed it in. She opened a door she'd kept locked all day, and suddenly, there it was as if it had been waiting for her. It unfolded itself into a colorful cloud of memory, of light, and she saw it all.

"Lila," she said to the window, stunned and knowing she was with the safest person she could ask, "what did you do last night?"

"A deep conditioner and watched *Schitt's Creek*. You?"

Gemma bit her bottom lip as they turned into Lila's complex. She'd crossed many barriers that day, but there really was no turning back if she said what was on her mind.

She spoke slowly as if not to frighten away her own timid thoughts. "I went to your birthday party, and I met Jack at the bar. We talked for an hour. He ordered me my favorite drink, we heard this song, and then we kissed on the sidewalk. It was the best kiss I've ever had in my life."

Lila parked and remained quiet until Gemma turned to

face her. The bare certainty in Gemma's voice hung between them. "You really remember all that?"

Gemma knew she could tell her the truth that she had finally accepted. "Yeah. I do."

Lila fiddled with her key fob and hesitated. Gemma's mood had tempered her enthusiasm for the bizarre, it seemed. Now that Gemma was taking it seriously, Lila stowed all her gasps and declarations. She spoke at a metered, cautious tempo like saying it too fast might make Gemma change her mind. "So, do you think that means he's . . . right?"

"About what?"

Lila snapped back to her normal self and dramatically groaned. "Gem, come *on*. I heard what he said to you back there. He's in *love* with you. Who cares if he's got a clingy ex-girlfriend and might be moving to Europe. He wants *you*. And I think if you remember what happened between you guys last night, *truly remember it*, that means his theory is right, and you have to love him back." She snapped her wrist like she was putting a point on her statement and proudly tilted her chin.

A warm rush started in Gemma's chest and filled her face. "It's not that easy, Lila."

"Of course it is! You have to trust him. And trust yourself." She reached out and put her hand above Gemma's heart. "Trust what you feel, Gem. Believe that this thing in here knows what it wants."

For a fleeting second, Gemma was tempted. Tempted to take the risk of letting herself feel something and admit that Jack was right, not just about her unhappiness but about everything.

"Too bad I told him to move to Scotland."

Lila shrugged. "Sounded like he's willing to renege on that little situation."

Gemma studied her friend with a moment of seriousness. "Don't you think that's a little irrational? I mean, that's his *life*, and—"

"Love is irrational!" Lila chirped. "Gemma, that guy is head over heels for you. Why can't you see that?"

She turned to stare at the stucco wall out the windshield. Jack had known her longer than she'd known him, sure. He knew his feelings and trusted what he wanted. But what if he was wrong? What if when he got to know her outside of a single day, he regretted rearranging his life around her? She had been hurt too badly to trust herself not to fall for someone who would hurt her again.

The insecurities were too big, and she secretly hoped he was on his way to the airport for a red-eye to Europe.

"I don't want to talk about this anymore," Gemma said. She shook her head to erase the bulk of it. The thought of going home and hiding under a blanket in front of the TV with Rex all night tempted her, but Lila's party was still on the docket, and she was worried a certain rock star would take it personally if she didn't show up to his concert after he had done her the favor of securing her whole team tickets. "Listen, Lila, I know we have plans tonight for your party, but Nigel Black gave me backstage passes to his show, and I'm wondering if you'd rather—"

Lila gasped so loud that Gemma flinched. She threw her elbows up and leaned against the side window as if Gemma had a tarantula on her lap. *"You have passes to Nigel Black's show and you're just now telling me?"*

Gemma threw a hand over her heart. "Lila, you scared me! I thought something happened!"

"Something *did* happen! You were holding out on me! Yes, I want to go. Yes, I'll go. *Yes*, we are going to go upstairs to get ready for *backstage freaking passes to Nigel Black's sold-out show at the Hollywood Bowl*." A smile almost broke her face. "Do you even hear me right now? People would *kill* for this! I mean, this is, like, holy grail rock god territory. This is the *best* birthday present you've ever given me!" Lila reached for her purse where she'd stuffed it by Gemma's feet and threw her other hand at the door to open it.

Gemma actually hadn't thought of the passes as a birthday gift, but she silently let the assumption go without comment.

Lila stopped halfway out the door, visibly vibrating with excitement. "Oh." She suddenly paused and leaned back in, where Gemma hadn't even unbuckled her seat belt. "My party. Well, that was going to be people stopping by the bar later, so no biggie, but we should keep the dinner res because they're going to charge my card if we don't show." She grimaced, and Gemma laughed, knowing the threat was real. And expensive.

They moved upstairs and Gemma opted for a shower. She had been running around all day, and despite a new shirt, she did still smell a little bit like coffee. Standing beneath the hot water was a cleanse she needed, a fresh start from everything from that morning.

Once the last remnants of her latte bath had been washed away, she got out and wrapped her hair—which did not smell like smelly shampoo because Lila had thrown it away—in a towel and assessed the outfit Lila had laid out for her to wear. A short black romper that tied at the waist with long sleeves waited on the bed. The neckline dipped a tad lower than she was used to, but she figured it was fit for a rock-'n'-roll show. As were the pair of wedges sitting on the floor with a heel of reasonable height that looked like they hadn't been worn. She shopped in Lila's jewelry collection and borrowed a simple gold necklace with a pearl pendant that fell in a timeless teardrop. Once she was dressed and had blown out her hair, she messaged her dog sitter to confirm she could swing back by and take Rex for an evening walk and give him a scoop of food since her plans had changed. If they had to pick up the passes back at the radio station, make it to dinner, and haul it up to the Hollywood Bowl, she would not have time to run home in between.

She found Lila at her dining table in front of a lit-up round mirror, carefully underlining her left eye with black liquid liner. Gemma could see she had already painted her lids using the open shadow palette of shimmery shades of purple and rose. The set was called Glamour Goddess and came from a celebrity makeup line, and Lila would surely turn to Gemma once she finished with herself.

Lila spun in her chair and gave Gemma a once-over with a smile. "You look hot."

"Thanks. You look like half a raccoon. Are these new?" she asked, and held up the wedges.

Lila waved a hand. "Yep, and all yours if you want them. Sponsor sent them, and they're too short for me."

Gemma smiled to herself, figuring that was the exact reason Lila had picked the chunky suede shoes with ankle straps for her. She would add them to her pile of free Lila castoffs and probably never wear them again after that night. "Thanks. Can I get something to drink?"

Lila turned back to her mirror to line the other eye. "Help yourself."

Gemma saw more cans of the seltzer Lila had served her that morning, orange-mango flavor from a line of all-natural drinks that she had never heard of, and she wondered, honestly, if Lila had to shop for anything at all or if she subsisted entirely on free samples.

She popped the top and pulled out her phone to call Carmen.

"What's up, Gem?" she answered.

"Hey, are you still at the studio? Did Nigel's people ever drop off the passes?"

"Sure did, Gemstone. Are you going to come get them? Or do you want to meet me at the Bowl?"

Gemma tossed the options around in her head. Going to get them would eat time out of their evening, but meeting at the Bowl would be easier said than done in a sea of concertgoers.

"We'll come get them."

"*We* as in you and that guy you were climbing like a tree in the booth earlier?"

A flash of heat scorched Gemma's face. She almost choked on her sip of orange-mango bubbles.

"*No.* I mean *we* as in me and my friend Lila. I'm taking her to the show for her birthday."

Lila overheard her conversation and blew Gemma a kiss through the cutout wall connecting her kitchen and dining room by way of the breakfast bar.

"So, you're *not* taking the writer dude to see the rock star after he saved our show by getting you to do the interview with said rock star."

When Nigel had offered them the passes, Gemma had visions of attending with Jack. Maybe they would even hold hands in the stage wings as they listened to her favorite songs. But that was before things had fallen apart.

"No. He's not coming," she told Carmen.

The clunk of chair legs hitting the floor told Gemma that Carmen had been rocking back as usual and had sat up to pay attention.

"Cool if I use that extra pass, then?"

Her request snuffed out any remaining fantasy of hope Gemma had.

"It's cool," she said, and took another sip of the addicting seltzer.

"Thanks, Gems. I assume whatever went down at Urban Light didn't end well if you're not granting him exclusive access to your old-man crush."

Gemma was midswallow when she started to gasp. The seltzer shot up her nose and tried to come out her eyes in a painful fit of carbonation.

"What?" she asked Carmen, choking, unsure she had heard her correctly. "What are you talking about?"

"That little tiff you guys had; it's all over the internet. Well, I *assume* it was a tiff if you've got him pouring his heart out to you like that. It's a shame. I was hoping for the best for you two. Seemed like a nice guy. I gotta go. This set is almost over, and not all of us got the day off today. Back to work."

She hung up and left Gemma blinking burning seltzer from the backs of her eyeballs. Her mind was a fog of confusion and the seltzer had lit a fire in her throat. Nothing made sense. How could Carmen know about her and Jack's conversation outside the museum?

She set her drink down and coughed to try and recover. She braced herself against the counter as she fought for breath.

"You all right over there?" Lila asked without looking, still painting her face.

At the sound of her voice, something Carmen had said clicked into place.

All over the internet.

Gemma stopped hacking and looked at her best friend innocently dusting her cheekbones with rouge.

She wouldn't, Gemma thought at almost the same time she thought, *Yeah, she would.*

"Lila," she said slowly. "What did you do?"

She paused with the dusting and looked at Gemma. "What are you talking about?"

Gemma stared her down from inside the kitchen. "Carmen told me that she saw my and Jack's conversation from Urban Light. How could that even be possible if she wasn't there?"

Lila's jaw tightened and her lips pursed in a look that said *guilty* so clearly, Gemma had no doubt what she had done.

"Lila," she said like she was scolding a toddler, "*what* did you *do?*"

They both remained frozen, Lila turned sideways in her chair at the dining table, blush brush in hand, and Gemma braced against the counter inside the kitchen. The only thing that moved was Lila's eyes as they darted to her phone perched on the breakfast bar between them.

Like someone fired a starting pistol, they both leapt into action.

Gemma lunged at the breakfast bar, reaching over the sink and clawing at the cold granite right as Lila sprang from her chair fast enough that it fell over backward. They both reached for the phone—Lila's connection to hundreds of thousands of followers—and Lila's hand slapped down first. Gemma's landed with a hard smack right on top of it.

"Gemma, wait!"

"You posted a video of us?!"

Lila tore the phone away and dashed for the living room. Gemma burst from the kitchen and nearly jumped on her.

"Lila! Take it down!"

"No!"

They fought like sisters over a favorite toy.

Gemma tackled her onto the pink velvet couch as Lila tried to play keep-away. She held the phone as far away as her arm could reach.

"Show me!"

"Stop it!"

Gemma realized as she tore at her friend's arm that she could just as easily use her own phone to assess the damage. She only needed Lila's to remove the damage once she knew what it was.

She climbed off her and sat back with a huff.

"Calm down, Gem," Lila said as she smoothed her hair. "I didn't do anything bad. I only edited a little snip of your conversation and put it on the internet, that's all." She innocently shrugged and Gemma scowled at her.

"That was a *private* conversation, Lila." She opened

Instagram and saw Lila's post right at the top of her feed. A panicky rush felt like pins and needles sticking into every inch of her at the sight of herself and Jack standing amid the streetlamps. The video had been posted twenty minutes before and had over ten thousand views.

Gemma's voice rose into a squeak. "You posted this while I was in the shower?"

Lila tsked and reached for Gemma's phone. "Oh, relax. It's no big deal. Look, I got the best part." She poked the little square to unmute it, and Jack's voice came from the phone's small speaker.

"It's *you*, Gemma. *You* are the center of everything. My whole universe has shifted to revolve around you. I'm literally stuck on you and only you."

The words put a hard lump in Gemma's throat at the same time they filled her chest with warmth. Her eyes washed with mist. She'd heard Jack say the words to her face but hearing them again hit differently.

"See?" Lila said with a smile as she gently elbowed her in the ribs. "I figured since you can't seem to see it on your own, maybe you'd be able to see it through the internet's eyes. And look, everyone loves it." She tapped the screen with a manicured finger to scroll the comments.

This is sooo sweet!

Omg. LOVE.

Do I recognize that guy from somewhere?

I was there! I saw them talking today!

Girl, marry him.

Find someone who looks at you like this guy looks at her.

My whole universe has shifted to revolve around this couple. Who are they?

Is this from a movie?

A soft smile broke out over Gemma's face. She tried to chew it away while Lila sat beside her beaming, proud of her handiwork.

The truth was, what Jack had said was very sweet and sincere. But people commenting on the sound bite didn't know the whole story. They didn't know the whole helping of absurdity behind why he was claiming to be stuck on her and why she was the center of his universe. If Lila had posted the ten or so seconds before or after that brief pass in their conversation, the internet would have been campaigning to have Jack committed.

But she hadn't. And that was the point.

Gemma watched the short snip again. The scene had been captured from Lila's standing tripod at an angle over her shoulder. Gemma and Jack stood behind her in profile, with Jack's face slightly more open to the camera. All Lila had to do was zoom in and increase the background volume to edit their conversation into the video's main attraction. Gemma realized with a start that the whole scene had also been captured on Lila's livestream. Who knew how many viewers had caught it in real time. That damage seemed lesser, given that the now fifteen-thousand-and-counting viewers who'd watched the video since it was posted had the option to watch it on repeat if they so desired.

She fought the discomfort of exposure and studied Jack's

face. Even with having seen it in person, she realized the pleading look was somehow more powerful on the small screen. He *really* believed what he was saying, that much was clear. A moment of hope sprang to life in her chest, the memory of their day together and encouraging thoughts about what it might lead to. But then she remembered the look that had crossed his face when she suggested he leave for Europe. How he appeared to take the option seriously— and he *should* take it seriously, she thought. He had a literal way out that he hadn't tried, and not taking it was even more irrational than spending another one hundred and forty-seven days looping through the same routine with her. Anyone could see that.

"Oh," Lila suddenly said as she looked at her own phone. "It's getting reposted."

"What?"

Lila's eyes widened, fanning her blackened lashes. "Oh, wow. Hello Happy just picked it up. They've got like three million followers."

"What?" Gemma shrieked. Of course she followed Hello Happy; they posted a collection of the most joyous content the internet had to offer. She never in a million years thought she would have been featured in their feed.

"'Cheering for this mystery couple in L.A.,'" Lila read from the post's caption. "Oh! The Net's Best reposted it too." She looked at Gemma with a guilty grimace.

Embarrassment flared from Gemma's head to her toes, but she saw right through Lila's thinly veiled ploy. "Shut up," she said with a knowing and playful glare. "This is exactly what you hoped for."

Lila bit her lip, blushing slightly, and gave her a confirmatory smile. "Of course, the thing that finally goes viral isn't a video of *me*, but I'll take it."

Gemma grumbled and stood up off the couch. "*Ugh,* Lila! I don't want to be viral! I don't want everyone to know our business! What am I going to do now?"

Lila stood and pressed her palms into her shoulders. "You're going to take a breath, realize this isn't the end of the world, and finish getting ready for dinner so that they don't give away our table."

Gemma took the prescribed breath, though it wasn't at all soothing.

CHAPTER

12

FOR ECONOMICAL PURPOSES, they ordered a rideshare to the radio studio, where they retrieved both the concert passes and Gemma's car. It was, after all, Lila's birthday, so Gemma offered to chauffeur.

After a quick chat with Carmen and a dash across town, Gemma and Lila folded themselves into the dinner crowd of Angelenos enjoying a dimly lit meal in a trendy restaurant a stone's throw from the Hollywood Walk of Fame. The vintage glam dining room was all purple velvet and chrome, with beaded chandeliers dangling from the vaulted ceiling like enormous jellyfish. The lighting made everyone look ten times sexier.

Lila sat across from Gemma in a pair of leather pants and a tasteful tube top with her hair tumbling over her shoulders. She had forgone her originally planned birthday party outfit of strapless minidress for something more practical for their new plans for a backstage adventure. She still looked hot as hell and wore vertiginous heels, as always.

"Thank you for changing plans tonight, Lila," Gemma said, and sipped her fizzy pink cocktail. They'd finished their appetizers and were on to their main courses.

Lila bulged her eyes at her. "Are you kidding me? I wouldn't miss this for anything. And it's about time you use your connections to get us somewhere good." She lifted her matching pink cocktail and sipped as Gemma narrowed her eyes at her implication. She smacked her lips. "*That's* not the connection I'm talking about. I know you did this on your own."

Gemma had done it on her own, really. Sure, Nigel knew her father, but he invited her to the show because of the conversation he'd had with *her*. She smiled about it all over again. Her smile quickly faded when she remembered a detail she hadn't yet shared with Lila.

"Nick is going to be there, you know."

Lila gave her a flat, loyal stare of annoyance. "So I've heard."

"Yeah, well, the part you didn't hear is that my dad set it all up."

Her eyes widened again.

"I know. When I went to visit him, he told me he pulled some strings to get Azalea as the opener tonight, and then he asked me how Nick is doing because apparently Nick told him we are still together."

"*What?*"

"Exactly. See, that's an appropriate reaction. When I told my dad, he tried to spin it into somehow being my fault that he didn't know because we never talk." She rolled her eyes, feeling her anger return and doing her best not to let it ruin dinner.

Lila took a sip of her drink. "Well, Gem, you do hardly see him. Can you fault him for not knowing what's going on in your love life?"

She gaped at her friend. "Me not talking to my father is different than my ex-boyfriend *lying* to him, Lila."

"Of course it is. I'm only saying that the lie worked because you don't see your dad enough to correct it. You know I'd shove Nick in front of a bus the first chance I got. Or maybe take clippers to his ridiculous hair. Or stomp on his hand with some heels so he couldn't play guitar anymore." She pumped her eyebrows and devilishly grinned over her drink like she couldn't decide which vicious option was her favorite.

Gemma forgave her for her comment. Still, she sipped her drink in hope that it would wash down the uncomfortable cocktail of guilt and annoyance souring her mood.

Lila's phone buzzed on the table. Another notification. The video of Gemma and Jack was certified trending by that point, and the more popular it got, the more Gemma felt like it was a reminder that she had ruined things with him.

"I'm sure my dad knows about my love life now," she said, and nodded at the glowing screen. "*Everyone* knows." The mere thought of however many hundred thousand people had seen the video by then made her want to hide under the table.

Lila smiled at whatever she saw and turned it screen down.

"I don't know what you hope to achieve with that. Jack probably never wants to see me again."

Lila looked up and rolled her eyes. "I hardly think that's true, Gem. He's probably—" She suddenly sucked in a

sharp breath and cut herself off. "Oh god. Don't look behind you. *Don't look don't look don't look*," she said in a
rush. Her eyes were pinned to a point near the restaurant
entrance, and it took everything in Gemma's power not to
turn around.

"Lila, you know saying that is only going to make me
want to look."

"Okay, but don't. Trust me, you want to sit this one out."

Gemma's heart thumped against her ribs. She could
only imagine what was happening over her shoulder that
would warrant such a warning.

Lila quietly cursed under her breath. "*Damn it.* This is
what I get for having such good taste in restaurants."

Worry bubbled up Gemma's throat like her fizzy drink
was making a reappearance. She had to assume someone
notable had walked in, as they were, in fact, dining in a
known celebrity hot spot. Based on the look on Lila's face
and the sharp swear words licking from her mouth like little
flames, Gemma knew it was someone she would not want
to see. Her father, perhaps. Or, god forbid, *Nick.* Or maybe
even . . . Jack?

Her heart skipped on the last thought. The sensation felt
important if not profound.

She took a breath and prepared herself for some kind of
grand, middle-of-the-dining-room gesture in case he had
come to win her back, again, but the diameter of Lila's cau-
tionary eyes told her it was not Jack behind her.

"If I can't turn around, can you at least narrate what's
happening?"

Lila nodded. "Yes. Don't freak out, I'm sure it's coincidence, but Angelica Reyes just walked in."

The past minute of Gemma's resistance evaporated into irrelevance as her head involuntarily whipped around.

Lila snapped her fingers at her. "Hey! Eyes forward, Gem."

Gemma's heart had begun beating uncomfortably hard. She could have ignored Nick, dismissed her father, perhaps run away before Jack could find her, but Angelica freaking Reyes had to be the *last* person on the planet she wanted to walk into the restaurant.

A sudden, horrifying thought hit her like a gut punch. Maybe Jack hadn't run off to Europe; maybe he had run back to Angelica.

"Is she here by herself?"

Lila picked up the panic in her voice and quickly shook her head. "No, but she's not with him." She knew without Gemma needing to say it that she was afraid Angelica had come with Jack. "She's with an entourage, though. Shit. That's Hayley Palmer with her, and some other girl I don't recognize." Lila sat up straighter and mindlessly smoothed her hair. It was already perfect but being in the presence of a supermodel often made one want to preen.

Gemma slouched deeper into her chair. As if she didn't already know that Jack's ex-girlfriend was ten thousand miles out of her league, she didn't need the reminder that Angelica and living goddess Hayley Palmer were BFFs.

"They're coming this way," Lila whispered.

Gemma sat up and leaned forward, still fighting the urge to turn around as well as all the unpleasant thoughts swimming through her mind. "How does she look? Is she glowing? Like, *I just had make-up sex with my boyfriend, and we're moving to a quaint European village to ride bikes and eat impractical meals of only cheese and bread together glowing?"*

Lila tore her eyes from the approaching party and looked at Gemma. "That's *very* specific."

Gemma shrugged.

"No, she's not glowing. She's got—god, she's still so hot, though—she's got, like, a full-tilt Elle-Woods-just-got-dumped-by-Warner-in-*Legally-Blonde* vibe going on."

Gemma's heart suddenly soared to the ceiling. "Really?"

"Big-time. She's going to need a cold compress in the morning to take care of all that." Lila waved her hand in a small circle, then sucked in another breath. "Oh god, they're coming closer. They're going to walk right by us. Want me to trip her?"

"Lila!" Gemma hissed.

"The offer stands for three more seconds. Yes or no."

Tempted—and knowing Lila would do it if she asked—Gemma counted to two and a half in her head before she said, "No."

Lila slid her foot, which Gemma had not even noticed she'd stuck into the aisle, back beneath the table. She lifted her drink and casually turned her head toward the wall as Angelica and company passed in a fragrant burst of weepy chatter. Gemma caught the nasally drone in her usually lovely voice and words like *He's gone* and *Who even is she?*

Clearly, she was talking about her and Jack.

Gemma wished the large plant behind her would eat her like it belonged in a shop of horrors. Instead, the man of the young couple being seated at the table directly across from them chose that moment to recognize Lila and blurt out her name.

"Hey! You're Lila in L.A.!"

Lila, usually one to indulge adoring fans, shot him a de-mure smile and nodded, not wanting to draw attention to their table, but the damage had been done.

Angelica had walked past their table and out of Lila's line of sight, but Gemma had a full view when she suddenly stopped and turned around. As if he was trying to make it worse, the man at the next table over—who had to be a tourist because no local would shout about a celebrity sight-ing in a dining room full of guests—called out, "Babe, it's Angelica Reyes! And *Hayley Palmer*?" His eyes were sau-cers glittering with stars. His girlfriend pulled out her phone for pictures.

In that moment, Gemma hated every last thing about L.A. and famous people. She wanted to slide from her chair like jelly and disappear through the floor, but she and Lila were trapped with dozens of eyes on them.

Lila nudged her with her toe beneath the table and shook her head. "It's fine," she muttered in reassurance, but Gemma could not think of one possible iteration of the im-pending scenario that would turn out fine.

Angelica stopped at their tableside wearing a white, flowy dress with bodice and skirt hooked together by small golden rings that showed off her bronze midriff. Hayley Palmer stood beside her like an illogically proportioned, curvy pillar in a minidress that made her legs miles long but probably would have hit Gemma's knees, and glowered down at them. Their friendship had been tabloid fodder for years. Their joint Instagram posts nearly broke the inter-net every time. And with the way Hayley was glaring at

Gemma, she knew she was every bit as loyal to Angelica as Lila was to her.

"Excuse me," Angelica said to Lila, "are you that influencer who posted—" She cut off when she turned to see Gemma. "*You*," she said on a breath. "You're her! That girl from Jack's house!"

Gemma didn't know what to say, so she just stared up at Angelica.

Angelica turned to her very tall, very beautiful friend and pointed at Gemma as if she weren't sitting right there. "This is the girl I told you about, Hay. I thought she was Jack's assistant, but apparently *not*, based on *her* video." Her voice cracked into a soggy whimper.

Hayley Palmer glared at Gemma as if she had committed an act of treason.

"Who even *are* you?" Angelica demanded. The pitch of her voice turned any heads that weren't already staring from when the man at the neighboring table had made his announcement.

Gemma's tongue grew heavy in her mouth. "Um, I'm Gemma."

Angelica glared at her through her swollen eyes running with makeup. "Gemma who? What do you do? Who are you?"

"I-I'm no one," she stuttered.

Lila scoffed, offended. "Like hell you are!" She stood and held her hand out palm up as if Gemma were a prize on display. "This is Gemma Peters—yes, as in *that* Peters you are thinking of. She's a radio producer with an impressive résumé and happens to be friends with Nigel Black, and we are on the way backstage to his show tonight by special invite. Not only that, but she's also one of the greatest people on the planet. She's loyal and kind and scary smart. Anyone would be damn lucky to have her even look their way, and too bad for you, Jack can't keep his eyes off her. Yes, she's *that girl* from his house and the now viral video, and if you spent two seconds thinking about it, you'd realize she's not some random assistant, and he is in love with *her*, not you!"

Angelica, Hayley, the third nameless yet equally beautiful woman with them, and Gemma all blinked at her, stunned.

Angelica eventually scoffed and pulled a hand to her chest. She glowered down at Gemma. "Well, if he's so in love with you, then why is he leaving the country?"

Lila snapped back on reflex. "Because he— What?"

Gemma's heart took a flying leap to her toes.

Angelica nodded a big bobbing motion that sent her flowing hair bouncing. "I went to find him after your little video went viral to remind him of what we have together, and he's at his house packing to leave for London. Tonight. He said he has to get out, to go, and things are completely over between us because of what happened the other day. I mean, it's not even that big of a deal. Joey and I are only friends. It was an accident." Her voice clipped up again, and she turned into Hayley's chest. Hayley wrapped an arm around her and cast them a glare that landed somewhere between devoted fury and runway chic.

Lila glanced at Gemma and mouthed *Joey?* in confusion, but she was too distracted to respond. The clatter of the restaurant dulled to a buzz as her hearing momentarily went offline.

Jack was leaving?

She couldn't believe it.

The contemplative look on his face when she suggested he move as a way to end the loop came back to her in a rush. He must have honestly considered it and realized it was a viable solution.

Something soft and delicate unexpectedly cracked in her chest.

"He didn't even mention you, but if he's leaving the country, then I assume it's over between you too," Angelica warbled. Hayley shushed her and patted her back.

How like a celebrity to go out in public to have a meltdown, Gemma thought. She herself was moments away from tears at the thought that she really had ruined things with Jack, and all she wanted to do was go home and hug a pillow and hide. And there was Angelica Reyes, wailing in the middle of a packed restaurant.

Hayley rubbed her back and cast Gemma and Lila a spiteful look. She guided them off toward their table and left the dining room muttering in their wake.

Gemma saw Lila sink back into her chair and her mouth move, but she was not processing anything coming out of it. All she could think of was the single moment that had put the day in motion: when Jack crashed into her at the coffee shop. She could still feel it, the jolt like an electric shock. His hands on her arms. The concerned look on his handsome face and the shine in his eyes. And then everything that had come after. His kindness, his certainty. How vulnerable he'd made himself in his attempts to get her to believe him. Seeing her unhappiness, her problems, and trying to help her. The way she'd opened up to him. Their kiss. The thought that she would never experience any of that again, anything with him, suddenly and completely broke that delicate thing in her chest that had cracked.

"Lila, I think I made a mistake."

Lila paused, fork halfway to her mouth. Gemma realized at the sight of her having resumed eating that she'd lost track of how long she had been staring into space. "What, you wish you got the pasta instead?" She nodded at Gemma's half-eaten plate.

Gemma looked down and realized she no longer had an appetite. There were more important matters to tend to.

"No," she said, determined. She lifted her napkin from her lap and set it on the table. "I think I made a mistake with Jack."

Lila's attention refocused in a snap. "What do you mean?"

She stood with a resolve that surprised herself. She'd been telling Jack he was delusional all day, and suddenly, the thought of losing him felt like the most absurd part of it all. If he left and the loop broke, she'd never see him again. If him leaving wasn't the solution and they woke up back in the same day, even if she remembered him—which was no guarantee—what incentive did he have to start all over when she'd told him to give up on her and go on to his new life?

Either option filled her chest with a tight sense of panic, not at being stuck in the loop but at the thought of letting him go.

Lila gazed up at her, still waiting for an answer.

A swell of determination filled her like a balloon, pushing the panic aside and assuring her of what she needed to do.

"I have to stop him. I can't let him leave."

Lila gaped up at her with her mouth open. "You're going to go after him?"

Gemma nodded once, assuring herself of her plan. "Yes."

"Like, we're going to storm the airport and try to stop him from getting on a plane?"

Gemma heard how rash and desperate it sounded. But still. "Yes."

Lila knowingly, and a bit smugly, grinned at her. Then she shot out of her chair again and danced. "I knew it! I *knew* you were in love with him. *Yes!*"

Gemma's face shyly burned as she threw her valet ticket at her. "Go get the car while I get the check."

LILA JUGGLED TAKEOUT containers in her lap as they sped across the city. Their waiter hadn't even blinked when they claimed a sudden emergency and asked for to-go boxes and an early check. As far as he'd been concerned, they'd cleared up a table for him to fill with another paying customer. Gemma apologized profusely for cutting Lila's birthday dinner short, but Lila assured her she had no qualms by running for the valet while Gemma had shoveled all their food into boxes and paid the check.

Gemma had no contact information for Jack, so finding him at the airport was her best bet. Angelica said he was leaving for London, so she'd put LAX's international terminal into her GPS and they took off.

She had no plan for what to say to him, how to explain that she'd been wrong and convince him to stay. She hoped the words would come when the moment presented itself— *if* they got there in time.

She pressed her foot harder into the gas to make a yellow light. She had one eye on the clock too; it read 7:15. Nigel's show started in under two hours. The show felt far less important than stopping Jack. She had two chances of a lifetime in front of her, she realized, and she knew that both her seven-year-old self and Nigel Black would want her to make the obvious choice.

"What are you going to say to him?" Lila asked.

"I don't know. I guess I'll figure it out when we get there."

"That's perfect. Don't plan anything. Let your heart do the talking," Lila said like she would have offered the same advice if asked.

The thought of what was in her heart had Gemma brimming and terrified at once. Grand gestures were not in her comfort zone by any stretch of the imagination. But neither were such strong feelings after a single day. She hadn't let herself feel anything in so long, she almost forgot what feeling even felt like. But Jack had her feeling all sorts of things. Big things. Why else would she be speeding into the night to try and stop him from making a huge mistake?

She smiled to herself as they flew down a busy street. They were minutes away, according to her GPS. But of course they had to make it *in* to the airport once they got there.

On its best day, LAX was a total nightmare. On a random Thursday evening that may or may not have been repeated one hundred and forty-seven times, there would be no exception.

When they arrived, Gemma parked in a middle layer of the concrete garage housing an endless maze of cars. She and Lila skipped the elevator and dashed down an outdoor stairwell that spilled them out on the far side of two multi-lane, one-way streets that they risked life and limb to cross even with all the lights flashing and walk signs on. They made it under the dim eaves, lit by fluorescent overhead lights and smelling like exhaust, cigarette smoke, and who knew what else. The air inside the terminal was only an ounce fresher.

Of course, they couldn't get anywhere without buying tickets, but the first step in their plan was to figure out which flight he was on. Then they would figure out how they might try to stop him from getting on it.

As they pushed through passengers and dodged luggage, Gemma realized that after everything they'd been through since that morning, she was finally the one chasing him. It put a smile on her lips at the same time a desperation tightened her chest with worry that she wouldn't make it in time.

They found their way to a board with a dizzying list of departures and arrivals.

"What are we looking for?" Lila asked over a telltale chirp of a camera.

Gemma turned to see Lila with her handheld tripod pointing her phone directly at her. Where it had come from, she had no idea. "What are you doing?" she demanded.

"Giving your fans the happy ending they deserve," Lila said with a smile.

Gemma gulped at the thought that thousands—maybe tens of thousands—were on the other end of the little glowing dot of light aimed at her. Anxiety pushed thoughts of protest to the front of her mind, but she realized with a thrilling sense of wonder that Lila's obsession with broadcasting her life might have been of benefit in that moment.

She squared herself and looked right at the camera. Lila took a cautious step back like Gemma might repeat the scene from her living room and tackle her, but instead, she took a steadying breath. A rush of nerves came over her. Then she threw caution to the wind and let her heart do the talking.

"Hi, um, whoever is out there watching. It's Gemma from earlier. I want to say thank you for helping me see something I've been missing all day—missing for a long time, actually." She quietly laughed to herself. "Missing for about five months, I guess."

Lila knowingly smiled as she kept filming.

Gemma pushed on. "I know there are a lot of you out there, but I really want to talk to one person." She swallowed what was left of her nerves and carefully thought about how to say what she needed to say without sounding senseless. "Jack, I'm here at the airport. I . . . I made a mistake when I told you to leave. I think you're right. It *is* us. I'm just as stuck on you as you are on me, and we need each other to get out of this. You've changed me today. You've made me feel things that . . ." Emotion caught her voice and made her pause. She took a breath and kept going. "You've helped me realize a lot of things that I needed to realize, and I think you're right that that's an important part of this, and it wouldn't have happened without you. So, I guess if you can somehow see this, please don't leave. Don't go. I need you too." She looked at her surroundings as if he might be nearby. Her voice pinched up with worry. "I'm going to try to find you, but I might run out of time. *Please.* If you're on one of these planes, get off while you still can."

She turned away from the camera and looked back at the departures and arrivals board. Her heart pounded at the thought of her declaration and how many people had seen it, and she desperately hoped one of them was Jack. They were in uncharted waters, though; he had never tried to leave during the day, so he wouldn't know Lila would be producing content relevant to him at that moment. On the very likely chance he was oblivious, she scanned the board with newfound determination. Lila chattered into her camera, which she had swiveled around to point at herself, narrating the scene.

Gemma scanned the alphabetized board as quickly as she could before it changed over to the next screen. An overwhelming number of flights came and went in a matter of minutes. She threw her eyes at the *L*s and saw a direct flight to London currently boarding and due to take off in a half hour.

Her heart surged. She shook with excitement.

"Got it!" she shouted at Lila like she'd discovered the answer to a complex puzzle. She spun in a circle looking for the correct airline's counter, and, thank god, saw it within jogging distance and not a full terminal away. "Come on!" she called to Lila as she took off.

Lila clutched her camera in one hand and trotted after her.

Gemma skipped the line of people laden with luggage and arrived at the counter out of breath. Lila explained to the disgruntled passengers she'd cut in front of that it was an emergency.

"Hi," Gemma said to the stern-faced woman behind the

counter. *Helen,* her name tag read. "I'm looking for a passenger. He's on that flight that is boarding for London right now."

Helen eyed her up and down and wasted several seconds before responding. "Ma'am, I don't have information about individual passengers."

Gemma didn't know enough about airline regulations to know if she was telling the truth or trying to get rid of her.

"Please, it's an emergency. I need to stop him from getting on the plane."

Helen's eyes grew a fraction. "Do you need to report something to security?"

"No! Nothing like that. Everything is fine. I just need to find him before the plane takes off."

Helen paused and then nodded at the angry passenger behind Gemma who had stepped closer to the counter.

"What's going on here?" he asked in a Boston accent. Based on his oxfords and the suit unbuttoned over his round belly, Gemma reasoned some kind of business was taking him to London on a Thursday night. "The rest of us have been waiting in line, and she cuts to the front?"

"I'm sorry, sir," Helen said. "I'll be with you in a moment."

"What kind of emergency gets you to the front of the line?" he sourly asked. "'Cause I might have one too." He looked over his shoulder with a laugh and received some supportive nods from the queue behind him.

Lila turned and glared at him. "It's an emergency of *love,* sir."

He snorted and scooted his rolling suitcase closer like he might try to push them out of the way. He eyed her camera.

"What is this, some kind of internet stunt? You doing this for views?"

Not at all, Gemma thought as she turned back to Helen. She didn't want an audience for this part if she could manage. "Please," she begged, "I need your help."

"Ma'am, like I said, I can't help you."

Each denial was wasting time she could be spending trying to stop Jack.

"Nobody cares about you and your boyfriend, sweetheart!" the man in line called. It earned him another glare from Lila.

Gemma turned back to Helen and mustered all the plea she could. "Please, can you call him over the PA system? His name is Jack—" She paused and realized that even after everything they'd been through, she didn't know his last name. A wave of embarrassment hit her.

"Ma'am, I can't do that. Now please, step out of line so I can help our ticketed passengers."

She considered buying a ticket on the spot and going through security to try her luck at the gate, but she would never make it in time.

"Wait! Please, just . . . let me think." She tried to remember if his last name had come up at all during the day. Had she seen it on the receipt when he paid for their lunch? He had swiped the check away too soon for her to offer to pay and tucked the receipt in his pocket after. It wasn't anywhere inside his car, and Dr. Woods had only called him Jack. She realized with a sinking feeling that she was at a loss.

"Oh!" A thought struck her. "He writes for the TV show *Mac Drake!*"

Helen arched a brow at her. "That doesn't help any-thing, ma'am."

"We can look him up online!" Lila blurted, obviously keeping up.

Gemma's heart pounded as she whipped out her phone and attacked her screen, suddenly thankful for such easy access to information and feeling foolish for not thinking of it earlier.

"Let me see . . ." she muttered as she scrolled. "*Mac Drake . . .* written by . . ."

And there it was.

"Lincoln!" she shouted. "Jack Lincoln!" She held out the phone for Helen to see.

She flinched at the bright screen and frowned.

Jack Lincoln, Gemma thought. What a solid name.

"I still can't tell you if he's on that plane, ma'am. And I'm not making a PA announcement. Now please, step aside." She held out her hand as if she were pushing Gemma and beckoned the unhappy man in line.

He stepped forward and jostled her with his shoulder.

"Wait! Please, I—"

"Ma'am!" Helen said sternly. "There's nothing I can do to help you unless you want to buy a ticket, and to do that, you need to go to the end of the line and *wait* like everyone else."

Gemma flinched at the bite in her voice. She couldn't see over the counter but assumed there was a phone back there that would connect her to someone who could help. Reaching for it would surely get her tackled by security, as would making a run for the gate.

She silently cursed the factors that had made airport security so insufferably tight. Yes, it stopped all sorts of malicious intentions, but it scooped up noble ones in the safety net too.

Gemma took a deep breath and made one final stand. She looked right into Helen's eyes. "Please, Helen. I'm begging you. The man who might be the love of my life is on that plane, and I'll never know if we're meant to be together if I don't stop him from taking off. I'm asking for your help. Please."

Helen eyed her as her jaw clenched. Gemma could see a decision processing in her cold eyes, and she hoped she had earned her sympathy.

Her heart surged when Helen reached for the phone that was indeed hiding behind the desk. Her face split into a smile and hope buoyed her spirit.

"Can I get security to the counter, please?" Helen said, and Gemma's soaring heart fell to the floor. "We have someone who needs to be escorted out." She paused to listen. "Thank you." She hung up and returned her gaze to Gemma. The look on her face said she took satisfaction in snatching away the fleeting hope that she had actually planned to help. "You have about twenty seconds to leave on your own before someone comes and forces you to."

A chill shook Gemma's body at the threat in her voice. She did not want to risk being escorted out, but she was so close. And she was still reeling from admitting what Jack meant to her. She had let her heart do the talking and what had come out . . . it assured her she was in the right place doing the right thing.

Lila suddenly threw herself at the counter, camera still in hand. "Who hurt you, Helen? Don't you believe in love? This woman is here grand-gesturing and you're creating a needless barrier!"

Helen flinched, and Gemma grabbed Lila's arm before she *really* got them in trouble. She tugged her away to a mix of applause and groans of sympathetic support from passengers.

"Love will win, Helen!" Lila shouted, somehow still managing to hold her camera and capture it all live. "Love always wins!"

"Lila! You're going to get us in trouble!" Gemma scolded right as a large man in a TSA uniform approached them. She took a sobering breath.

"Is there a problem here?" the security agent asked. The name badge resting on his broad chest said *Raul*.

"No," Gemma began. "We're just leaving—"

"*Yes*, there's a problem!" Lila snapped, camera now trained on Raul the TSA agent. "My best friend is here trying to stop *the man she loves* from boarding a flight out of her life forever and we *need* to get to the gate! But *Helen* is a bitter—"

Raul held out a gentle arm. He was tall and bulky with light brown skin that Gemma imagined would have set off a nice smile if he weren't frowning at them. "Ma'am, please lower the camera."

"I'm sorry," Gemma muttered on behalf of them both. She felt not only the eyes through the camera on them, but everyone in the airport was staring at the scene.

"Don't apologize, Gemma!" Lila scolded, and lifted the camera back up. "You've done nothing wrong."

Raul's eyes flashed as if someone had turned on a light. He took a step back and looked them both up and down. "Wait, Gemma?"

Time loop or not, and despite what had happened with remembering Jack, Gemma was one thousand percent positive she had never met Raul before. She scanned her memory as deep as it went for any indication that they'd stumbled into a new iteration of something she'd already done to explain why he recognized her and came up empty.

And then it clicked.

"You know me from the viral video," she said with a glimmer of hope like the sun turning a rain cloud's edges gold.

His face split into the wide, brilliant smile she knew was in there. "Yeah!" He turned to Lila. "And that would make you Lila in L.A.!"

Lila's scowl instantly flipped into the charming, appreciative smile she wore whenever she met a fan. "Indeed, it would."

Raul laughed a jolly sound and spread his arms. "No shit! I love you!" He stopped and cleared his throat, his cheeks going rosy. "I mean, your content is great." He shyly smoothed his hair with a hand, and Gemma realized that they had met a *fan* of Lila's.

Lila flushed and flirtatiously shrugged her chin into her shoulder. "Thank you."

Yes, Gemma thought at the chance this man might help them. *Flirt your butt off, Lila.*

Raul continued smiling at them, mostly Lila, as he put the pieces together. "So wait, you're here for the guy? The guy from the video?"

"*Yes!*" they said at the same time.

Lila stepped forward and put her hand on his arm. "He's leaving, Raul. He's getting on a plane, and Gemma is here trying to stop him before it's too late. Can you please help us?"

Raul looked over his shoulder at the staring crowd and swiped his hair again, obviously reluctant. "Can't you call him or something?"

"I don't have his number," Gemma confessed. "I know it sounds ridiculous, but we only met today, and I don't have any contact information for him. I actually just learned his last name a few minutes ago. But what I *do* know is he's getting on a plane to London, and it will be the biggest mistake of my life if I let him go."

It came straight from her heart again, and the warm swell of it—the truth—made her dizzy in the best way. She couldn't fight the smile on her face despite the dire situation.

Raul took another glance over his shoulder. "Damn. This story is even better than I thought."

"Isn't it, though?" Lila crooned. She rose up on her toes and squeezed his left biceps like she was testing a piece of fruit for ripeness. "That's why we need you, Raul. You *have to* help us. Gemma *has* to make it to Jack, and you're our only hope."

She was selling it so hard that even Gemma was buying it.

Raul took a tense breath and scanned the room. Most everyone had gone back to their own business of lugging suitcases and looking all-around miserable. In the thick of it all, would anyone notice if he helped them bypass the rules?

Gemma chewed her lip, acutely aware of how much time

had passed since she had looked at the flight directory and seen that Jack's plane was going to take off in thirty minutes. They were down to the wire.

Raul looked at their pleading faces, mostly Lila's, and made a decision.

He gently pushed her camera down and nodded his head to their left. "You'll have to stop filming, but you can come with me."

Gemma's heart surged.

Lila squealed and flipped her camera to face herself. "I'll be back, my loves. Don't go anywhere!" She clicked off the video and deftly collapsed the little tripod like a telescope. "Where are we going?"

Raul discreetly shuffled them toward the hall behind the counter. The security lines frothed like a boiling pot as passengers removed shoes and belts and loaded bins. Gemma couldn't believe they were actually side-skirting it all. What they were doing was most definitely illegal.

They arrived at a door with *AUTHORIZED PERSONNEL ONLY* screaming at them in large block letters, and Raul paused with a hand on it.

Gemma counted the loss of a few more seconds as they waited.

"You don't have any weapons, do you?" Raul said.

"Of course not!" Gemma blurted.

"Only the burning flame in her heart!" Lila chirped behind her.

Gemma would have rolled her eyes, but she could not deny the heat rippling from her chest into her every limb.

They were so close, and they were going to make it.

"Right," Raul said, and swiped his badge. The door beeped and let them into a dim hallway that smelled of luggage conveyor belts. Gemma thought she heard him mutter something about *going to federal prison* behind them and chose to ignore it.

She started walking faster, though she didn't know where they were going. Raul caught up at a slow jog and turned them down another hall with a set of double doors at the end. They popped out into the light of a busy hub of gates. Passengers who'd cleared security sat in rows of chairs waiting for flights and milled about on their phones, snacking and stretching their legs.

"It's that easy?" Lila said what Gemma was thinking. Given the hassle of security, it seemed unfair that a short hallway was the solution to bypassing it in under a minute. She felt like they should have had to fight a dragon or solve a riddle to get by.

"Yep," Raul said. "But don't tell anyone. What gate?"

Gemma thought back to the numbers she'd seen on the flight directory and glanced at the protruding signs up above. Her heart sank.

"One fifty-six," she said. They were in the 130s.

Raul pivoted to their left and beckoned them with a hand. "Better hustle, then."

They fell into step, and Lila pulled her tripod back out like she was deploying an umbrella. "Can I film again?"

Raul glanced sideways as she hurried to keep up with his long strides. A smile spread across his face. "Sure."

She squealed. *"Oh!* This is so exciting. You're totally getting a supporting credit in the love story of Gemma and Jack. MVP Raul!"

Raul beamed so hard Gemma thought his face might break. Lila's flirting seemed wholly genuine by that point, but maybe it had been all along. He was a very attractive security agent.

Lila resumed her video by greeting her fans. Gemma tried not to think about the hordes of them who'd been anxiously waiting while her livestream went dark.

She tuned it out and looked for gate 156 as they hurried through the airport.

"Please please please," she began to mutter under her breath.

She realized that despite the crushing nerves that she wasn't going to make it in time, her primary feeling was one of happiness. She knew, finally, how she felt and what she wanted.

Jack.

It was all irrational, but Lila had been right: strange didn't have to mean bad. She laughed to herself as tears misted her eyes and she ran—*ran*—through the airport to get to him.

Lila hurried to keep up, surely giving her viewers a bouncy account of the journey as she held her tripod. Raul set a steady pace in front of them, darting his eyes side to side and clearing a path. Gemma wondered how long until someone caught on to what they had done, and she realized it made better sense to have Raul out in front leading them than behind as if he were chasing. That might get them tackled by an intervening security agent. Though, surely, they would all have to answer for their sins at some point. Gemma hoped that point would be after she found Jack. Maybe he would bail her and Lila out of jail. She smiled at the absurd though not entirely out-of-the-question thought and kept running.

They'd made it to the 140s and were getting closer to the correct gate. She had no plan for what to say to Jack but was ready to let her heart do the talking since that had seemed to work in her favor earlier.

"Please don't go, Jack," she said on a breath. Her eyes shot to the numbers on the signs at each gate. The even gates were on the right.

She cut across the aisle flowing with passengers, dodging suitcases and nearly tripping over a dog on a leash. Gate 154 was within sight, which meant 156 was right past it.

"Sorry! Excuse me!" she said to everyone and no one as she pushed through. The crowd at gate 154 was headed to Mexico City, and she wondered at how two starting points could begin so close together and end half a world apart.

She was so close. Almost there.

Her heart was in her throat as she tore around the corner to gate 156.

It promptly fell as she watched an airline employee close the doors leading to the jet bridge. The woman smoothed her hands over the seam at the sealed opening and turned with a satisfied nod. A man tapped a keyboard behind the desk and looked out over the empty seats awaiting the next set of passengers.

"Wait!" Gemma shouted. "Wait! Please!"

Both employees jumped when she came hurtling at them, arms desperately waving.

Gemma stomped to a stop and fought for breath. Out the dark window, she could see the pilots in the lit-up cockpit turning knobs and talking with each other. A man in an orange jumpsuit stood on the tarmac below waving a light stick at them. They would be pulling away any minute.

"No no no. *Please*, I need to stop that plane!" Gemma said to the employees.

They looked at each other in confusion.

"Ma'am," the woman who had shut the door said, "the doors are closed. This flight is cleared for takeoff." She looked at Raul in alarm as if there were a true threat to assess.

Gemma expected him to heroically demand they open the doors and let them through, but when he stayed silent and cast her an apologetic look, she realized he hadn't expected them to get there too late. He had helped her in hopes of a grand-gesture reunion at the gate. Going any farther would set off a cascade of events that no one wanted to be responsible for: opening the gate, delaying the flight, changing everyone's agenda. For as much of a nightmare as LAX was, Gemma knew it ran on a strict schedule.

And she had missed her chance.

"I'm sorry, Gemma," Raul said, and the sincere disappointment in his voice knifed into her still-pounding heart.

Everything, all the optimistic rushing of the past five minutes, came to a screeching halt. Gemma felt as if a wave had slammed into a seawall and left her battered in the surf.

Lila murmured something into her camera and stopped the video. She dropped her tripod to her side with her brow furrowed in sorrow. "I'm sorry, Gem."

Gemma felt like she was under water as the sad scene slowly unfolded around her. The airline employees cast her concerned looks. Raul scanned the nearby gates for signs of trouble. Lila stared at her feet. The man on the tarmac waved his light stick, and the plane pulled away from the jet bridge.

She walked to the window and pressed her hand to the glass. Night had fallen and bulbs of every color lit up the runways like a neon flower garden in neat rows. She had no idea what was going to happen when Jack left. She might wake up in the same day and be none the wiser. Or, perhaps worse, she might wake up tomorrow, actually tomorrow, and remember everything.

Raul quietly cleared his throat. "Uh, Gemma? Listen, you have to leave now before we all get in some serious trouble. I thought this was going to end differently, but . . ."

She turned to the forlorn look on his face. The fanfare of an emotional reunion might have at least distracted them from the penalty coming their way for breaking the rules, but they were basically sitting ducks standing at the empty gate. He was right; they had to go.

Lila said something to Raul that Gemma didn't hear and then looped her arm through her elbow. "Come on."

She led her through the bustling throng in a daze. They casually joined the stream of travelers heading to baggage claim and disappeared into the crowd like they had been a part of it all along. When they emptied out into the cooled night air back on the sidewalk, Gemma hardly remembered leaving the gate. The journey blurred into broken pieces she couldn't put together for the sudden feeling of the piece that made everything whole having gone missing. Vanished into the night on metal wings, never to be seen again.

The pain in her chest was like a chord that had never been struck before. Deep and resonant and connected to a part of her heart she didn't know was capable of such feeling. She stopped wondering how it was all possible and trusted that the ache over losing Jack meant that everything he'd told her was true. Every last bit.

And now he was gone.

"Can we stop for a second?" she asked, suddenly overwhelmed and tired.

Lila turned to her in surprise after her having been silent for the past several minutes. They had crossed the busy street and made it to the parking garage. "Sure. We can stop."

Gemma had already started to sit on the small curb near the elevators. Their arms remained linked, so she pulled Lila down with her.

"Uh, Gem, it's kinda gross here. Do you want to maybe—? Okay." Lila gave up trying to talk her out of sitting on the ground. Instead, she sat down beside her and patted her arm.

"I ruined it, Lila. I ruined everything."

Lila's dauntless optimism seemed to have left with Jack's plane. She let out a heavy sigh and leaned her head into Gemma's shoulder. "Yeah, that didn't end up the way I hoped it would. I'm sorry, Gem."

Gemma shrugged in defeat. "I don't know what's going to happen now. Is tomorrow actually going to be tomorrow? Or are we stuck forever?" An uncomfortable sense of panic tightened her throat. She thought about Dr. Woods's spinning globe and how it had stopped when he poked it with his stylus and suggested that all of reality might have been stuck as well thanks to her and Jack.

A wave of guilt washed over her. She groaned and held

her face in her hand. Her mistake may have had consequences beyond only herself, and that was too much to bear.

"Unfortunately, I don't have an answer for you, Gem," Lila said. "But I *do* know there's nothing we can do about that plane being gone. I also know we still have passes to Nigel's show . . ."

Gemma lifted her head to give Lila an ashamed look of remorse. "I'm so sorry, Lila. I've totally ruined your birthday."

She shook her head with a small, forgiving grin. "Nonsense. The only way you could do that is by staying here in this gutter. The night is young and who knows, this might be our only chance to live this version of it. Come on." She stood and wiped her hands on her bottom before holding one out to pull Gemma up.

"You're way too optimistic for someone stuck in an endless loop."

"And you're way too cynical for someone who fell in love in a single day."

As much as the reminder stung, Gemma knew she was right. She had fallen. Completely.

CHAPTER
13

SEEING THE LIGHTS of the Hollywood Bowl lifted Gemma's spirits a fraction. The outdoor amphitheater wedged into the hills like a giant clamshell sent waves of sound pulsing through the night. She knew by the tone of the voice ringing into the dark when they arrived that Nick's band was not yet onstage. There must have been two openers. That at least meant they had not missed the start of Nigel's set, but it increased the chances of running into Nick backstage.

"*Ooh*, this is so exciting!" Lila squealed from beside her as they approached the back entrance.

Gemma felt the beat of the song vibrating her rib cage the closer they got, and it felt like a drug. She might have worked in a quiet studio where they mostly talked, and she considered herself a connoisseur of recorded music because it ran in her blood, but nothing rivaled a live show. Nothing.

She knew once they got inside, select people would recognize her, ones knowledgeable of her father, but as they passed through the initial security, she and Lila were simply another pair of lucky guests flashing their lanyard passes. At the first gate, a burly man in all black wearing an earpiece aimed his flashlight at their passes and let them in with a nod.

Lila squealed again and deployed her mini tripod.

"I don't know if they're going to let you stream in here," Gemma warned.

Lila tossed her hair with a tsk. "Let them ask me to stop, then." She greeted her followers for what had to have been at least the fifth time that day, and Gemma wondered how many were still tuned in after the scene at the airport.

Her heart dipped at the thought. She shook it away and vowed to enjoy the opportunity at hand.

The song onstage finished off with a frantic rush of drums and guitars. The crowd cheered. Gemma felt it all rising from the ground, pushing in from the air itself, like the energy entered every cell of her body. A small smile spread across her face.

They made it to the next set of doors, where their passes were scrutinized with more care. Another burly man granted them passage. When they crossed inside, the sound waves that had been thundering and sharp outside dulled to a muffled but still strong pulse. The walls vibrated. Gemma could feel it tingling her scalp.

Immediately inside the door, a woman with an earpiece and a tablet looked at their passes and pointed down a long hall. Lila squeezed Gemma's arm in excitement. The music got louder the closer they got to the stage. Crew and staff hurried up and down the hall talking into earpieces and carrying all manner of items: amp cords, guitars, water bottles. Gemma saw a bag of Taco Bell go by. The chaos of live entertainment was intoxicating.

They rounded a corner into a new hallway right in time to see a folding chair come flying out of an open doorway. It smashed into the opposite wall, gouging out a chunk of drywall, and clattered on the concrete floor.

Gemma gasped and held out a hand on reflex to stop Lila. Raised voices poured from the doorway; something was obviously not going well inside. They glanced at each other, unsure if continuing forward was safe, when a man draped in lanyards and wearing a headset stepped backward through the door with his hands raised. Another man followed him with his finger angrily pointed at the first man's chest.

"This is *bullshit!*" the man with the angry finger said, and Gemma recognized the voice.

Her blood went cold at the same time her heart pitched up into her mouth.

"Listen, I don't make the rules. I just follow them so that I don't lose my job," the man with his hands up said.

They were fully in the hallway now, the man with his hands raised looking both apologetic and agitated. And the other man, a man Gemma knew very well, was beet red with anger. His disheveled hair fell in shiny blond waves to his broad shoulders. He wore a tight black tee shirt and had a sleeve tattoo that Gemma was endlessly thankful did not contain any ink dedicated to her. He had the chiseled cheekbones and jawline of someone created for the spotlight. He looked taller, somehow, but maybe that was because Gemma was stunned to see him. Or perhaps because he was furious and puffing himself up to intimidate the other man.

"Who did this, then?" Nick, the ex she never wanted to see again, demanded, and poked the man in the chest.

The first man stood his ground despite the poke looking like it had hurt. "Someone with a lot more sway than I have," he said through gritted teeth.

Nick dropped his hand and shook his head with an annoyed groan. "What does that mean? Tell me where this came from!"

The commotion was causing a scene. Other doors had popped open, and a few people leaned out to see what was happening. Another man Gemma recognized came marching up the hall from the other direction with his phone pressed to his ear.

"Billy!" Nick shouted at him. "What the hell is going on? They're trying to cut us at the last second!"

Gemma stiffened and felt Lila do the same beside her. No one had even noticed them standing in the hall with all the drama.

Billy Jackson, the band's manager, a man who worshipped Gemma's father and had played a pivotal role in the destruction of her relationship by getting Nick everything he wanted, joined the standoff. Gemma loathed him, which she realized wasn't entirely fair since he was only doing his job. But still, she'd cast him and his slicked-back hair, gold watches, and devilish good looks as a secondary villain in the story. He held up a hand to Nick and kept his phone pressed to his ear with the other.

"Nick, I just heard. I'm trying to—" He cut off to listen to whoever was on the phone. He looked up at the ceiling like he was thinking. He nodded. "Shit. Okay, yeah. Yeah, we got it," he said into the phone. He ended the call with a press of his thumb and shook his head. "I'm sorry, man. It's not happening."

"*What?!*" Nick bellowed.

His bandmates had slowly seeped out of the doorway to join. Gemma tilted her head down when she saw the familiar faces, trying to hide. She held the drummer and bass player in the same esteem as Billy the manager, but the rhythm guitar player, Jimmy, was a great guy with a lovely wife who'd been unfortunately swallowed up in the pool of unpleasantness. Still, running into any of them at all had definitely *not* been in her plans for this evening.

"What the fuck, Billy," Nick demanded. "Who is making this call? We're supposed to go on in ten minutes. They can't—"

"They can, Nick," Billy said, holding up a hand to calm him. "Trust me, we gotta let this one go."

Nick exhaled a sharp breath and balled his fists. A vein pulsed in the side of his neck. Gemma knew the look on his face; he was not going to give up easily. Despite the favors he'd been granted, tenacity ran thick in his blood like any artist fighting for a shot. "Well, what are they going to do, stop us from going onstage? There are thousands of people out there. They're going to leave a gap in the lineup?"

"The first openers are extending their set," the man who had been poked in the chest said. He had to be the event organizer, Gemma reasoned. "They were told after the last song to run up until nine p.m. for Nigel."

"Oh, well, that's perfect," Nick spat. "People came here to see us! You can't—"

"*People came here* to see Nigel Black," the first man said, sternly cutting him off. He folded his arms and gave Nick a nasty, exhausted glare. "You're just an interchangeable ap-petizer who thinks he's a god like every other small act pig-gybacking on a big name. It's not happening tonight, so I suggest you leave. Don't trash the room on your way out." He pivoted on his heel and walked away in the direction Billy had come from.

Nick stared after him, fuming. Then he yanked free one of the drumsticks sticking out of his drummer's folded arms and hurled it down the hallway after him. It bounced off the wall, then the floor, clanking. The man didn't even flinch or stop walking.

Gemma had never seen Nick behave violently, but some-how the scene did not surprise her at all.

Nick combed a hand through his hair and gestured after the man. "What the fuck, Billy," he repeated, evidently out of ways to express himself.

"Nick, man, calm down," Billy said. He tapped his phone with a thumb as if he was messaging someone.

"No! Not until I get some answers. Who would do this to us? Who even has the clout to pull strings like this at the last second?"

Billy looked up at him and took a breath. His eyes grew serious. "The same person who pulled strings at the last second to get you *in* the lineup, Nick."

A heavy silence settled over the hallway, save for the music from the stage reverberating through the walls.

Gemma could not believe what she had just heard. She knew who had pulled strings to get Azalea in the lineup, but her mind could not make sense of how that same person could have also done this.

Billy put a hand on Nick's shoulder and squeezed it. He

looked him in the eye like a coach instructing a player. "Nick, listen to me. This is a very small industry, and there are people who you don't want to piss off. Roger Peters is at the top of that list. I don't know his motivation here, but all the same, let this one go." Billy patted his back and turned to take a phone call.

The rest of the band headed back into the dressing room, and Nick looked like he might punch the wall. He even made a motion to do it but thought better of it at the last second and dropped his hand. Instead, he crossed the hall to pick up the chair he'd thrown. When he bent down, right before his golden hair tumbled into his face and he left the chair alone, he saw Gemma.

For the past several moments, she'd felt like she had been watching a movie play out in front of her; something she wasn't truly a part of. With his eyes suddenly on her, she was pulled into a spotlight she did not want to join.

She ducked her face and quickly turned around.

"Gemma?" he said, disbelief evident in his voice. "Is that you?"

The sound of him saying her name felt like an old wound flaring up in cold weather. The memory of something powerful pulsed under her skin, and along with it, a reminder of the pain it had caused. But still, it was Nick. The once-keeper of her heart. A bond that strong took a long time to die.

She was going to turn around and allow herself a moment of poisonous indulgence in his magnetic presence, but a tone slipped into his voice and stopped her.

"Wait," he said as if something had dawned on him. "Did *you* do this?"

The accusation snapped her out of whatever delirious and short-lived relapse she'd had thinking he was worth her time. And it served as a plain reminder that he knew exactly what he'd done, how he'd used her. To think she could have influenced her father's decision to pull his band from the lineup said clearly that he knew he deserved something of the sort. That Gemma had reason to use her father's influence the same as he had done to get where he was.

"Seriously, Gemma. Did you tell him to do this?"

She hadn't turned around, but she knew he was coming closer. She sensed the heat of him. The power and allure he wielded radiated in waves. It was part of what she had fallen for—what his fans fell for. But in that moment, it bounced off her like it had hit a shield.

She hadn't told her father to do anything, not explicitly, but clearly, she'd finally gotten through to him on some level, so, in a way, the gesture was her doing.

She turned to Nick, subconsciously bracing for the brunt of his raw appeal, but when she saw him straight on, his eyes, his lips, that perfectly messy golden hair she used to tangle her fingers in, all she felt was satisfaction at his frustration.

He, on the other hand, nearly did a double take at her in Lila's romper. His eyes traveled up her bare legs and lingered on her chest with what looked like a pang of regret before finally meeting her angry gaze.

"So what if I did, Nick? Are you going to stand here and tell me you don't deserve it?"

His jaw clenched. He still looked shocked to see her there at all, but he clearly hadn't been expecting her to say what she had. "This is my *life* you're messing with, Gemma."

Back when they broke up, there hadn't been much ceremony to it at all. One day soon after his band had signed their record deal, Nick told her he didn't have time for their relationship anymore. When she realized she had been but a stepping-stone, a necessary ticket for admission into the world he so badly wanted to enter, her heart had been too crushed to fight back. She'd surrendered out of self-preservation and kept her emotions close. She'd never really told him how it had affected her.

But after the day she'd had, the revelations and confrontations, seeing him face-to-face felt like it was up next in a line of things a long time coming.

"And what about *my* life, Nick? What about the fact that you used me to get to here, to get to all of this"—she circled her arms with her index fingers pointed up, gesturing at their surroundings—"and never once looked back when you made it? What about that? Not to mention, you *lied* to my dad about us still being together."

He blinked at her. Surprise briefly flashed in his eyes, and in that split second, she saw a glimpse of the guy she had fallen for. But just as quickly, whoever he had become chased the old Nick away, and Gemma realized the guy she thought she knew might never have existed at all. He narrowed his gaze. "You of all people should know what it takes to survive in this industry. I did what I had to do."

Gemma snorted in disgust. "Hell of an apology, thanks."

He stepped closer and lifted a hand like he might poke her the way he'd poked the event organizer. "Listen, you can't—"

"I'd think *very* carefully about the next thing you say, Nick." Gemma nodded at Lila standing beside her, still streaming.

Lila's lips peeled into a devious grin like exposing him was even better than shoving him in front of a bus. She lifted her hand and wiggled her fingers in a wave. "Hi, Nick. It's been a while. Say hi to the internet because we're live."

His face paled when he realized their conversation—the whole scene in the hallway—had been broadcast online. Gemma could not fight her satisfied smile. Nick quickly pivoted away from the camera, mortified, and headed for the dressing room.

At the same time, a herd of people rounded the corner and moved quickly up the hallway.

"Oh my god!" Lila said on a dramatic breath. "It's *him*."

Gemma had the same reaction, though she reined it in, having already seen Nigel Black in person that day.

He led the pack with long strides, looking like the legend he was in all black. His boots clicked on the concrete. The entourage behind him wore earpieces and juggled tablets and garment bags and phones. They chattered and hurried while Nigel glided out in front, appearing unfazed by it all.

Everyone in the hall froze as they approached. His presence was nothing short of stunning.

Gemma, Lila, and Nick were still standing in the middle of the hall, blocking the way. Instead of plowing past, Nigel came to a stop when he reached them. The crew behind him halted like a flock of ducklings.

"Gemma, love!" he said when he saw her, his face brightening in a way that made her melt. "So glad you could make it!" He reached for her to kiss her cheek, and the melt turned into a full-body swoon. "And this must be the birthday girl. Hello, love," he said to Lila.

Never, not once in a decade of friendship, had Gemma seen Lila speechless. She stood with her mouth hanging open. Nothing but a small squeak came out.

"This is my friend Lila," Gemma said in her silence. "Lila, this is Nigel."

"Nice to meet you, Lila," Nigel said. "Happy birthday."

Lila kept gaping in shock.

Nigel laughed a warm, rough sound that turned Lila a shade of pomegranate. Nick was staring in an equal shade of shock. Gemma was the only one managing to keep her cool.

Nigel made note of the chair on the floor and the dent in the wall. He cocked his head toward Nick and furrowed his brow. "Everything all right here?"

Gemma waited to see what he was going to do. Was he going to fess up to his fit in front of Nigel? His manager had just told him not to piss off powerful people, and if her father was high on the list, Nigel was even above him.

Eventually, Nick heaved a defeated breath and shook his head. "All good. We have to drop out tonight, though. Sorry not to get to share the stage with you, man."

The fact that Nigel expressed no surprise put a warmth in Gemma's chest. Perhaps he already knew the reason for the last-minute change. "Tough break, kid. Maybe next time." He turned back to Gemma. "Glad you'll get to stick around, though, love." He leaned in and gave her cheek another kiss. When he pulled back, he winked at her. "You won't want to miss this show. Happy birthday, Lila."

They parted so he and his entourage could pass by. It wasn't until they had rounded the far corner that Lila finally spoke.

"Nigel Black knows it's my birthday."

Gemma laughed. "Yes, he does. And however many people are watching your livestream know that he knows too."

Lila gasped like she suddenly remembered her camera was in her hand. She flipped it around to address her viewers with an important message. Gemma turned to see Nick pick up the chair and walk back into the dressing room. She had nothing else to say to him, so it didn't matter. He'd revealed his true self to her and to everyone on the other side of Lila's camera, and that was enough. She realized she would never get an apology because he wasn't sorry.

But there was someone she wanted to talk to. Someone who had apologized in a roundabout way, and she needed to acknowledge it.

She walked farther down the hall, past where Lila was rambling into her livestream and the dressing room where Nick had closed the door. She pulled out her phone and called a number she so rarely dialed that she could not have entered it by memory.

"Hello?" her father answered.

Her throat instantly tightened with emotion. She turned to face the wall and leaned her head against it.

"Hi, Dad."

He paused. "Hi, Gemma. Is everything okay?"

She wasn't sure if he asked because of the emotion straining her voice or because she never called him, ever, and a desperate emergency was a likely scenario for reaching out.

"Um, yeah. Everything is okay." She paused to find her voice and the right words. "I'm at Nigel's show, backstage, and I wanted to say . . . thank you."

She settled on those two words alone because what he had done ran deeper than having Nick's band pulled. He had finally put her first. He had chosen her after a lifetime of prioritizing himself. It would take her time to figure out how to fully acknowledge the sudden appearance of something so important, but she could at least start.

He released a heavy breath that sounded like relief on many levels. "I'm sorry, Gemma. For earlier. For . . . too many things I could possibly ever make up for. You deserve better than I've treated you your whole life. You're right: none of this is worth it without the people I love to share it with. I don't know that I deserve your forgiveness, but I'm going to work for it."

Her throat squeezed tighter, and she felt liquid warm her eyes. Her mother's words about forgiveness came back to her. It was up to her, she knew that. She'd always known that. Her father had just always made it so easy not to forgive. But this gesture meant something. It meant something big.

"I think it's going to take a while, Dad, but this is a good start."

A weight settled on the line as her words landed. She heard her father breathe in deeply as if a chronic ache was easing ever so slightly. "Thank you for being honest with me, Gemma. I'm sorry if I ever made you feel like you couldn't be. And I'm sorry for not seeing how Nick hurt you."

She realized in that moment that she was getting an apology from someone who really mattered in her life. Despite all the pain he'd caused her, she didn't need one from Nick. She didn't need anything from Nick. The realization felt like liberation from the previous year of being heartbroken over him. A weight she didn't even know she'd been carrying lifted from her shoulders. She felt free.

She quietly laughed and pressed her fingertips into the cool wall. Sounds from the stage vibrated inside it. "You should have seen his face, Dad."

Her father echoed her quiet laugh, and she liked that they were sharing a secret. "Oh, I'm sure he wasn't happy." He paused and came back on a serious note. "I'm sorry I didn't pay closer attention, Gemma. I should have seen the role I played in all this. When you left this afternoon, you were so upset, and it was the only thing I could think of to do. I had to make some calls, but sounds like it all worked out?"

"It did, yes. And I ran into Nigel a minute ago; he didn't seem surprised by the lineup change."

Her father paused again. "Yes, well, news travels fast in this industry, doesn't it."

She smiled at the thought of all the calls her father had made for her benefit—and against his own. And she realized that giant, expensive, outlandish gestures like asking rock stars for favors and offering to charter private flights was how her father knew how to fix things. The world he lived in had different rules than hers, but he was trying to bridge the gap between them in the ways he knew how.

Perhaps she could start to make room for it.

"Thank you, Dad. Really."

"Of course, Gemma."

It was a tiny step, but it was in the right direction.

"Have you talked to your brother lately?" he asked. "He

texted me a while ago to say he's still on standby in New York."

"Oh my god, Patrick!" Gemma said with a gasp. In all the mayhem of the evening, she had forgotten to check in with him. Again. Guilt washed over her. The poor guy was still stranded at the airport, trying to get home to her.

"I have to go, Dad," she said in a rush.

"All right. Have a good time at the show."

"I will, thank you!" she said, and ended the call. She furiously tapped her screen to bring up Patrick's number.

"Gemma?" He answered after three rings, sounding like she'd woken him up.

"Patrick! Are you still at the airport?"

Muffled sounds of him moving around came through the phone. He grumbled and took a deep breath. "What time is it? Ouch! Shit, these chairs are not made for sleeping . . ."

She pictured his lanky body pretzeled into a ball on an airport chair, his hair sticking up from having fallen asleep at an angle. "It's almost nine here, so you're close to midnight."

"Oh god," he groaned.

"Patrick, listen—"

"What's that sound? Where are you?" he said through a yawn.

She realized the sounds of the show were carrying over their call. "Believe it or not, I'm backstage at the Bowl. I got passes to Nigel Black's show tonight."

Patrick paused as if he was taking a moment to understand. "I'm sorry, *what*?" he replied, wide awake. "You wait until *now* to tell me this?! I would have started sprinting home on foot if I had known! You told me it was sold out, and now you're backstage?!"

Gemma laughed at his reaction. "It was sold out."

"How did you get passes? Did you ask Dad?"

"No. I did this one all on my own. Nigel was on our show today, and I interviewed him because my boss was out."

Patrick was gaping; she could hear his mouth hanging open from three thousand miles away. "You hosted the show?"

"Believe it or not, I did."

"And you interviewed Nigel Black?!" He nearly shouted the question in his excitement.

"Yes again."

"That's amazing, Gem! And then Nigel Black was like, 'Hey, love, want some passes to my sold-out show to-night?'" He put on a horribly campy British accent that made Gemma laugh.

"Pretty much."

"Damn. Well, good job to you."

"Thank you."

Patrick yawned again, and she knew it was time to set him free.

"Listen, Patrick. The reason I called is to tell you that you can give up trying to get here tonight. I'm sorry I've held you hostage all day." She wasn't sure if they were going to wake up in the same day again and it would all be moot, but in this version of the day, she needed him to know that she had come to an overdue realization. "And I want to apologize for all the times I've made you play peacekeeper between me and Dad. I've put a lot of unfair pressure on you, and I'm really sorry for that."

He grew quiet for a long moment and came back with a serious tone. "I just want you to be happy, Gem. And I worry about you being alone out there. I know things were different for you growing up than they were for me, and it's up to you what you want to forgive, but I hope you can give him a chance. Yes, he made mistakes, but we only get one family, and I'd hate to see you miss out on a member who's right there willing."

His words resonated in a way that Gemma would not have been receptive to on another day. "I'm going to work on it."

"Good—wait, really?"

She softly smiled at his surprise. "Yes, really. I ended up going to see him today, and things . . ." She thought back to the scene at his house, how she'd left so angry, and where they had ended up. "Things worked out better than I expected them to."

He didn't say anything for a moment. "Wow, Gem. That's really great."

"Yeah, it is. Turns out you were right, and I could do it on my own."

"*See*, I told you," he said proudly.

"Yes, you seem to have grown very wise."

He laughed. "I think it happened somewhere between my third and fourth missed standbys today. I can't wait to get out of here."

"Okay, but promise me you'll come home before you move for good, please?"

He paused again. "I'm sorry, am I dreaming right now?

You're making up with Dad *and* you're not upset about me moving?"

Gemma smiled. "You're awake, I promise. And I'm sorry for my reaction earlier. You caught me completely off guard, and I can't believe you told both Mom *and* Dad before you told me, but I'm really happy for you."

A beat passed.

"You are?"

"Of course I am. You totally deserve that job, and you will be amazing at it. The institute is lucky to have you."

He was speechless for long enough that Gemma heard a PA system in the background call out a passenger's name.

"Get out of there, Patrick. Go check into a hotel and sleep for a week like you said you wanted to."

"I might need two weeks after all this . . ." She heard the smile in his voice.

"Take as long as you need but let me know when you're heading home."

"I will. Have fun at the show, Gem."

"Bye, Patrick. Love you."

"Love you too."

They hung up, and Gemma hoped they weren't fated to communicate only by phone and video calls for the rest of their lives.

She took a breath, satisfied with the loops she had closed with both her father and brother. Around her, she noticed the hall had cleared out and the walls had stopped vibrating. The dulled roar of a live show had shifted to the much softer sound of the background music pumped through speakers between acts.

The openers had finished their set.

Nigel was on next.

Electric anticipation filled the air, and Gemma could almost taste it. Her heart rate picked up and she smiled. It was a once-in-a-lifetime opportunity for more than one reason, and she wasn't going to miss it for anything.

CHAPTER 14

GEMMA AND LILA stood in the wings, stage right, as Nigel opened the show. She'd had front-row tickets to plenty of shows plenty of times in her life, but watching the set from behind the scenes was an unrivaled experience. It was like being inside a living thing. She was standing right on top of the source of the lights and sounds filling the air. Her heart beat in sync with the drums, and every lyric felt like it originated inside her own head. Nigel was mere feet away, giving his all to a screaming crowd of thousands. Her inner seven-year-old self was overwhelmed with excitement, and her thirty-two-year-old self could hardly contain it.

Nigel's set looked like a shabby living room assembled onstage: antique rugs covering all the power cords lacing the floor like veins, a couch no one was sitting on, an array of funky floor lamps. It didn't really make any sense and yet it was perfect. The drummer sat up on a small platform behind the couch; the keyboards were to his right along with a trio of backup singers. The bassist and guitar players roamed their respective sides of the stage, moving with the music, and Nigel stood in the center of it all, the star and source of light.

For his second song, he launched into the one Gemma's father had put on the record player that afternoon. The memory it always filled her with, something sweet and delicate, took on a new flavor that made it even better. She gripped Lila's hand as they belted out the lyrics with Nigel, completely drowned out by the deafening amplifiers and lost in the delirium of his performance, which was good since Gemma did not pride herself on her singing voice.

Lila had stopped streaming because, as she had shouted to Gemma as they'd entered the stage, it would rob the moment of exclusivity, and Gemma had to agree. Broadcasting their backstage access to hundreds of thousands of people who weren't there would defeat the purpose of the experience being special. Lila had been taking pictures and videos to post later, but the moment they were in was for them and them only. It was one of the most thrilling things Gemma had ever experienced.

She looked out over the crowd at the seats carved into the hillside that disappeared into the night. The stage lights shined pulses of color, turning all the faces and raised arms into a glowing, swaying rainbow. The energy coming from them was as powerful as what was leaving the stage, the two meeting in the night air with the force of an electrical storm. Gemma studied a few faces in the front row. Each of them sang along like she did, adding their voice to the chorus of fans caught up in the spirit of it all. Though they'd never met, she felt like she knew every one of them. In that moment, their love of Nigel unified them, strangers from all walks. And that was the ultimate beauty of music.

When the song finished off with a crash and a roaring cheer from the crowd, Nigel paused to address the audience. His question of "How's everybody doing tonight?" was met with thunderous cheering. He wiped his brow with his arm and gulped at a water bottle he then tossed back onto the couch. He moved back to the microphone and Gemma, Lila, and seventeen thousand strangers hung on his every word.

"Thank you so much for coming out tonight!"

The crowd screamed. Gemma cupped her hands around her mouth and joined them.

"Now listen, listen," Nigel said, holding up a hand to calm them. "We don't normally do this, but we've decided to add a song to the set this evening. You see, there's someone very special here, a new friend of mine, and I've been asked by a *very* persistent young fellow to dedicate this song to her. I have to say, this one is a bit of a stretch for us, but what the hell. Gotta love love, right?!"

Nigel turned and pointed right at Gemma and gave her a wink. She didn't even know he knew she was standing there. Then he turned around to face his bandmates and bobbed his head to count off the song.

When the opening notes of Gemma's favorite song—the one that had been following her all day—came out of Nigel's guitar in a roughed-up, sexy cover, she almost fainted.

"No. *Way*," Lila said beside her, her jaw unhinged. She sucked in the biggest gasp of her life before she screamed, *"THIS IS OUR SONG!"*

Gemma was too stunned to process what was happening.

Nigel Black, rock legend, was covering a fifteen-year-old Top 40 pop hit. The moment was beyond special. It was the one and only time the song would ever be played this way. The only evidence of it would be stories from people who'd been at the show and the several thousand social media posts that would come later, and none would be as good as being there in the moment.

Nigel kept singing the saccharine pop lyrics in his gravelly voice. They'd slowed the tempo and scratched it up like someone had taken car keys to a shiny paint job, and it had no business sounding so damn good. Gemma would have pulled out her phone to record it if her heart weren't suddenly pounding.

It was a message. For her. And only one person could have sent it.

Jack. He was somewhere nearby, he had to be. He wasn't on that plane to London. He was *here*, at the show, convincing Nigel Black to dedicate a song to her. And not just any song. *The song.*

She looked out at the audience. The younger faces sang along; the older ones looked confused yet no less entertained. Glowing phones lit up the rows and rows of bodies swaying and singing, but she didn't see Jack.

Gemma turned to Lila, who was lost in a craze of beloved lyrics, and gripped her arm. "Lila!" she screamed over the noise. "Lila, he's here!"

Lila bobbed her head and punched the air to the hardened lyrics. She finished singing along to the chorus before responding. "Who's here?"

"Jack!" Gemma shouted. "It's Jack! He knows this is my favorite song! He dedicated it to me as a message!"

Lila's eyes went full-moon size and her mouth fell open again. "Are you *serious*?!"

"Yes! I have to find him!" Her heart was going to beat out of her chest. Her whole body might have been about to explode.

She eyed Nigel centerstage, singing his heart out to a song she never would have imagined he knew the lyrics to. Rosy lights pulsated off him. The whole stage had become a sea of swirling, warm red glow. He hit the second verse with as much passion as if he'd written it himself. She felt like she was in a dream: her favorite singer singing her favorite song—for her, by special request.

She scanned the crowd again, desperate. She had to find Jack.

The chorus came back around, and she threw her eyes across the stage. The band was giving the song one hell of a rock-glam glow-up, and everyone was enthralled. Even the techs and roadies lingering in the wings looked entertained.

And there he was.

On the opposite edge of the stage, right inside the wing like she was, stood Jack. He gave her a small but eager wave, as if he'd been watching her the whole time and patiently waiting for her to see him.

She almost collapsed with relief, excitement, joy, and another very strong feeling she wasn't sure she could articulate without seeing him up close.

Her body thrummed with exhilaration. She suddenly ached to touch him, to speak to him. To tell him everything she now knew she needed to say. But a raging, live performance stood between them.

She waved back and pointed upstage. She'd meant it as

I'll come to you, but when she stepped over cords and wires and managed not to trip as she rounded behind the drummer's platform in a hurry, there he was waiting for her.

They reached for each other, gripping each other's arms, and the relief she felt at his solid form stole her breath.

"I thought you left!" she shouted over the song still pounding on.

He looked bewildered. "Left?"

The panic she'd felt at the airport, the crushing loss, came back to her but only to intensify her relief. "Yes! I ran into Angelica at a restaurant, and she told me that you were leaving for Europe."

His eyes, still shining in the swirling lights, grew wide as if he realized how close he'd come to disaster. "No! I only told her that to get rid of her! I didn't think you were going to run into her!"

Gemma's heart surged with understanding. It had been a decoy. If only she'd known.

But if she had known, she thought, would she have gone chasing after him and realized her true feelings? Probably not. But she had—she *had* realized how she felt—and it had led them to this moment like it was all meant to be.

As if she had been running on a wheel or a fixed belt, Gemma suddenly felt that she had been set free. No longer stuck in a rigid track of her own making, of denial and cautious self-preservation, in admitting the truth, she felt a freedom she had never known before.

Her words came tumbling out. "Jack, when I thought you were leaving, I realized I'd made a huge mistake, so I went looking for you to try and stop you. I went to the airport—"

"You went to the airport?" He watched her with wide eyes, eager and interested, and looking both surprised and thrilled she'd gone to such lengths.

"Yes! And this horrible woman at the ticket counter wouldn't listen to me, and they called security on us, and then Lila convinced this TSA agent to help us sneak in, but we were too late! I thought you were on a plane to London, and I watched it leave! I thought I had ruined everything. You're right; we need each other. And the truth is, I haven't let myself feel anything for so long that I was holding back. But you make me feel everything, Jack. All this time I was protecting myself by walking away because I was afraid. I was afraid of what I felt, but I'm more afraid of losing you. I don't want to walk away from you. Ever. I—"

He gripped her arms and pulled her into a kiss. He kissed her and kissed her, and it felt as enormous as their kiss at the bar. The whole world—maybe the universe—tilted and put Gemma right where she knew she was supposed to be. She threw her arms around him and leaned into the feeling.

And just like that, it was as if a door opened in her mind, and she could walk through the past one hundred and forty-seven days.

She saw the first coffee collision, Jack's smile, his eyes. Sitting with him in the coffee shop, talking to him on the sidewalk. He'd told her about his job; she'd shared about hers. She saw their dates: the sweet, embarrassed flush in his cheeks when he took her to a barbecue place and she told him she was vegetarian; him gently swiping a dribble of strawberry ice cream from her lip when she'd ordered it to go after lunch and the zing his touch shot through her body; them attending Lila's birthday party and keeping to themselves in the corner as if they were the only two people in the world. She could even feel, somehow, through the stretch of time and mystery her urge to be near him on all those previous days. To know more about him, this beautiful, alluring stranger who somehow felt like an old friend. But as strong as that pull had been, she also felt how her own resistance had met it like an anchor.

As much as she'd wanted to know him in all those days, she hadn't allowed herself. And she realized, wrapped in his arms now, that she'd fully welcomed him, that it had had everything to do with her and nothing to do with him.

While her mind tumbled down a chute of sweet, recovered memories, she also saw all the times she'd walked away. She saw texts from Patrick saying he was stranded at a new airport and couldn't make it home, despite her demands. She saw herself turning down the interview at work, not visiting her father. She saw dozens and dozens of different versions of Lila's birthday party, all of them with her alone and in a foul mood after a bad day. She saw herself stuck in the same day over and over again, refusing to see that much of it was her own doing.

She opened her eyes and saw Jack, face flushed and a shine in his beautiful eyes, and knew that he was the key— her key—to seeing that she needed to change.

Happy tears washed her eyes and made her vision sparkle in the spinning lights. She wiped one away and smiled up at him. "I remember, Jack. I remember everything."

He jerked in surprise and tightened his grip. "You do?"

She nodded. "I do!"

"Oh, thank god!" He lifted her off the ground to spin in a circle. Her dizziness was not helped at all when he set her down and went back to kissing her.

The song roared on in front of them; the crowd kept cheering. Gemma wondered at how her heart could withstand so much emotion in one day, so many ups and downs, because it currently felt primed to burst.

She pushed back from Jack and smiled at him with a shake of her head. "How did you do this?" She gestured at the band.

His eyes flashed in a signal that it was no small feat, but he smiled like he'd do it again. "I had to think of a way to keep you from walking away. This is the first time you've ever gotten passes for this show, and I knew you weren't going to miss it because of what Nigel means to you. You've walked away every other day, no matter what I do, so I figured I should pull out the biggest stop I had. I had nothing left to lose."

Gemma gazed at him in wonder. "And how did you get in here? I gave your pass to my coworker."

He shyly smiled and ran a hand through his hair. "Turns out I know some people too. Also, I guess there's a video of us from outside the museum that went viral? People kept recognizing me from it." He held out his arms in a shrug like he was confused but would take the easy win.

Gemma rolled her eyes. "Yes, you can thank Lila for that."

"Thank me for what?" Lila shouted from behind Gemma.

She turned to see her standing there with her phone at the ready. The little camera light was not glowing, but the look on Lila's face said that was only because she was wait-ing for permission to record.

Gemma grinned at her and reached for the phone. She pressed the white button to *Go live* and handed the phone back to her. "This," she said.

She grabbed Jack and kissed him for everyone online to see. The song crescendoed into its ending. The drummer only feet from them thrashed and kicked as Nigel's vocals rang out the final lyrics. They cut off in unison, and all the lights snapped out with a dramatic beat.

The crowd went wild, Lila kept recording, and Gemma kept kissing Jack.

CHAPTER

15

THE AIR RANG with sounds of the show long after the stage
lights had gone out, as if the hills themselves were singing
in the dark. Gemma, Jack, and Lila—along with Hugo,
Carmen, and her girlfriend, who eventually materialized in
the mayhem—ended up backstage with the band. They
crammed into a crowded green room hot as an oven and lit-
tered with bottles and body odor and wisps of smoke from
those going in and outside. It was a grungy rock-'n'-roll
mess straight out of a movie, and they were living for it.

Through the clinked glasses, dozens of once-in-a-lifetime
photos that Gemma would blow up and hang on her walls,
and conversations that made her sure she was dreaming,
Jack's hand remained quietly but firmly in hers. He hadn't
let go of her, and she hadn't let go of him. The warmth of
him beside her and the sight of Lila's head thrown back in
laugh after laugh as she flirted her way through the room
filled Gemma with a dizzying sense of happiness so overwhelming, she knew they'd landed on the best iteration of

Lila's birthday party to date. If only Patrick had been there to put all of Gemma's favorite people in one place.

She hoped he was sound asleep in a New York City hotel, given that it was nearing midnight on the West Coast.

After an hour of noise and booze and bodies pressing up against her, Gemma found herself slowly drifting to the fringe of the party, as she was prone to do. Jack had gone to find her a bottle of water. When he returned with it, he slipped the cool, damp tube into her hand and leaned close to say something over the blaring music.

"Not really your scene?" His lips brushed her ear and sent a tingle to her fingertips.

She smiled, knowing that he'd said the same thing to her the night before at Lila's party. He knew she was not a fan of small, loud places full of strangers getting drunk, and she knew that he wasn't either, yet there they were again.

"No, not at all," she said, turning to him and reciting the same thing she'd said in the bar.

He held her gaze with a satisfied comfort, like the game they were playing was a physical and precious thing between them. "Mine either."

Instead of asking him what he was doing there like she had the previous night, she took a swig of her water, the smooth nothingness like a balm on her throat after shouting all evening, and grinned at him. "Do you want to get out of here, then?"

Jack's eyes flashed at the reroute in conversation. The corners of his mouth lifted, and he nodded. The sight sent Gemma's heart tumbling. They'd never made it so far together, and what came next was entirely up to them.

Gemma searched the room for Lila, ready to give her

notice that she was in fact leaving with Jack this time. She found her on the couch against the back wall, halfway on someone's lap, laughing and tossing her hair. She took one step in her direction when the man of the hour appeared in her path.

"Gemma!" Nigel Black sang with his arms out. He'd changed shirts after the show, but he still smelled like hard work and liquor mixed with a heavy dose of cologne dashed on to compensate. "Not leaving, are you?" He glanced down at her and Jack's clasped hands and smiled at the flush in her face, which only made her flush more.

"Oh, well, actually, we—"

Nigel tutted and shook his head. "Say no more. I will not stand in the way of this beautiful union after all the hard work Jack put into it." Gemma thought she heard Jack murmur something that sounded like *You have no idea.*

"Thank you, Nigel," she said. "For everything."

He casually lifted his shoulder. "Made for one hell of a memorable show, didn't it?" He thrust out a hand at Jack. "Jack, I'd tell you to be faithful to this one, but if even half of what you said to convince me to play the song is true, I know I won't have to worry."

Jack turned a sweet shade of pink that made Gemma desperately want to know what he'd said. "Of course, Nigel. And thank you again. I really can't thank you enough."

Nigel didn't release his hand. He stopped shaking and squeezed it. A serious note dropped into his tone. "Thank me by not fucking this up, yeah?"

Jack swallowed hard, and Gemma felt a surprised swell of affection. Nigel Black was acting more paternal than her own father ever had.

"No—I mean, yeah. Yes. I won't fuck anything up, sir," Jack said, stumbling.

Nigel laughed like it was all a joke and clapped him on the shoulder. "Good." He turned to Gemma and kissed her cheek. "Gemma, love, hold on to this one. He's a good man. And give your father a chance. He means well even if he has his head in his ass from time to time. Happens to the best of us, god knows."

She smiled at the feel of his scratchy face against hers once more. She never thought she'd meet Nigel Black again, let alone be kissed on the cheek by him multiple times in the same day.

Or have him cover a pop song for her live.

Or have him give a warning to her new boyfriend like they were teens going on a date.

All of it filled her brimming heart and more than compensated for her freeze-up of shame. Her inner seven-year-old self was proudly beaming. "I will, Nigel Black."

He winked at them and folded himself back into the crowd.

Jack let out a heavy breath like he'd been holding it.

"What did you say to him to convince him to play the song?" Gemma asked, too curious not to.

"I'll tell you once I recover from being threatened by Nigel Black. Holy shit." He put his hands on his thighs and bent over for another deep exhale.

Gemma laughed and rubbed his back. He'd swapped out his tee shirt for a button-down the same color of the shirt she'd spilled coffee all over that morning. She glided her hand over the smooth, pale blue fabric and taut muscles and felt like her fingertips were sparking.

Jack stood back up and shook his head. "Can we go for real now?"

"Yes. I just need to tell Lila first."

Jack slipped his hand back into hers as if he didn't want to get lost in the crowd. They fought their way through the tangle of bodies and found Lila still on the couch. She sprang up as soon as she saw them.

"Gemma!" she gushed, and threw her arms around her neck. The heat of her curvy body pressed into Gemma in a clear signal she'd had plenty to drink. "This is the *best* birthday I've *ever* had! Thank *you!*" she sang. She released Gemma and sucked in a big gasp as if Jack were a long-lost friend, which, in a way, he was, even though she'd seen him minutes before. "And *Jack!* I'm *so glad* you're here too!" She hugged him and let out a little squeak of affection. Her reaction made it feel like they were at her party rather than backstage at a show, and it didn't surprise Gemma, seeing that Lila could turn about any situation into a party. "Are you guys leaving?"

Gemma expected a five-star pout, but instead, Lila smiled when she saw their clasped hands. "Yes. Will you be okay on your own?"

Lila rolled her eyes. "Of course, Gem."

"Good," she said, and fished her keys out of her bag. She held them out to Lila. "I know you're smart enough not to drive yourself home tonight, but when you do leave here by whatever other means, can you please stop by my place and check on Rex?"

Lila slowly blinked at the dangling fob and set of keys. "Where are you going?"

"Not home," Gemma said with a sly grin. She was intensely aware of Jack's hand in hers. She felt him squeeze it.

Lila's face lit, and she snatched the keys with an excited and coordinated swipe that told Gemma she wasn't as tipsy as she'd thought. "Yes. Yes, I fully support this decision and will help enable it. Go. Be gone!"

Gemma laughed, her face warmed with gratitude and chagrin, and hugged her best friend again. "Thank you, Lila. Have fun and be safe."

"Always," she said with a flirty tilt of her chin. She turned to Jack and held up a finger like she was going to lecture him. Instead, her words seemed to get stuck in her throat. She swallowed, and the momentary moisture that glossed her eyes put a hard lump in Gemma's own throat. Lila turned her hand to point at Jack and tapped her finger right on his heart. "Be good."

It was a command and a wish all at once.

"Always," Jack said to her with a smile.

Gemma and Jack slipped away and skirted the edge of the room to make their exit. Breaching the hot pocket of the doorway was as refreshing as jumping into a cool swimming pool. Gemma inhaled a breath of much fresher air and felt the flush in her cheeks ease like a fever breaking. The tension in Jack's hand, which she hadn't noticed until right then, loosened into a more relaxed grip. She shot him a smile, realizing he'd been holding on to her so tightly at least in part because he was as uncomfortable in the crowded room as she had been.

They entered the hall and should have turned right to wind their way to the exit. Gemma was already buzzing with anticipation of where they were going to go together when a door to their left—toward the stage—banged open and caught their attention.

They turned to see a man with a headset looped around his neck carrying a box out the door. He looked dead on his feet and ready to be done for the night. He crossed the hall into another doorway, and the door he'd come from stood open long enough for Gemma to see the inky black hollow inside it.

A wild idea struck her.

"Come on," she said to Jack, and pulled on his arm.

They hurried down the hall, Gemma keeping an eye on the doorway the man had entered, and dove into the doorway he'd left open before he noticed.

Thick darkness instantly swallowed them whole. Gemma couldn't see a thing. She knew they'd entered the wing of the stage where light went to die.

"What are we doing?" Jack whispered. His voice close by in the dark shot a thrill through her veins. "Can we be back here?"

She took a cautious step forward, one arm out in front of her so they didn't crash into a wall. "Probably not, but if we get caught, I'll play the Dad card."

Jack quietly laughed. "Is that on the table now?"

She took a few more steps farther into the dark. Her hand brushed what felt like an amplifier. "Should the situation call for it, yes."

"*The situation* being getting caught trespassing at a world-famous concert venue?"

"That would be the one."

She tripped over something unseen on the floor. Jack blindly reached out to catch her and, in the dark, landed with his hand high on her ribs. The contact shot that same thrill from before through her veins at about a million times the intensity.

"Careful," he whispered, and didn't move his hand.

Gemma felt it there, warm and firm, each of his fingers like a live wire. It was minimal, but his touch was . . . everything. She found herself slowly sinking back into him until her shoulders met his chest.

He pulled in a breath, pausing for a second, before softening and easing into her like he'd been holding back all day but desperately wanted to touch her in that exact way. He wrapped his arms around her, encompassing her with a warmth that was at once comforting and exhilarating. Her entire body came to life in a way she hadn't felt in ages, if ever at all. She reached her arm up behind her and pushed her hand into his hair. It was as soft and thick as she imagined. At the feel of her fingers tugging, he slowly exhaled, melting into her, and sank his lips to her neck with a small sound from deep in his throat that made her knees weak.

They'd been reserved in public, minus the make-out behind the drummer during the show, but the restraints of polite-enough company were off.

Gemma turned in his arms and dropped her bag. He walked her backward up against the object that was in fact an amp; she felt its wiry mesh screen on her back when he leaned into her. He at first held her face in his hands, kissing her softly and slowly like someone tasting a delicious new food. When she hungrily ran the tip of her tongue over the swell of his bottom lip, he opened his mouth like he was suddenly starving.

As if they'd flipped a long-waiting switch, everything began moving faster.

His hands went to her shoulders, her waist, her hips like he was outlining her body in one fluid motion. He pulled her close and kissed the breath right out of her. She'd never felt anything like it. Something so soft yet powerful and limitless. It was as if he'd reinvented making out. But it was really a matter of how perfectly their lips fit together, she realized. How complementary he was to her in shape and taste and other ways she couldn't wait to explore. She fisted her hands in his hair and then ran them over his shoulders, memorizing the form of him. She wanted to touch him all over and felt the same need in his grip, his kiss. She heard it in the desperate, heated sounds coming from him like he couldn't get enough. Neither of them could.

"Is this okay?" he paused to ask once she was disheveled and dazed.

Her eyes had hardly adjusted in the pitch black, but she saw the wet flash of his, the shine on his lips. She grabbed a handful of his shirt and pulled him flush up against her. "Definitely."

She saw his teeth when he smiled. "Good, because I've been dreaming of it for five months." He went back to kissing her, his hands in her hair, the taste of him like a glass of fine wine she wanted to sip with great care and never reach the bottom of.

Through the hazy fog, she could sense she'd wanted to do this for months too. It was as if a box opened inside her, one filled with hidden, piled-up pining that exploded and hit her all at once. Her desire for him, this man who had suddenly appeared in her life but had also been there all along, was bone deep. She knew it in every cell. And she had the instant gratification of him right there in her arms. She didn't have to wait for his mouth, urgent but soft against hers, or his whole body pressing into her.

He firmly gripped her hips, his hands hot through the thin fabric of her romper, and moved so that his leg pressed between her thighs. Her breath caught in her throat and she felt every nerve in her body reach out for him.

Just like that, he lit her on fire.

He put his hands against the amp on either side of her head, crowding in, while hers were pressing into the muscles of his lower back. They felt as tight as they'd looked when she saw them earlier. A little moan of appreciation escaped her throat. Wanting more and unable to stop herself, she flipped her hand beneath his shirt and laid her palm against his skin. He was feverish beneath her fingers, and the smooth, delicious heat of him sent her senses into overdrive. At the same time, he slid a hand from her shoulder to her hip, blazing a trail, to cup under her bare thigh and hitch her knee around his waist.

She gasped into his mouth, completely drunk on him and ready to fully surrender, when the door they'd passed through suddenly shut. A loud *clunk* followed the sound and echoed into the dark loudly enough to startle them both.

Their lips parted, and they froze. Gemma's heart hammered in her chest, pumping blood to parts of her body that made her dizzy. They stood perfectly still, wound around each other like vines, and waited.

No lights flipped on. No one shouted at them. No one appeared to tell them to leave.

Jack stepped back, and Gemma set her foot back on the ground. Every place where he'd been touching her screamed for him to return. "Did we just get locked in here?" he asked.

A sudden sense of panic hit Gemma like they were trapped in a closet. But then she remembered they were standing in the dark corner of an enormous open space.

She slipped away from him and carefully walked in the direction of the stage. "You mean, *out* here?" Her voice carried like a small bird flapping into the endless night.

She stepped into the moonlight on the empty stage and looked out at the dark hillside. Row after curved row of abandoned seats sat silent under a dusting of stars. With the stage lights hanging from the domed ceiling turned off, they were far enough into the hills for the night sky to twinkle above them. Gemma gazed up at it and had a sudden vision of herself as the tiny speck she was. Not more than a grain of sand in a boundless expanse.

Jack came to stand beside her. She felt his eyes on her face, outlining her profile, before he too looked up at the sky. "What are you thinking about?"

"The universe."

Her mind tended to telescope when she thought of the unknown. It zoomed from the infinite space on all sides of everything down through the solar system, the atmosphere, the sky, the clouds, all the way to her own two feet on the ground in her shoes. The rapid in-and-out gymnastics that she let her mind do sometimes made her dizzy. Not in a way that physically challenged her balance, but one that left her mind tumbling down corridors of *why* and *how*. She struggled to comprehend how it all existed, what was beyond it, and her purpose in it.

But then people like Jack turned up, and she realized that maybe connections in life were all that really mattered.

She slipped her hand into his and looked back up at the sky. "Do you think we're spinning again?"

Jack released a heavy breath, knowing she was referring to the globe demonstration in Dr. Woods's lab. If Jack's theory was right, all the axes should be back in motion. "I certainly hope so."

She couldn't feel anything different. Gravity hadn't felt like it shifted in any direction other than pulling her more toward Jack.

She nervously squeezed his hand and turned to face him. "Jack, what if—"

He shook his head before she could finish asking the thing that she was sure neither of them wanted to consider. The silent question hung between them with the weight of a thousand unsaid words. She looked up into his eyes and was struck with sudden, paralyzing fear that she might not recognize them the next time she saw him. Her tongue grew thick, and she couldn't voice the question that had been on it moments before.

Jack sensed her worry, perhaps feeling it himself, and reached for her other hand. The certainty she'd seen on his face every time he'd tried to explain what was going on throughout the day settled into place. His jaw muscle twitched and his eyes focused. "I have another theory."

"Oh?" she said, intrigued.

"Yes. I think we should stay awake all night, just in case."

A laugh popped from her lips.

"I'm serious! It'll be a precaution. We've made it this far. Do you really want to risk having to start all over?"

"Of course not. Though I have to admit, your eleventh-hour worry has got me a little concerned. You don't think it's a midnight thing—which we are *well* past by now?"

He shook his head. "It can't be. I regularly stay up past midnight, and it never made a difference."

Even the thought of such a late bedtime made her tired.

"I go to bed before eleven every night."

He unthreaded their fingers and held out his hands. "Well, there you go. That's why it never worked."

"Because I was asleep?" she asked with an arched brow.

He laughed. "When are you going to start believing me about all this?"

He made a fair point. Even though she was exhausted and probably would have been out like a light seconds after her head hit a pillow, he had been right about everything else that day. Maybe they both had to stay awake all night. She would hate to risk falling asleep and undoing all their hard work. Though she was pretty positive that if his original theory was correct—the one where she had to fall for him to break the loop—they could skip off into the moonlight together worry-free.

She sighed and wrapped her arms around his neck. She rose on her toes to kiss the corner of his mouth, still lifted in a little grin. "Fine, Jack Lincoln. I'll stay up with you all night."

His grin widened. "How do you know my last name? I've never told you before."

The question would have sounded absurd under any other circumstances.

"Oh, because I googled *Mac Drake* when I was trying to convince the World's Most Heartless Ticket Agent to call your name over the PA system at the airport, and I realized I didn't know it. Luckily, a TSA agent helped us through a back door instead. I could have gotten arrested for you today, sir." She playfully poked him in the chest.

He smiled again. "Well, that would have been an interesting turn of events."

She impishly scowled at him and folded her arms. "Yes, never would I have thought I'd risk going to jail over some guy."

"Oh, I've done all sorts of things I never would have done if I hadn't met you," he said like it was a challenge.

"Oh yeah?"

"For sure."

"Like what?"

He pursed his lips like the list was long and he was considering where to start.

She poked him in the chest again, jaw slack, as if she were scandalized by the mere suggestion that she'd caused him trouble.

"Ouch!" he said with a laugh. He grabbed her hand and looked at her finger. "Speaking of ouch, what happened here? I've never seen you with a Band-Aid before."

Gemma had forgotten about the small wound in the day's events. The cut was so tiny, she probably didn't even need the bandage anymore. "Oh, I accidentally cut it earlier. It's totally fine."

Jack frowned like he didn't like the fact no matter how slight. "I guess add minor injury to things that would have otherwise not happened." He chastely kissed the tip of her finger. "Okay, here's another one: If I hadn't met you, I never would have choked down Negronis trying to impress you."

Gemma's head fell back in a laugh. "Valiant of you. I promise I'll never make you do that again."

"Thanks. Those things are truly awful."

"They are not. What's your favorite drink?"

"Scotch. I'm a writer."

"Is that really a thing?"

"Indeed. They handed me a bottle when they inducted me into the club."

"Hmm. I think you're telling tales, Mr. Lincoln," she said, and narrowed her eyes.

"Doubt me if you want. I can't say any more; they'll revoke my membership."

Gemma laughed, and he squeezed her hand. "Well, if I hadn't met you, I never would have lost my favorite shirt to coffee stains." She pushed out her bottom lip in a dramatic pout.

Jack pinched it with a grin. "I'll get you a new one. You look amazing, by the way. I've never seen you wear anything like this." He appreciatively eyed her head to toe. "I almost passed out when I saw you from across the stage."

Gemma normally would have blushed at such a statement, but his eyes on her made her feel radiant. She playfully pointed her toe and put a hand on her hip. "You like it? Lila picked it out for me."

He answered by pulling her into a deep, slow kiss. She almost lost her balance.

By the time he let her go, she was positively spinning. She couldn't believe she'd wasted so much time not kissing him. "If I hadn't met you," she said, keeping their game going, "I never would have made out with anyone on the stage at the Hollywood Bowl—*during* a show, no less."

"I think that's a pretty safe bet," he said with a smile. "And I never would have begged Nigel Black to cover a pop song at said show."

Gemma threw her head back and dramatically groaned in appreciation, channeling Lila. "That was *amazing*. Seriously the coolest thing ever. You've set an incredibly high bar for sentimental gestures, you know."

He shrugged and laced his fingers back between hers. "I look forward to topping it someday."

They still stood centerstage, alone in the pale moonlight. Gemma marveled at how quiet their voices sounded in the exact space that had been raging with noise not three hours before.

"I don't know if that's possible."

His lips pulled into a mischievous grin. "We'll see."

Gemma gripped his hands and leaned back, swaying against the sturdy weight of him holding on to her. "Okay, here's another one: If I hadn't met you, I never would have had the guts to interview Nigel."

He reeled her in by the arms and released a hand to tuck her hair back. "I don't think you needed me for that; you only needed a little push. I just happened to be the person in the position to give it to you."

She softly smiled at him. "Well, thanks for giving it to me. It's my dream to do something like that someday, and I've always been afraid to . . . I don't know." She felt a swell of honesty rise in her chest, and before she knew it, she was confessing one of her biggest secrets. "I'm afraid I'll be bad at it, at anything in music, and with everyone in the industry knowing my dad, it's like the stakes are higher. They have expectations. And at the same time, I don't want anything handed to me because of him, so I've been holding myself back in multiple ways."

He smoothed her hair again and lifted her chin with a hooked finger. "You're not bad at it, trust me. I think you will be an amazing host, so you should go for it. And anyone who judges you because of your family, for any reason, can fuck right off."

She laughed. "Have you been holding back swearing in front of me all day? I've seen *Mac Drake*; I know you've got the vocabulary. But I've hardly heard it other than when you told Nigel you aren't going to fuck up—and when you called him *sir*!" A cackle burst from her throat, bouncing her chest. "Oh, I'd forgotten about that until right now!"

Jack's face turned an adorable shade of rose. He buried it in his hands. "Please don't remind me of that. It just came out!"

Gemma kept laughing and grabbed his wrists to pull away his hands. "Well, he *is* knighted, so technically, you weren't wrong. Sir Nigel William Orville Black."

Jack shook his head with an embarrassed smile. "A, why do you know that? And B, there's a difference between addressing someone with their honorific and unknowingly slipping it in because you're terrified. I'm officially more afraid of him than your father."

"Good. You should be."

Their laughter died down and they held each other, his hands on her hips and her arms around his neck, slowly swaying to a song only they could hear. Gemma thought of all the songs that had been played on this stage over the decades of live performances. Some of the most famous musicians in the whole world had stood right where they were standing. She knew their private, quiet moment was all the more special for that reason.

"Here's another one," Jack said. "If I hadn't met you, I never would have become a viral internet sensation."

Gemma's laughter returned in giggly bubbles. She wondered how far the video of them had spread, and how many people had tuned in to the grand finale of Lila's livestream. "Is that something you wanted?"

"No!" He joined her in laughing. "That's the *last* thing I want."

"Good. And same. I'll leave that life to Lila. Fame of any sort is not on my bucket list. *Oh!*" she blurted. "I've got another one: If I hadn't met you, I never would have known that Duncan Miles—who is ridiculously hot in person, by the way—is a diva." She flipped her hair and jerked her neck back and forth for emphasis.

"Ah, yes. I'm sure that is vital information you are happy to have in your keep now."

"Completely vital. And on that note, I never would have met Angelica Reyes either, which, take it or leave it, honestly."

Jack grimaced. "Yeah, sorry about that."

Knowing that Angelica was out of the picture and given the fact that Jack's arms were looped around her and they were slow dancing to silent music on a grand stage, Gemma felt securer about probing. "How did you guys even end up together?"

He released a mighty sigh. "We met at a party last year and kind of hit it off. We started hanging out, and I thought

I was into her, but I think I was just lonely. And she was"—
he paused for another breath—"she was a lot. Jealous, demanding. Obviously unfaithful." Pain flitted across his face
and put an ache in Gemma's heart.

"I'm sorry, Jack. Catching her with someone must have
been awful."

A dark laugh puffed from his lips. He stopped swaying
and dropped his arms. The absence of his touch shot a pang
of regret through Gemma for bringing up his ex. "In truth,
I didn't remember it until she told me, and none of it matters now," he said. "But you know, I think all the wild things
that happened today really were meant to fix that part of my
life. I mean, you running into her at a restaurant? What are
the chances?" He wandered over to the couch still set up in
front of the drum platform and sat like the thoughts were
too heavy to carry. He looked up at her with shiny pools for
eyes. "The way it was all connected today—in ways *I* didn't
even see until *you* started remembering—it has to all mean
something, right?"

His certainty appeared to pull back like a curtain, exposing a look of raw wonder on his handsome face. His eyes
searched Gemma's for an answer. She didn't have one for
him because she found it all inexplicable too, but she did
have pieces of the story he didn't yet know.

She sat beside him and slipped her hand into his. "In a
weird way, yes. If I hadn't run into her, I wouldn't have
thought you were leaving and realized I couldn't let you go."
She pulled his hand to her lips to kiss it and softly smiled. "I
mean, I didn't really need the theatrics and public encounter, but it all served a purpose, I guess."

"I can only imagine what that looked like, and sorry again."

Gemma shrugged. "Speaking of difficult relationships, did you know that you are my dad's neighbor?"

He blinked at her in surprise. "I am?"

"Yeah. After the scene at your house, I started walking down the street, and I was suddenly right around the corner from the house where I spent half my childhood. I'd spent all day—one hundred and forty-six of them—refusing to visit my father, and there I was, right outside his door. Because I'd met you."

Jack looked like his head was about to explode. His mouth fell open. "So, what did you do?"

Gemma sighed, thinking back to how angry she'd been on that street. "I did everything to stall and bail out at the last second. I hid in someone's hedges and called Lila and my brother, and they both told me to go inside."

He watched her, waiting for more. "And?"

"*And* I went inside," she said with a soft smile. His hand tightened on hers with an encouraging squeeze. "We talked, and I may have unloaded on him because he told me that he'd pulled strings to get my ex's band in the opening lineup for Nigel's show tonight. He thought Nick and I were still together because Nick had lied to him and said we were." She shook away the unpleasant memory since it was in the past and they'd moved on. "I left really upset, and that's part of why I was so short with you at the museum; I'd just come from there."

He frowned like he wished he could go back and make it better.

"But," she went on, "what I said to him finally got through to him, because he made some calls and got Nick's band pulled at the last second as a favor to me."

Jack's eyes popped wide. "Seriously?"

She nodded.

"Damn. Maybe I *should* be afraid of your father."

A quiet laugh rocked her shoulders. "Nigel was in on it too, so you'll hold them in equal regard if you know what's best."

"Noted," he said, dazed. "And I thought I had connections."

"It has its perks sometimes," she conceded. "And that whole situation actually put me in a position to finally confront Nick about everything he's done to me. I ran into him backstage right after his act got pulled."

Jack pressed his palm into hers and squeezed. "And how did that feel?"

A smile spread across her face. "Fucking great. Even better, Lila caught the whole thing on her livestream."

His mouth fell open again. "Wow. How did I miss all this?"

"Oh, you were busy running around convincing your ex you were leaving for Europe and begging a rock star to serenade me."

"Both very time-consuming yet important activities."

"Surely."

"So, are you and your dad better now?"

Gemma leaned back against the couch's surprisingly comfortable cushions and sighed. "Not yet. But I think we can get there. Eventually."

"That's really great, Gemma. I'm happy for you," he said with genuine warmth.

She softly smiled. "I guess I should have realized that telling you about him in the first place was a sign I was ready to make changes. I never talk about him with anyone."

Jack gave her a look like he'd selflessly play the role of open ear in whatever way she needed.

"And because of all that," Gemma went on, "I finally set my poor brother free—both from the airport and from playing family peacekeeper. I apologized for the position I'd put him in all our lives and told him how happy I am for his new job in Lagos." Her voice caught on the last word. She'd temporarily forgotten that Patrick would be permanently leaving soon.

Jack threw an arm around her shoulders and pulled her close. He pressed his lips to her hair.

"Sorry," she said with a sniffle. "I'd kind of forgotten that news with everything else tonight."

"Don't apologize. That's pretty big news, even if it's not going to change your relationship."

She tucked into his chest and took a ragged breath, remembering their conversation from outside the radio studio and taking comfort in the way he smelled like woodsy fresh air. She hadn't yet pressed her face so close to the source. "I hope you're right."

"I know I'm right. And you know, that's one hell of a domino effect."

"What is?" she said, her voice nasally and clogged.

"If you hadn't met me, we wouldn't have gone to my house, and you wouldn't have ended up at your dad's house.

Then nothing that happened from there would have carried out like it did."

She realized he was completely right. She considered sitting up to look at him, but her shoulders fit so perfectly under his arm and her head so warmly against his chest, she didn't want to move. "I guess if you look at it that way, it makes sense, then, that Patrick was stuck in New York all day. It made it so I visited our dad on my own and finally said everything that needed to be said," she added, realizing yet another connection in it all. She quietly laughed in wonder.

Jack thoughtfully hummed, and she heard it deep in his chest. "That . . . seems to fit right in with everything else here."

"And what's more," Gemma went on, "we wouldn't have gone to your house if you hadn't quit your job." The last word turned into an audible yawn.

Jack tensed and leaned forward, so she sat up. "Hey, no yawning. We've got to stay awake, remember?"

She hadn't realized how tired she truly was until they sat on the couch. Its old, worn-in cushions cradled them like welcoming arms, and she would have given anything to lie down. "I'm awake," she promised Jack with a nod. "You're just . . . very comfortable." She lifted his arm and settled back beneath it. She stifled her next yawn, her eyes burning, before she spoke again. "Why did you quit your job? Did you ever figure that out?"

Tension lingered in his body like she hadn't hidden her yawn well enough, and he might have been about to scold her again, but he let it out with a breath. His arm settled warmly over hers. His hand rested on her hip. "As soon as you kissed me onstage, all my memories came back too. From before the loop. I was really unhappy, Gemma. I honestly did need a change. Don't get me wrong; I love *Mac Drake*. I love the characters; I love the cast and crew. It's been a great five years, but I felt bored and stuck. Running in place. I think I'd been thinking about a change for a while, and then Angelica . . . Anyway, that was the last straw, because we broke up about a week ago in real days, and Charlie got the offer for the new show right around that time too. I was ready to leave it all, and then I met you. I didn't know that the change I needed all along was you."

The way he said *you* made her sit up and look at him. The moonlight bleached them both colorless, but she could somehow still see the blue of his eyes.

"Do you think that's why you couldn't remember what came before the loop? Because of . . . me?"

On another day, she might have felt foolish for centering herself with such significance in someone else's life, but the way he looked at her told her the answer without him needing to say it.

"Yes. I've been in here for so long and so focused on you that nothing else mattered. And, Gemma, I'm so much happier with you than I was before."

Gemma flushed and tucked her hair behind her ear. She knew that no matter how long she had the fortune of it falling on her, she would never get over his unabashed flattery and his gaze like the universe began and ended with her.

"And what about your new contract?" she asked, reluctantly pulling a slice of reality back into her little bubble of comfort.

His lips pulled into a soft smile. "I had Charlie put it

through the shredder, figuratively speaking. I'm not going anywhere."

When he'd made the suggestion before, it threw her into a tailspin of self-preservation panic. She didn't want him to rearrange his life around her, but that was before everything he'd just said. Before she knew how sure he was of what he wanted, and before she felt the same certainty.

She leaned in and kissed him, softly and slowly. The warmth that filled her lulled her into a deeper state of drowsiness. She saw the same exhaustion mirrored in Jack's eyes when she pulled back. It had been a hell of a day, and a hell of a five months.

He grinned at her. "So, I guess I can say, if I hadn't met you, I never would have un-quit my job."

She hummed a laugh and settled back beneath his arm. "Yes, you're welcome for that. Though I'm sure you would have loved making up stories about dragons in the snow." She yawned again, and when Jack didn't scold her, she realized it was because he was yawning too. She felt his chest expand and contract in the telltale way. "I felt that," she said.

"I have no idea what you're talking about." His voice was watery and warm.

"Mm-hmm." Her eyes had slipped closed.

"I really don't know what I had been thinking either. I mean, to switch genre so dramatically . . . I guess that's testament to how desperate I was for change."

"Do you think you'll regret it?"

"No," he said immediately. "I don't regret anything that landed me right here with you." He shifted to lie back with his head propped up on the couch's pillowy arm. He hauled Gemma up beside him and lifted one leg onto the cushions.

"I thought we weren't sleeping," she said, eyes closed, once she settled into him with her back to the couch. She nuzzled her nose against his chest and took a deep inhale. The smell of him alone would have been enough to knock her out.

"We're not," he said through another yawn. "I'm just resting after five months of chasing you."

She laughed and her body bounced against his. He ran his fingers through her hair, and the gentle tugging bumped her down another level of consciousness. "Jack, that's a bad idea."

"Mm-hmm," he said, but didn't stop.

She curled into his warmth and looped a leg over his. In a dreamy haze, she thought back to that morning when they'd crashed into each other. To say the path that put them where they'd ended up was long was a careless understatement. It had started with one hundred and forty-seven coffee crashes and wound its way through science and a psychic, exes and celebrities, a viral video, missed flights, flights that never were, reunions, a rock concert. A kiss. A few kisses actually.

They really had flicked a domino that knocked everything into place, but what had been the first piece? Where did it start? Which decision put it all in motion? Had it been her decision to get coffee that first morning? Or had it been Jack's when he chose to kiss her in the bar that night? Or was it something bigger, perhaps. Something outside them that couldn't be pinpointed or backtracked to an origin.

Perhaps it was all as Dr. Woods had said and they were objects in random motion that had coincidentally collided and gotten stuck.

Whatever it was, Gemma knew it had led her to where she was supposed to be. To him. The catalyst to the changes she needed to make for her happiness.

"Jack," she said, her voice quiet and her mind moments from slipping under. She reached her arm across him and heard his heart steadily beating inside his chest. "If I hadn't met you, I never would have fallen in love in one day."

He squeezed her against him and kissed the top of her head. His voice was warm and soft. "Today was the best day of my life."

CHAPTER
16

JACK WOKE WITH a crick in his neck and a chill at his back. The front of his body was curled around the warm, soft shape of the woman of his dreams. And he finally had her. Right there in his arms. She smelled like flowers and vanilla. On instinct, he wanted to press his lips into her shiny golden hair, but he didn't want to wake her. In all the times he'd seen her, all the months he'd spent trying to get her to remember him, he'd never seen her sleep. She was so beautiful and peaceful, her lashes gently closed, her perfect lips in a soft bow, that he forgot to panic for a moment.

Realization of where they were and what had happened shot through him like an electric shock. He sat up quickly but carefully and looked around.

They'd fallen asleep onstage at the Hollywood Bowl.

Pale morning light layered the empty amphitheater in a gauzy L.A. haze. Birds chirped somewhere nearby, braving returning to the trees now that the stadium wasn't blasting music. The warm summer night had cooled into a fresh new day.

"No, no, no, *no!*" Jack whispered in a panicked rush.

They weren't supposed to fall asleep! They were going to stay up all night to make sure it worked, to make sure the loop didn't reset! Even if they woke up where they'd fallen asleep, there was no telling what might have happened while they were unconscious. Everything could have been ruined.

He looked down at Gemma still sleeping, her cheeks flushed from the warmth of their bodies pressed together, and felt sick with worry that she'd wake and not know who he was. He'd lived it one hundred and forty-seven times, and it was the worst kind of heartache. The cruelest trick that fate could play on him. The open and willing but perpetually unfamiliar look on her beautiful face that he saw every day haunted his dreams.

From the moment he'd met her, that first day in the coffee shop, he'd done everything in his power to erase that look from her face, to replace it with one of recognition—and he had! He'd succeeded the day before by kissing her. He knew it the moment their lips had touched. He *knew* kissing her would work because he was completely, helplessly in love with her by then, and even the universe's cruelest game couldn't fuck with something like that.

But staring down at her soundly sleeping, he couldn't shake the fear that it had all gone away again. That a wicked hand had reached into her dreaming mind and stolen it.

He couldn't bear the thought. He couldn't stand to think of starting over, not after yesterday, last night. He'd convinced Nigel Black to sing her favorite song, for god's sake!

Jack was a good person; he knew that about himself. Sure, maybe he could have volunteered more often or donated to more charities, but altruism wasn't the singular hallmark of a good man. He was kind and thoughtful, liked in both professional and social circles. He spent every Sunday on the phone with his mother. Back at the start of the loop, he'd thought he was being punished or perhaps tested in some way, and he'd spent many weeks resentful about it. But he'd realized over time that the loop wasn't some sadistic prison sentence or test that he had to pass. It was an opportunity. An opportunity to point his life in the direction it needed to go.

He'd honestly lost track of when he stopped remembering the days before the loop began, but he wasn't sure it mattered. Gemma had been the catalyst all along. He now knew that she'd entered his life the day after he'd made a life-altering decision that would have left them worlds apart, and as a consequence, he was given the chance for a redo.

One hundred and forty-seven redos.

He couldn't be mad about that because he was a million times happier than he'd ever been before her—even if all the redos had been the most exhausting experience of his life and the single greatest challenge to his sanity.

But if it hadn't worked . . . If all the life-fixing they'd done, the closure-finding and path-resetting, didn't sum up to breaking the damn loop, he was out of ideas.

He watched her continue to sleep, the woman he knew undoubtedly was the love of his life, with a gut-wrenching fear that she'd forgotten who he was.

Hesitation curled around his throat as if it might choke

him. As long as she was asleep, she was still in love with him after their long, life-altering day that finally—*finally*—put everything in place. If she woke . . .

He didn't want to consider the other half of the thought experiment.

He sighed and looked out at the still morning bathed in blue light. It occurred to him that he had a second source of information to confirm if they'd broken the loop: the date on his dad's watch. But even then, if he looked down at his wrist and saw that the date had moved forward, that didn't guarantee Gemma would remember him. There were no rules in this game. *That* fact he had learned well.

There were no rules about how he'd ended up in that coffee shop that first morning, a place he'd never been but randomly decided to check out on a whim. No rules about how the first time he'd crashed into Gemma, he felt the significance in his bones, and by the second time, he knew she was the missing piece in his life. No rules about how chasing after her every day left him both heartbroken and determined to get it right the next time. No rules about how she got more beautiful every time he saw her, and how every new thing he learned about her, no matter how small—her favorite drink, her favorite song, how she picked the blueberries out of a muffin—felt precious. There was nothing logical about any of it, other than the fact that he loved her.

There were no rules. Only decisions, big and small, that shaped any given day and accumulated into a life.

The first day they crashed into each other, a decision had been made for him. He wanted her—*needed* her—in his life. And there was nothing he wouldn't do to keep her. It was still true, he realized as he looked down at her now.

He knew it with the same certainty he'd felt every previous iteration of the day. A dogged determination to hold on to her because he knew she was the one, and he couldn't give up.

Even if it meant living through a one-hundred-and-forty-eighth version of the same day.

He made another decision and quietly moved from the couch to kneel in front of it, facing her. He listened to her softly breathing for a final, perfect moment before he reached out and pressed his hand to her arm.

"Gemma," he whispered so as not to startle her. His heart had shoved up under his collarbone and squeezed like an angry fist. He had to steady his hand from trembling. "Gemma," he said again, and gently shook her arm.

She peacefully woke and filled her lungs with her first conscious breath of the day without opening her eyes. Jack held his own breath as her brow furrowed. Her face pinched as her body registered that she'd spent the night on an old couch. She took another, deeper breath, and her eyes fluttered open like a bronzed sunrise. Jack had never seen a shade of brown so beautiful.

He held stiller than a statue, watching her wake and feeling his heart pound in anticipation.

She blinked several times, her face betraying nothing. When her gaze fell on his, her eyes widened a fraction. She pushed herself up to sitting, her hair mashed on one side and her cheek rosy. She stared down at him kneeling in front of her, and Jack couldn't remember the last breath he took.

"You," she said.

A tiny sip of air slipped into Jack's lungs, but he wouldn't fully breathe until he was sure. He held her gaze, willing her to remember and silently begging.

"Yes, me."

Gemma didn't take her eyes off him. He felt her probing his face, his chest, his arms, and his hands resting on his thighs. He sensed himself standing on the edge of an abyss. She could push him into it with a single question, *Who are you?*, and the words would feel like a temporary death sentence exactly like they had every day before as he fell. But then, ever determined, he would start the torturous climb out of the dark abyss back into the light that was Gemma Peters.

He felt her light already like a patch of sun bursting through the clouds, and he silently hoped with all his strength that he could stay in it. He kept quiet, waiting, *hoping*, and feeling his battered heart soldier on until Gemma's face split into a brilliant smile.

She flung herself off the couch and landed in his lap. He fell over backward, and suddenly she was on top of him, kissing him breathless with the stage floor at his back.

He threw his arms around her and held on with everything he had. Relief washed over him like a downpour after endless drought. The feeling was so profound, he felt his throat tighten and a tiny tear pinch out of his eye. He let her envelop him, her warm body small but solid on top of his, her hair a curtain around them. He kissed her and kissed her and was so consumed, he kissed the empty air where she had been before he even noticed she'd scrambled to sit up.

She straddled him and reached for his arm. Her fingers closed around his wrist and she jerked her hips to twist her upper body in a way that stirred something near the base of his spine. "What day is it? You told me this thing is never wrong, right?" she said.

He was too dazed from being tackled to realize she was looking at his watch.

She sucked in a gasp and turned to him with her mouth agape. Her hair was a golden, tousled nest around her flushed face. He'd never seen her so beautiful before. "Jack." Light danced in her eyes, setting the bronze shimmering. "It's Friday."

He snapped out of his daze and sat up. "It *is*?" He reached for his own wrist and looked at his watch, the most accurate piece of technology he'd ever owned.

She was right. The date had moved.

"It's Friday!" he shouted right in her face.

She rocked back laughing but didn't make it far before he grabbed her and kissed her senseless. He held her in his lap, her knees pressed into the stage floor on either side of his legs and his hands in her hair. They clung to each other in a delirious tangle of joy and relief.

"For a second, I thought you didn't remember," he slurred against her mouth.

She pulled back and smiled at him, wiping a tear off his cheek, and not even asking why he was crying. "Of course I remember! I was just confused as to why I woke up outside with a kink in my back," she said with a laugh. She let go of him to push her fists into her spine. It loudly popped and he leaned forward to press a kiss to her chest, which she'd shoved in his face. "I can't even remember the last time I slept on a couch."

Jack bent his neck to the side and felt it crack. "Yeah, I'll be paying for that one for a while too."

"Part of the endless bounty of being in your thirties."

Jack laughed as she buried her hands in his hair, which he was sure was as messy as hers, if not worse. He held on to her hips and felt her wiggle against him. He knew he needed her to get off him soon unless they planned to completely defile the stage at the Bowl—which, he realized, they probably wouldn't have been the first couple to do.

Gemma placed her hands on his shoulders. "So, now what? We're free. What do we do?"

He lifted a hand to smooth her hair and shrugged. "Anything we want."

Her smile would have knocked him down if he hadn't already been sitting. "Hmm," she said as she looked out at the stadium over his shoulder. Her optimistic gaze seemed infinite, as if she were looking off into an unknown but thrilling future of possibilities.

Jack desperately wanted to be part of every one of them.

She turned her smile back to him with a promise in her eyes that he would be. "How about we start with breakfast? I know a great coffee shop nearby."

EPILOGUE

THE MOMENT GEMMA had been dreading for two weeks was finally upon them. She'd tried with all her might to pretend it wasn't looming over everything like a big, sad cloud—and she'd done a really good job of it for the most part—but there could be no more pretending. The time had come.

Jack pulled to the curb at the airport and put the car in park. Rex stood up on the back seat, always alert and ready to jump out the door when he sensed a stop in motion. Except he wasn't the one who'd be getting out of the back seat. The other much taller, much more human passenger was preparing to depart.

Gemma considered jamming her finger into the child-safety button that kept the back doors from unlocking at all, but she knew Patrick had a plane to catch.

Jack opened his door first, risking his life to step out into the unloading zone at LAX's international terminal. Patrick was flying over to London, for real, then hanging a

right down to Nigeria. The airport was as chaotic and frantic as ever on a Sunday morning in honor of his departure.

A light hangover still throbbed in Gemma's temples
from all the wine she'd had at Patrick's farewell dinner the
night before. Their father had hosted, and Jack came along
to meet him. Jack had in fact met her entire family in the
span of two weeks thanks to Patrick being in town and
them needing to squeeze half a year's worth of visits into
the same fortnight that happened to overlap with her falling
madly in love with the new man in her life. Her mother had
come up for a few days during the first week, and Jack had
gone to lunch with them. Patrick had of course been in the
thick of it all each day, hanging out at her apartment while
she was at work and spending most every afternoon and
evening with her. She wouldn't let him get a hotel, but she
had spent a few nights at Jack's house to give him some
space. The whole lot of them, plus Lila and Raul the TSA
agent, who she'd apparently been DMing since that day at
the airport, had gone out one night at Lila's insistence
and gotten roaring drunk and sung karaoke. Gemma had
learned that Jack had an amazing voice. Which, of course
he did.

She'd learned that he had other amazing abilities as well
on those nights she'd spent at his house.

Ever since the loop broke, she'd spent every day wrapped
up in a delirium of new and exciting things and people she
loved. Her heart had been brimming so full, she'd been
able to stave off the impending crush she'd feel over her
brother leaving. Though she had on purpose stored a little
bit of the overflowing happiness to soothe her aches later.

"Yes, you're a good boy. Rex is a good boy," Patrick cooed

from the back seat. Gemma heard Rex's tail excitedly thumping against the leather seat. "You take good care of my sister, okay?" Rex's collar jangled and Patrick's voice grew muffled as he leaned in to hug him.

Gemma heard the back of the SUV pop open where Jack had gone around to retrieve Patrick's luggage, and things were suddenly moving too quickly for her.

Her throat tightened with emotion. She'd promised Patrick she wouldn't cry, and she'd borrowed an enormous pair of face-shielding sunglasses from Lila in case she couldn't keep her promise and had to hide it.

Patrick reached over her seat and squeezed her shoulder. "All right, Gem?" He said it with a note of worry in his voice, both asking if she was okay and reminding her it was time to go.

She swallowed a fiery lump and nodded without turning around. "Yeah. Yes."

Patrick opened his door and unfolded himself onto the curb. Gemma pressed the button to lower his window so that Rex could stick his head out when he closed the door. She stayed in the car trying to gather herself.

Jack rolled over Patrick's suitcase and parked it at his feet. How her brother managed to move across the world with a suitcase and a backpack, she couldn't figure, though Patrick had always been a man of limited needs. A tee shirt, jeans, and a notebook, and he was happy. She'd forced a new phone upon him with a ridiculously overpriced data and messaging plan that she was footing the bill for, with strict instruction to keep in more frequent contact. But she knew, deep in her heart, that just as Jack had said, no matter the distance, Patrick would always answer when she called.

She lowered her own window but didn't chance getting out to say goodbye. She feared she would become a puddle and ruin it for everyone.

"It's been great meeting you, Patrick," Jack said, and held out his hand. "Good luck getting everything set up over there."

Exactly as Gemma had known they would, they got along like old friends.

Patrick, never shy with his affection, pushed Jack's hand away and pulled him into a hug.

The sight made the lump in Gemma's throat tighter.

"It's been real, dude," Patrick said, and slapped him on the back. "I'm glad Gemma met you."

Patrick had laughed until beer nearly squirted out his nose when they shared the story of Nigel Black threatening Jack. Gemma didn't know what private conversations her brother might have had with her boyfriend in her absence, but there were no parting sidewalk reminders of how he should treat his sister in that moment. She assumed he'd either already told him, trusted that Nigel had scared him straight, or perhaps trusted that Jack was a great guy and Gemma could take care of herself. Or maybe a combination of all three.

Rex poked his head out the window and gave a whimper.

Patrick turned to give him another scratch on the ears. "Oh, Rexy, I'll miss you too. Be a good boy."

That only left Gemma, and she wasn't sure she could actually do it. In all the times she'd said goodbye before, she'd felt like she was shipping him off with a return-to-sender label; he always came back to her. This time, he was leaving on a one-way ticket.

Patrick stepped sideways to expectantly stand outside her door. She couldn't see his face because he was so tall. He held out his hands, and she stared at the faded image on his shirt of a band she hadn't listened to since high school. "Well?" he said.

Gemma could feel hot tears welling up her throat, ready to fall, and she knew he was going to chastise her for it. Staying in the car would have been safer, but she couldn't stand the thought of not hugging him goodbye.

Before she changed her mind, she shoved open the door and threw herself at him. She instantly burst into tears.

Patrick wrapped his arms around her with a laugh. She heard it rumbling in his bony chest where she pressed her ear. He always reminded her of a giraffe: a head taller than everyone and long-limbed. She squeezed him hard enough to make him gasp.

"*Gemma*, come on! You promised you wouldn't cry."

"I know. I know. I'm sorry," she said, and wiped her eyes. The giant sunglasses were pointless, so she took them off. She looked up at him and reeled all over again at the sharpened features of his face. His jaw was stronger, his eyes wiser. He even had tiny crow's feet at their corners from squinting in the Nigerian sun. Every time she saw him after a half year, manhood seemed to have taken a chisel to the boy he once was. He was a full-fledged adult, she knew that, but he'd always be her little brother. "I'm going to miss you so much."

He let out a heavy breath. She'd had the same breakdown the night before, thanks in part to all the wine at their dad's house, and Patrick had been drunk enough to cry with her. They'd walked up the street back to Jack's house, and Jack let Patrick crash in his guest room. Now, on the sidewalk in public, Patrick tried to put on a brave face, but she heard his breath stutter in his chest.

"I made you promise not to cry because it's going to make *me* cry, Gem," he said only for her to hear.

Gemma gave him a final squeeze and pulled away. She fluttered her hands and wiped her eyes. "Okay, I'll stop. I'm sorry." She took a deep breath and blew it out her mouth. "Be safe over there."

Patrick reached for his backpack and threw the strap over his shoulder. "*Me* be safe. I'm not the one who stopped reality for five months so I could fall in love. *I'm* the one who should be worried here, honestly. Who knows what's going to happen to you two." He winked at her, and she felt her face flush.

Once he was safely in L.A., she had to tell him the truth of how she'd met Jack. She could tell the story to precisely two people who wouldn't think she was making it up, and Lila already knew. She'd told Patrick on her own, without Jack there, in case Patrick worried that Jack, a man he'd never met, had somehow coerced her into telling him such a wild tale. He'd struggled at first, but when they stayed up an entire night snacking on junk food and theorizing about why and how and all the pieces that had to fall into place to break them out of the loop, Patrick was a converted believer. The same as Lila, he had no memory of the one hundred and forty-six trips through the same day, and only remembered the final version of it. All the others slipped back into the pocket of time they'd spilled out from, as if they never existed at all.

Jack came to stand beside Gemma and hooked an arm around her back. She leaned into him for support.

Patrick extended the handle on his suitcase, ready to roll away, and adjusted his backpack. "Call me if you guys get sucked into an interdimensional vortex or anything. Otherwise, see you at Christmas." He shot her a crooked smile, and she knew she couldn't hug him again because she'd never let go.

"Bye, Patrick. Let me know when you get there!"

"I will, Gem!" he sang at her tenth reminder. "Gotta go now!"

He grabbed his bags, and they watched him roll to the automatic sliding doors and disappear inside.

Gemma released a big breath and turned in Jack's arms. He pinched the end of her ponytail and tugged on it, tilting her chin up. She and Patrick had woken late after all the wine and crying, and Jack made them breakfast. She didn't have time to do anything other than pull up her hair and brush her teeth before they had to leave for the airport.

"You did it," he told her, and chastely kissed her lips. "You saw him off."

She softly smiled at him. She knew her face was puffy from the hangover and tears, and she wasn't wearing a lick of makeup, and still, Jack was looking at her like she was the only girl in the world.

"I did. Thanks for coming."

"Of course. I'm glad I got to spend so much time with him. Though I'll be honest and say I'm happy I finally have you to myself." He leaned over and pressed his lips to her neck. It shot sparks through her swollen body and woke her up more than the two cups of coffee she'd had with break-fast.

Once the loop broke, they'd only had three days before Patrick arrived in town. Gemma spent most of the first one sleeping, having stayed up almost all night at the Bowl, and the other two in Jack's bed. The thought of crawling back there for the rest of the day sounded like the greatest idea of all time.

"Yes, I could use a day of rest before my first day at my new job," she said, and bounced her hips in excitement.

After her interview with Nigel, she'd been promoted to afternoon host. Starting Monday, she'd have her own show. She'd spent two weeks prepping and was an anxious ball of excitement and nerves for her first official hours on the air the next day. She'd finally made the leap, and she was ready to fly.

"I'm thrilled for you," he said. "But I have to warn you, there won't be much resting going on today."

Heat flashed her cheeks. The promise in his voice made her hold on to him tighter so she didn't lose her balance. "Is that so?"

He leaned in and slowly ran his nose along hers, bring-ing his lips whisper-close but not actually touching hers. "Yes, that's so."

One of Jack's many talents was making her wait in the most deliciously tempting ways. He did things with his mouth and hands and even his eyes that left her begging before he ever really touched her. She sometimes wondered if it was playful payback for the five months that he spent chasing her.

They'd reasoned that Jack's theory had been right from

the start: they had to fall in love to break the loop. He'd started remembering from the beginning because he was ready to fall. A man on a ledge in many senses looking for the piece in his life he didn't even know was missing. The piece was Gemma, but she hadn't been ready. She had been stuck in so many ways and unwilling to see that she needed to change until he came along and helped her. It took one hundred and forty-seven days and the best kiss of her life for her to be ready.

And now she was ready for anything with Jack.

She stole a kiss against his lips and went to turn for the passenger door right as a woman approached them.

"Excuse me, ma'am? Sir? You can't be parked here."

Gemma turned and saw a familiar woman standing on the curb in her airline outfit. "Helen?"

Helen the ticket agent briefly narrowed her eyes and resumed her stern look of disapproval.

"Helen, it's me!" Gemma said. She hung from Jack with an arm around his neck still. "And this is the guy!" She pointed at him.

Helen sourly eyed them both.

"Jack, this is the ticket agent I told you about. The one who wouldn't let us—"

"Ma'am, you can't be parked here." Helen cut her off with a sharp command.

Gemma flinched. She looked side to side, and in truth, they were the only car idling at the curb. All the others quickly pulled away as soon as the passengers were dumped out onto the sidewalk like cargo. "Aren't you a ticket agent?" she asked Helen. "What are you doing out here policing traffic?"

Helen smoothed her hand over her prim uniform. "As an employee of this airline and a tenant of this airport, it's my duty to address problems where I see them," she said robotically, and Gemma considered checking her back for a battery pack. Or an off switch. "Now please, move your vehicle."

Gemma smiled at her, half laughing that they'd run into each other again. "Okay, we will, but don't you care that I found him? This is him!" She pointed at Jack again, hoping they could crack Helen's frosty exterior with a happy ending. "We told you love would win!"

Helen narrowed her eyes once more. Her mouth flattened, and Gemma realized that she knew better than to think she could melt this ice queen of a woman.

She stopped smiling and poked Jack in the side as if they had to escape a bomb about to go off. "Get in the car," she said to him, feigning a deadly serious tone worthy of a scene from *Mac Drake*. "It's futile, and we should run before it gets worse."

He caught on to her teasing and cast her a dramatic look like they were in true danger. "How much time do we have?"

"None. You don't know this woman, Jack. She's going to call security in three . . . two . . ."

"If you don't move your vehicle, I'm going to call security," Helen said right on cue.

Gemma and Jack exchanged a glance of fabricated fright, trying not to laugh, and pushed off from each other. Gemma threw herself at her door, and Jack sprinted around the hood, shouting, "Go! Go! Go!" Rex barked for dramatic effect at all the commotion.

They slammed their doors and Jack hit the gas on the car, which had been running the whole time. They left a bit of rubber on the road and turned heads as they sped off into the sunny day, cracking up, in a dramatic escape worthy of a Hollywood ending.

ACKNOWLEDGMENTS

I FEEL LIKE lightning has struck twice now that I'm here writing acknowledgments for a second book.

Melissa Edwards, my agent, thank you for getting behind this quirky little love story from day one. Your guidance helped it shine before anyone else ever saw it. I can't thank you enough for your advocacy and partnership in this business.

Cassidy Sachs, editor extraordinaire, thank you for falling for these characters as hard as I did, and for helping me find the heart in their story. Working with you is a dream. I can't wait for what we do together next.

Everyone at Dutton, thank you for giving another one of my books a home. Special thanks to Hannah Poole, Isabel DeSilva, and everyone else on the publicity and marketing teams for getting this book on readers' radar.

Sarah Horgan, thank you for another stunning cover that I will never stop swooning over!

The Bookstagram community, thank you for supporting authors and celebrating books in all your creative ways.

The boys of the real Azalea, especially the rhythm guitar player, for letting me fictionalize you as villains. None of you are Nick.

Stella and Penny Lou for inspiring Rex. You're all the best doggies.

Dr. Leily Kiani and Dr. Cyprian Czarnocki for inspiring the spirited physicist character in this story. I probably should have fact-checked my time-loop science with you, but I was afraid you would tell me it's all wrong. (I know it's all wrong; I made it up.) Thanks for some of my best grad school memories.

Morgan Weaver for letting me borrow your name for the friendly old man character who we both know secretly lives inside you. Stay salty, friend.

Dr. Sharon Danoff-Burg for inspiring Patrick's career in wildlife conservation with stories about your James's travels and adventures. Thank you for being in the know during business hours and for the continuous support and friendship.

My uncle Dan Rus for naming Nigel, and my aunt Krista Rus for transmitting the message. Thank you for being fans and always talking books. Drinks on the beach anytime!

My agent siblings. I honestly don't know what I would do without you. The unconditional support, information, and friendship is more than I could have ever hoped for. I wish only the best for every single one of you.

Natalie Bell and Nathan Grebil for being my ride-or-die fan club. Thank you for making my first novel feel like such an important big deal. You two are the best hype team and friends anyone could ask for.

My in-laws, Anne and Geoff Clifton, for always dog sitting and for selling my books to everyone you know.

All my Rus, Orsi, and extended family members, and friends who buy multiple copies of my books. What do you do with them all? Please don't stop! Thank you for a lifetime of love and support.

My nephews for eagerly asking when my books will be out even though you're not old enough to read them yet. When you see this someday, tell your parents hi. They're pretty great.

My parents, always. Little did you know when you got married in 1983 that you'd have a weird kid who would write a novel and dedicate it to you forty years later. Thank you for always cheering.

My husband for helping me dream big and for keeping me grounded. You inspire me every day.

And thank you to all the readers out there who believe in love, happy endings, and maybe a little bit of magic.

Holly James holds a PhD in psychology and has worked in both academia and the tech industry. She loves telling stories with big hearts and a touch of magic. She currently lives in Southern California with her husband and dog.